Little Goody Two-Shoes and Other Stories

Palgrave Macmillan Classics of Children's Literature

This series brings back into print some of the most important works in children's literature first published before 1939. Each volume, edited by a leading scholar, includes a substantial introduction, a note on the text, suggestions for further reading, and comprehensive annotation. While these full critical editions are an invaluable resource for students and scholars, the series is also designed to appeal to the general reader. *Classics of Children's Literature* presents wonderful stories that deserve a place in any adult's or child's library.

Series Editors:
M. O. Grenby, Newcastle University, UK
Lynne Vallone, Rutgers University, USA

Maria Edgeworth, *Selected Tales for Children and Young People*
Edited by Susan Manly

E. Nesbit, *The Story of the Treasure Seekers* and *The Wouldbegoods*
Edited by Claudia Nelson

Little Goody Two-Shoes and Other Stories: Originally Published by John Newbery
Edited by M. O. Grenby

Hesba Stretton, *Jessica's First Prayer* and Brenda, *Froggy's Little Brother*
Edited by Liz Thiel

Little Goody Two-Shoes and Other Stories: Originally Published by John Newbery

Edited with an Introduction by

M. O. Grenby

Professor of Eighteenth-Century Studies,
Newcastle University, UK

First published 2013 by
PALGRAVE MACMILLAN

Palgrave Macmillan in the UK is an imprint of Macmillan Publishers Limited, registered in England, company number 785998, of Houndmills, Basingstoke, Hampshire RG21 6XS.

Palgrave Macmillan in the US is a division of St Martin's Press LLC, 175 Fifth Avenue, New York, NY 10010.

Palgrave Macmillan is the global academic imprint of the above companies and has companies and representatives throughout the world.

Palgrave® and Macmillan® are registered trademarks in the United States, the United Kingdom, Europe and other countries

ISBN 978-1-137-27427-4   ISBN 978-1-137-27429-8 (eBook)

DOI 10.1007/978-1-137-27429-8

This book is printed on paper suitable for recycling and made from fully managed and sustained forest sources. Logging, pulping and manufacturing processes are expected to conform to the environmental regulations of the country of origin.

A catalogue record for this book is available from the British Library.

A catalog record for this book is available from the Library of Congress.

Contents

Acknowledgments

This book would not have made its way into print were it not for the assistance of: Helen Stark, who undertook much of the preliminary research and read a draft; Gen Larose, who photographed the illustrations; Lynne Vallone, who read and commented on parts of the manuscript; and Brian Alderson, who, as well as offering wise advice, has been overwhelmingly generous with his time and his collection.

I would also like to thank staff at Palgrave Macmillan, past and present, who have encouraged this venture and shepherded the book into print, particularly Francis Arnold, Kate Haines, Felicity Noble and Jenna Steventon.

Introduction

This volume collects together three children's books published by John Newbery in the mid-eighteenth century. Who wrote them is uncertain; so too are the precise dates of their first publication. What is beyond doubt is the significance of Newbery's contribution to the history of children's literature. Children did read before Newbery began to publish for them in about 1744. And other publishers had already produced a handful of books designed to make children's reading 'a Diversion Instead of a Task' (as the sub-title of Mary Cooper's 1743 *Child's New Play-Thing* put it). But Newbery's achievement was to make children's literature *work*. That is to say that Newbery made children's literature work for him, so that it became a profitable part of his business and, once his descendants and his competitors had followed his lead, a thriving and secure sector of print culture. But it is also to say that his books worked for their readers in ways that we still think children's literature should. They have strong characters, amusing antics, and an engaging address. They look attractive, with decorative bindings and appealing illustrations that synchronise with the text. They entice children to read, and unobtrusively induct them into the prevailing social value system. They successfully fuse their fun with their educative content.

This introduction looks first at Newbery himself and at his career as perhaps the most important of all pioneers of children's publishing. Then it explains the selection of the three titles included here and (presenting new evidence) considers the complicated questions of who wrote them, and when. The third section examines in more detail the texts themselves, placing them in their eighteenth-century cultural contexts. And the fourth section explores their economy and politics: something not always associated with children's literature. Indeed, it is clear that the boundaries of what was 'proper' for children's literature were still being negotiated in the mid-eighteenth century. Newbery and his authors, having few models to follow, were experimenting.

Sometimes the results can seem rather unruly and unsuitable. But even if these books can appear rather odd and old-fashioned today, it is no surprise to find that Newbery's contemporaries spoke of his books with huge affection, nor that the best of his publications became literary classics, remaining in print, and in children's hands, for more than a century after their first appearance. The final section of this introduction examines their readership and this remarkable legacy.

Newbery's children's books are worth our attention for a number of reasons then. They are one of the foundation-stones of the whole children's literature canon. They provide a unique insight into the society and culture, and even the politics and economy, of the mid-eighteenth century. But third, and surely no less importantly, they remain a joy to read.

John Newbery

Newbery himself is an intriguing and rather enigmatic figure. Born in 1713, the son of a farmer, in Waltham St. Lawrence in Berkshire, he was employed by a newspaper proprietor, William Carnan, in the nearby town of Reading. Carnan died in 1737 leaving some of his property to Newbery. Two years later Newbery married Carnan's widow. He was thus able to set himself up as a printer in Reading, and entries in his 'Private Memorandum Book' show that he was casting about for books to publish.[1] In late 1743, he relocated to London, moving to the address at which he was to become famous, 65 St. Paul's Church-Yard, in 1745. From then until 1767, when he died, Newbery published around 500 titles.[2] The majority of these were primarily intended for adults, includ-

---

[1] Some entries from this 'Private Memorandum Book' are recorded in Charles Welsh's Newbery biography and bibliography, *A Bookseller of the Last Century* (London: Griffith, Farran, Okeden and Welsh, 1885), pp.14–18. Welsh evidently had access to a large cache of papers relating to Newbery's business, but the whereabouts of this archive are now unknown: see Terry Belanger, 'Where Are the Newbery Papers?', *Bibliography Newsletter* (*BiN*), 3, vii (1975), 2.

[2] This figure includes new editions and reprints and is derived from S. Roscoe's authoritative bibliography, *John Newbery and His Successors* (Wormley, Herts.: Five Owls Press, 1973).

ing poetry, periodicals, pocket-books and many other miscellaneous kinds of publication. But a substantial proportion were for the juvenile market.

Browsing through a chronological list of his publications makes it clear that Newbery was feeling his way in this unprecedented venture. After *A Little Pretty Pocket-Book* (advertised and apparently available for sale in summer 1744, though no copy earlier than 1760 survives), he seems to have concentrated for several years on a series of instructional books on grammar, rhetoric, geography, logic and so on, co-published with the Salisbury publisher Benjamin Collins and marketed under the title *The Circle of the Sciences* (1745–8).[3] In the 1750s, other individual volumes of stories, fables, pictures and poems sporadically followed, along with some rather sober dictionaries, scriptural adaptations and histories. Some were lastingly successful but Newbery still seems to have been trying out different kinds of products. It was only by the early 1760s that children's books began to form a consistent and sizeable proportion of the business, though even then Newbery's interests in various newspapers and journals, and his books for adults, probably took up most of his attention. Indeed, Newbery's growing prosperity, which allowed him to experiment with different kinds of literature, was not derived from publishing at all, but from a retail and wholesale trade in patent medicines (they are touted in *Goody Two-Shoes* and advertised at its close: pp. 93 and 157). Almost certainly the largest part of his income came from the 'Fever Powder' invented by Robert James, immensely popular as a cure-all in the mid-eighteenth century and available into the twentieth, for which Newbery had been appointed sole vending agent in 1746.[4]

---

[3] See Christine Ferdinand, *Benjamin Collins and the Provincial Newspaper Trade in the Eighteenth Century* (Oxford: Oxford University Press, 1997), pp.40–1.

[4] The logic of the link between the trades in books and patent medicines, because 'both dealt in products which were centrally produced and nationally distributed' which 'called for national advertising', is clearly set out by John Feather in his *History of British Publishing* (London: Routledge, 1988), pp.114–15. See p.229, note 9 for more on the composition and sale of Dr. James's Powder.

At Newbery's death in 1767, his son Francis, working in partnership with Newbery's stepson Thomas Carnan, took over the business, though Francis broke from the partnership in 1779 to concentrate on selling the patent medicines. John Newbery had already established his nephew, also called Francis, in the book trade, and a rancorous rivalry developed between the two publishing operations (as is amply demonstrated by the angry preface to *The Fairing*: p.161). It was in fact the nephew's business that survived longer, his wife Elizabeth taking it over on his death in 1780, and her manager, John Harris, continuing it, under his own name from 1801.[5] By the 1780s, children's books were probably dominating the list, an indication of the increasing specialism of the Newbery firm but also of the extent to which children's books had become established as a vibrant, and commercially viable, section of the print trade.

Choice of texts and questions of authorship and date

The three titles reprinted here – *The Lilliputian Magazine; The Fairing: or, a Golden Toy for Children;* and *The History of Little Goody Two-Shoes* – have been chosen chiefly to demonstrate John Newbery's astonishing capacity for innovation. *The Lilliputian Magazine* has the distinction of being the first known periodical for children.[6] *The History of Little Goody Two-Shoes*, probably Newbery's most famous work, has often been called the first children's novel (although it is a claim open to question). And *The Fairing* is perhaps the single title among John Newbery's productions that aims most obviously to amuse and delight its readers, subordinating its didacticism until it is only dimly visible in the background. These three titles, it should be stressed, are not representative of Newbery's entire children's list: the majority of his publications were more earnest and educational. Most were also pretty ephemeral. In contrast, the three titles reprinted here endured. Although only three issues of the *Lilliputian Magazine*

---

[5] See Marjorie Moon, *John Harris's Books for Youth, 1801–1843*, revised edition (Winchester: St. Paul's Bibliographies, 1987).

[6] See Kirsten Drotner, *English Children and Their Magazines, 1751–1945* (New Haven, CT: Yale University Press, 1988).

were ever produced, it was quickly repackaged in a single volume in 1752 (as was Newbery's custom with his periodicals) and published as such through until the late 1780s.[7] Newbery and his successors likewise published new editions of *The Fairing* from its first publication in the mid-1760s into the 1780s, at which point other printers, in England, Scotland, Ireland and America, began to produce their own editions, probably pirated (although, according to the usual interpretation, the law at that time granted copyright only for 14 years). As for *Goody Two-Shoes*, its success meant that, by the end of the eighteenth century, it formed a staple of dozens of British and American publishers' children's lists. Indeed, abridged, revised and re-illustrated versions were still being published for children in the second half of the nineteenth century.[8]

What is by no means clear is who wrote these books nor, except in the case of *The Lilliputian Magazine*, precisely when they were first published. Until the last quarter of the eighteenth century it was unusual for authors to take credit for children's books: this reflects their lowly status but may also indicate that children's books could be the work of several authors and sometimes perhaps the publisher. It is certainly possible that John Newbery wrote all or part of these three titles. His 'Private Memorandum Book' from his days in Reading indicates that he planned to compile books himself, and Charles Welsh (writing in the 1880s, but not the most reliable authority) quoted Francis Newbery saying that his father was 'in the full employment of his talents in writing and publishing books of amusement and instruction for children'. Welsh also printed an otherwise unknown epigram from Samuel Johnson: 'Newbery is an extraordinary man, for I know

---

[7] For a full account of the publication of the *Lilliputian* see Jill E. Grey, 'The *Lilliputian Magazine* – A Pioneering Periodical?', *Journal of Librarianship*, 2 (1970), pp.107–15. Grey draws on information from the ledger of its printer, William Strahan, to demonstrate that Newbery certainly first published the *Lilliputian* in periodical form, ordering from Strahan 4000 copies of the first two parts, and 3500 of the third. Since Newbery did not order a separate cover for part three, and since it was printed a year after part two, Grey speculates that it may never have been issued alone, but only ever appeared bound with parts one and two (p.112).

[8] See Wilbur Macey Stone, *The History of Little Goody Two-Shoes. An Essay and a List of Editions* (Worcester, MA: American Antiquarian Society, 1940).

not whether he has read, or written, most books.'[9] We know, however, that Newbery employed a stable of writers to produce the copy for his newspapers, journals and books, and it is likely that he turned to one or more of them when he decided to enter the juvenile market.

The most obvious candidate for *The Lilliputian Magazine* is the poet Christopher Smart. Born in 1722, Smart had been a high-achieving but also rowdy student, and then fellow, at Cambridge University before he became inescapably attracted to the more bohemian life possible in London. He moved there in 1749, and quickly began writing for Newbery, producing light, satirical verse, but also serious and religious poems, which Newbery was pleased to publish. He also wrote for, and edited, some of Newbery's periodicals: *The Student, or, The Oxford and Cambridge Monthly Miscellany* (1750–1) and *The Midwife, or, The Old Woman's Magazine* (1750–3). An offshoot of the latter was a comic theatrical show produced and largely performed by Smart, who appeared, in drag, in the character of 'Mrs Midnight'. Called 'Mrs Midnight's Oratory' or 'The Old Woman's Oratory', it was first seen in December 1751 at the Castle Tavern, near Newbery's shop, before transferring to the larger and more fashionable Haymarket Theatre. In 1752, Smart cemented his ties with Newbery by marrying his stepdaughter, Anne Maria Carnan. Although they had two children, it was not a happy marriage and it has been suggested that Smart's inconsiderate behaviour to his wife caused a rift with his father-in-law. Certainly it was Newbery who, in 1757, committed Smart to a madhouse, ostensibly because of a heightening religious mania (reports describe Smart praying loudly in public and urging others to join him), though bi-polar disorder, drunkenness and even political subversiveness have been suggested as the real reason for his incarceration.[10] It was only in 1763 that Smart gained his

---

[9] Welsh, *Bookseller of the Last Century*, pp.14 and 22–3.

[10] Chris Mounsey paints Newbery as a ruthless and perfidious exploiter who, 'acting either alone or in concert with unknown political figures, spread rumors about Smart's alcoholism, sexuality, and insanity after having had him locked away' either because of his mockery of government policy in print and on stage, 'or for reasons of commercial jealousy.' *Christopher Smart: Clown of God* (Lewisburg: Bucknell University Press, 2001), pp.17 and 200.

freedom (having written what is now his most celebrated poetry, *Jubilate Agno*, while in the madhouse). His last years were productive but impoverished. He died in debtors' gaol in 1771. He had separated from his wife, and had apparently become estranged from Newbery, although it was Thomas Carnan, Newbery's stepson, who supported him in his last days and published his plaintive *Hymns for the Amusement of Children* (1771).

Hymns is the only work for children known certainly to be by Smart. But, given the closeness of his relationship with Newbery in the early 1750s, and particularly his authorial and editorial contributions to Newbery's periodicals, it would hardly be a surprise to find that Smart was involved in *The Lilliputian Magazine*. Indeed, since the late-eighteenth century, he has been credited as its editor, though the evidence is not conclusive.[11] All that can for certain be said is that he wrote one or two of the pieces to appear in the *Lilliputian*, notably 'A pastoral hymn' (p.31), advertised in the newspapers as by 'Kitty Smart', and which, under the title 'The Hymn of Eve', would later become one of his best-known works.[12] On the basis of this and three other pieces (see pp.27, 29 and 30), Smart's most authoritative bibliographers go so far as to say that 'the *Lilliputian* was almost certainly edited...by Smart'.[13]

Yet close analysis of *The Lilliputian Magazine* allows us to go much further. It is riddled with hints of Smart's involvement. Stylistically it often exhibits the sort of sprightly, jocular writing that Smart was becoming known for in the early 1750s, but snatches of more boldly poetic writing also remind us of Smart's more elevated manner. '*Riches and titles...are like bubbles on a running stream, liable to be blown away by the first breeze, or jostled into nothing by the next wave*' (p.18), for example, is not the language

---

[11] The claim is made by James Pettit Andrews in his *Addenda to Anecdotes, &c. Antient and Modern* (London: John Stockdale, 1790), pp.18–19. William J. Thoms also speaks of Smart as the 'editor' of *The Lilliputian Magazine* in *Notes and Queries*, 2nd ser., 74 (1857), pp.425–6. On the former, see Andrea Immel, 'James Pettit Andrews's "Books" (1790): The First Critical Survey of English Children's Literature', *Children's Literature*, 28 (2000), pp.147–63.

[12] *London Daily Advertiser and Literary Gazette*, 29 June 1751, p.2.

[13] Robert Mahoney and Betty Rizzo, *Christopher Smart, An Annotated Bibliography* (New York: Garland, 1984), no.368.

usually to be found in Newbery's texts. Likewise the quasi-biblical language in the 'History of the Rise and Progress of Learning in Lilliput' ('Now liberty sprung up and displayed itself, like the tree of life in paradise...': p.21) is very much what we might expect from the pen of a poet who won the Seatonian prize five times for verses on the Supreme Being, and who would become obsessed by how best to articulate the praises of God that were, he felt, inherent in natural creation.[14] More concrete evidence comes from the fact that several of the putative child contributors to the *Lilliputian* are surnamed Smart (pp. 30 and 67), while one of the epigrams, said to have been written by Master Bridges of Bath, is actually, and incongruously, a flattering tribute to Smart's periodical *The Midwife; or, Old Woman's Magazine* (p.64).

Indeed, the *Midwife* and the *Lilliputian*, published at the same time, seem to share much the same frame of reference. In the former, for instance, Smart had printed the supposed will of Lemuel Gulliver, the protagonist of Jonathan Swift's *Gulliver's Travels* (1726), bequeathing 'the Property and Copy-right of all my Voyages, which she shall think proper to write Notes or Comments upon' to Mary Midnight (Smart's own alter-ego). It was an invitation avidly taken up in the *Lilliputian*: it is not only its title that alludes to Swift's imaginary world (first brought before the public only 25 years previously) but several of the fables and narratives are set there (pp. 5, 18 and 45). In one of these, the Angelicans (another fantastical species to rank alongside Swift's inventions) are described as 'a gigantic sort of *Lilliputians,* about the size of the fairies in Mr. *Garrick's Queen Mab* (p.42)'. This is a reference to the recently produced pantomime, written by Smart's friend David Garrick, which had been the subject of a glowing article in *The Midwife.*[15] Advertisements for the *Lilliputian* included endorsements from Queen Mab and 'Mother Midnight'.[16] And the two

---

[14] See Harriet Guest, *A Form of Sound Words: The Religious Poetry of Christopher Smart* (Oxford: Clarendon Press, 1989).

[15] *The Midwife, or Old Woman's Magazine,* 2 (1751), 151–5 and 1 (1750), 145–51. On Smart's 'puff' for *Queen Mab* see Min Wild, *Christopher Smart and Satire: 'Mary Midnight' and the* Midwife (Aldershot: Ashgate, 2008), p.50.

[16] *Salisbury Journal,* 61 (11 March 1751) quoted in Mahoney and Rizzo, *Christopher Smart, An Annotated Bibliography,* no.370.

periodicals even on occasion repeated exactly the same phrases. In its opening dialogue the 'Author' of the *Lilliputian* says that the book aspires to teach children 'the *great grammar of the universe*; I mean, the *knowledge of men and things*' (p.4). Compare the dedication to the first collected edition of the *Midwife* in which the author says 'A Gentleman who has read the *Great Grammar of the Universe*, and obtain'd an intimate Acquaintance *with Men and Things*, sends me Word that there is no Sense in my Book.'[17] Such, in fact, are the continuities between the two periodicals that it is difficult to avoid the impression that the same mind was behind them both.

What is curious is that similar cross-references appear in *The Fairing* too. One attraction at the fair which forms the setting and subject for the book are 'Dogs and Monkies brought from the Theatre in the *Haymarket*' which perform various human activities such as dining, dancing and storming a fortress (p.186). Mention of the Haymarket Theatre, and the precise roster of activities the animals perform, make this very evidently a reference to the 'Pantomime Entertainment by the Animal Comedians' which formed part of Smart's 'Mrs Midnight's Concert' for several weeks in 1752–3. Allusions in *The Fairing* to 'my old Friend the learned Dog' and to the use of blue powder on wigs (a preposterous fashion that 'would certainly have prevailed' had it not been ruthlessly mocked by Mrs Midnight) are also connected with Smart's *Midwife* (see pp.187 and 214). But what is so intriguing is that *The Fairing* was apparently published in 1764: over a decade after the *Lilliputian*, the *Midwife*, and the last of Smart's 'Mrs Midnight' performances.

Before pondering this oddity – the appearance of all those references to Smart's activities of the early 1750s in a book published ten years later – we need to establish the publication date of *The*

---

[17] 'Preface' (signed 'Fardinando Foot, Esq.'), *The Midwife, or the Old Woman's Magazine* (London: 'Printed for Mary Midnight and Sold by T. Carnan', no date but 1751), p.iv. By the 'Gentleman who has...obtain'd an intimate Acquaintance *with Men and Things*' Smart may have meant Newbery; certainly this 'Gentleman' seems to have a good knowledge of publishing, explaining that the *Midwife*'s lack of sense makes the book 'more likely to sell' and referring 'to several senseless Pieces that have been publish'd lately with Success'.

Fairing. The earliest surviving copy of *The Fairing* is dated 1767. But advertisements appeared in several newspapers in December 1764. Their characteristically playful text is worth quoting in full:

> The Philosophers, Politicians, Necromancers, and the Learned in every Faculty, are desired to observe, That on the First of January, being New Year's Day, (Oh that we may all lead new Lives!) Mr. Newbery intends to publish the following important Volumes, bound and gilt; and hereby invites all his little Friends, who are good, to call for them at the Bible and Sun, in St. Paul's Church Yard; but those who are naughty, are to have none:
>
> 1. The Renowned History of Giles Gingerbread, a little Boy, who lived upon Learning. Price One Penny.
> 2. The Easter Gift, or the Way to be very good: A Book very much wanted. Price Twopence.
> 3. The Whitsuntide Gift, or the Way to be very happy: A Book very necessary for all Families. Price Twopence.
> 4. The Valentine's Gift, or how to behave with Honour, Integrity, and Humanity: Very useful in a trading Nation. Price Sixpence.
> 5. The Fairing, or a Golden Toy, for Children of all Sizes and Denominations. Price Six-pence.
>   In which they may see all the Fun of the Fair,
>   And at Home be as happy, as if they were there.
> A Book of great Conscience to those whom it may concern.
> We are also desired to give Notice, that there is in the Press, and speedily will be published, either by Subscription or otherwise, as the Public shall please to determine,
>   The History of Little Goody Two-Shoes, otherwise called Mrs. Margery Two-Shoes. With the Means by which she acquired her Learning and Wisdom, and in consequence thereof her Estate.... [18]

There is no reason to doubt this advertisement's claim that *The Fairing* was published on 1 January 1765 (save to say that Newbery probably would have made it available in late 1764 to catch the

---

[18] *London Evening Post*, 25–7 December 1764, p.2.

Christmas market): the probability is that copies from this first edition simply do not survive. But in any case, why, in the mid-1760s, was *The Fairing* still alluding to Smart's productions of ten years earlier? Smart had gained his release from the madhouse in January 1763. Might he be the author of *The Fairing*, signing himself 'You Know Who' in the book's dedication (p.161)? Certainly there are compelling reasons why not. By the 1760s Smart was on very bad terms with Newbery. After all, it was Newbery who had had Smart incarcerated. And Smart was utterly estranged from his wife Anna Maria, Newbery's stepdaughter, who had been sent to Dublin and then Reading to manage Newbery's affairs. Indeed, Newbery's will, proved in 1767, specifically stipulated that Smart should not benefit from Anna Maria inheritance.[19] Yet on the other hand, Smart was prodigiously productive after his release: his *Song to David*, three volumes of poems, an oratorio, and translations of the fables of Phaedrus and the Psalms of David were all published in 1763–5, though none of them by Newbery. And one cannot help asking why, if Smart was not the author of *The Fairing*, Newbery would have countenanced the decision of whoever did write it to commemorate Smart's 1750s successes when their falling out had apparently been so acrimonious? The mystery remains impenetrable. Perhaps the most likely explanation is that work was begun on *The Fairing*, by Smart, in the early 1750s, but that the manuscript was set aside (coincidentally, or not, during the period of Smart's imprisonment) only to be completed, or prepared for publication, when Newbery was ready to release a substantial tranche of books, as the advertisement details, in 1764. By then, many of the incidents it alluded to were ancient history but Newbery presumably chose not to revise the text just as he chose not to go to the bother of expunging references to Smart.

The same advertisement also announces the forthcoming publication of *Goody Two-Shoes* and it now seems beyond doubt that this, Newbery's most celebrated production, was first published in late 1764 or early 1765, though the identity of its author remains a

---

[19] See Betty Rizzo and Robert Mahoney (eds), *The Annotated Letters of Christopher Smart* (Carbondale and Edwardsville: Southern Illinois University Press, 1991), p.125.

matter of debate.[20] Previously overlooked internal evidence sheds light on precisely when it was actually written, and perhaps who wrote it. 'Why, it was but Yesterday, that a whole House fell down in *Grace-church-street*, and another in *Queen's-street*', interjects someone calling himself the 'Man in the Moon' when the school run by Goody Two-Shoes collapses in the novel. This 'Man in the Moon' then goes on to call for Parliament to take action to prevent further disasters (pp.130–31). Intriguingly, what must surely have been the first of these events is reported in a July 1763 edition of *Lloyd's Evening Post*:

> On Saturday evening, about six o'clock, a melancholy accident happened in Gracechurch-street. The party-wall between Mess. Nash, Edows, and Martin, and Mr. Harrison's, being deemed very bad in the opinion of the workmen, they were ordered to repair it; but whilst they were about it, and before they could get it properly secured, and shoared up, both houses fell down in less than three minutes after they heard it crack; there were 16 people in the house at the that time, but providentially not one was hurt.[21]

The 'Man in the Moon', whoever he or she was, was evidently aware of day-to-day events in central London. Newbery himself comes to mind, especially since he was the largest shareholder in – and therefore perhaps had a hand in editing – the newspaper

---

[20]   The evidence for its first publication date is set out in Julian Roberts, 'The 1765 Edition of *Goody Two-Shoes*', *The British Museum Quarterly*, 29 (1965), pp.67–70, including a discussion of the unreliability of the date '8 April 1765' that appears on the dedication leaf of some editions from about 1770.

[21]   *Lloyd's Evening Post*, 22–5 July 1763, p.85. The Queen Street collapse may be that referred to in the diary of Jérôme Lalande for 3 May 1763: 'This morning I saw three houses which had collapsed, from a lack of good building regulations, there were several people crushed in Whitefriars' (*Diary of a Trip to England. Translated from the Original Manuscript*, ed. Richard Watkins (Kingston, Tasmania: Published by the author, 2002), p.28) – although Queen Street is actually a few hundred meters east of the area usually designated as Whitefriars.

that reported the collapse and its aftermath.[22] His shop was only half a mile away from Gracechurch Street. It seems not unlikely that he was the 'Man in the Moon', although perhaps interposing his plea for parliamentary intervention into a narrative written by somebody else.

Besides Newbery, the other main candidates for the authorship of *Goody Two-Shoes* are the printer and journalist Griffith Jones and the poet, playwright, novelist and much else, Oliver Goldsmith. The former's claim has been advanced on the basis of an assertion in John Nichols' *Literary Anecdotes of the Eighteenth Century* (1812–15) that it is 'to Mr Griffith Jones, and a brother of his, Mr Giles Jones, in conjunction with Mr John Newbery, the public are indebted for... The Lilliputian histories of Goody Two Shoes, Giles Gingerbread, Tommy Trip, &c., &c.'. In fact, Nichols was here reprinting a claim that had been made a little earlier, by the bookseller Henry Lemoine in 1797, but no further corroboration can be found.[23] Evidence to support Goldsmith's candidacy is a little more persuasive, but hardly overwhelming. Goldsmith had worked as a hack writer for Newbery since at least 1760 and from 1762 to 1764 – at the very time *Goody* was being written – he was living in Newbery's care (or perhaps custody) at Newbery's Canonbury House (just as Smart had done a decade earlier). During this period, amongst much other writing by Goldsmith, Newbery co-published *The Citizen of the World* (1762), brought out the extremely successful *History of England in a Series of Letters from a Nobleman to his Son*, and purchased the copyright of *The Vicar of Wakefield* (finally published 1766). It would hardly be a surprise if Goldsmith also had a hand in *Goody*, though the only substantiation his supporters have been able to adduce are various perceived similarities of tone, style, structure, humour and theme between *Goody* and some of Goldsmith's works, notably *The Vicar of Wakefield* and *The Deserted Village* (1770). In particular, the dismay

---

[22] Newbery's authors frequently wrote for *Lloyd's Evening Post*. See Arthur Le Blanc Newbery, *Records of the House of Newbery from 1274 to 1910* (Cambridge: Cambridge University Press, 1911), p.17.

[23] Nichols, *Literary Anecdotes of the Eighteenth Century* (6 vols., London: printed for the author, 1812–15), vol.3 (1812), p.466; Lemoine, *Typographical Antiquities: History, Origin, and Progress, of the Art of Printing* (London: S. Fisher, 1797), p.82.

expressed at the enclosure of land by the rich in the latter recalls the 'Introduction' to *Goody*. Goldsmith, in fact, had, as early as 1762, in Newbery's *Lloyd's Evening Post*, written angrily against the increasing rates of eviction of the rural poor by large landowners, and the appearance of very similar sentiments in *Goody*, written a year or two later, is striking.[24] But it does not prove Goldsmith's authorship of even the 'Introduction', let alone the whole book. Indeed, Charles Welsh, who had access to an archive of Newbery business records now lost, lists many of Newbery's financial dealings with Goldsmith but evidently found no record of a payment for a children's book.[25]

What seems increasingly likely is that *Goody* was the combined work of several different authors. Indeed, at the end of the introduction to *Goody*, 'the Editor' deliberately raises the suggestion that preface and narrative are written by different people ('Why, do you suppose this is written by Mr. Newbery, Sir? This may come from another Hand': p.93). Similarly, the history of Tommy Two-Shoes (pp.149–54), promised at the end of his sister's story (p.144), was added only in the second edition, as if Newbery (perhaps responding to a rival's opportunistic sequel) thought better of a plan to publish another complete book and commissioned one of his authors to add ten pages that could be tacked on to the end of *Goody*.[26] A letter purporting to be from the book's printer

---

[24] Goldsmith's essay appeared in *Lloyd's Evening Post*, 14–16 June 1762, p.571, and was later titled 'The Revolution in Low Life'. See Sylvia Patterson Iskander, 'Goody Two-Shoes and *The Vicar of Wakefield*', *Children's Literature Association Quarterly*, 13 (1988), pp.165–8. The debunking of Lady Ducklington's ghost in *Goody* (pp.108–12) may also be linked with Goldsmith's exposé of a 'real' London ghost in his pamphlet *The Mystery Revealed; Containing a Series of Transactions and Authentic Testimonials, Respecting the Supposed Cock-Lane Ghost* (London: W. Bristow, 1762).

[25] Partial records of the Newbery-Goldsmith transactions are given in Welsh's *Bookseller of the Last Century*, p.62n.

[26] See Roberts, 'The 1765 Edition of *Goody Two-Shoes*', p.70. David Hounslow speculates that Newbery's expeditious expansion of Tommy's story was a response to the unscrupulous publication, by Henry Roberts, of a book called *The Orphan; or, the Renowned History of Tommy Two-Shoes*, which appeared in 1765 or 1766. Hounslow, 'The Opie Copy of the 1766 Edition of *The History of Little Goody Two-Shoes*', *Bodleian Library Record*, 15 (1995), pp.136–9 (p.138, n.1).

adds to the impression of the text's hybridity (p.154). There is even the hint of a connection to Smart in *Goody*'s singing of the 'Cuzz's Chorus' which, David Hounslow has argued, Smart probably wrote in the late 1750s (p.103).[27] Quite possibly, irrespective of whether he was producing a periodical like the *Lilliputian* or a 'novel' like *Goody*, it was Newbery's method to collect material from a number of authors (and illustrators) and to compile it into a more or less coherent volume (either himself or employing an editor). It was a process that may sometimes have taken years, as appears to have been the case with *The Fairing*. Such a *modus operandi* would explain why the question of who wrote Newbery's books has remained so difficult to answer.

Genre confusion, the carnivalesque and politeness

Newbery's publications were also generic hybrids. *Goody Two-Shoes* is part moral tale and part fairy story, with a heroine who, like Cinderella, goes from riches to rags and back to riches again. *The Fairing* actually includes two nursery tales – *Dick Whittington* and *Puss in Boots* – both also tracing a child's journey from poverty to affluence. Though well-known now, these were fairly new in the mid-eighteenth century. The story of Dick Whittington circulated chiefly in the form of a seventeenth-century ballad while *Puss in Boots* (with *Cinderella*) had been in English only since 1729 when Robert Samber published his translation of Charles Perrault's *Histoires ou contes du temps passé*. Despite their novelty, the inclusion of fairy tales in respectable children's literature was already contentious. John Locke, in his *Some Thoughts Concerning Education* (1693), had associated tales involving the supernatural with servant culture – something the new children's literature was designed to displace – and he had condemned such stories as psychologically damaging to young minds. Newbery, though a disciple of Lockean rationalism in most ways, was evidently prepared to defy the widespread critical aversion to the fairy story. He and his successors published several volumes of Perrault's and Madame d'Aulnoy's tales and, in *Goody*, even went so far as

---

[27] David Hounslow, 'The Cuz's Chorus: Or, a Little Piece of Book-Trade Nonsense', *Quadrat*, 12 (2001), pp.3–7.

to license the inclusion of a speaking, reading and poetry-composing raven (pp.119–22). Some compromise is evident though. The Newbery edition of Madame d'Aulnoy's fairy tales received a subtitle that stressed the practical utility of the fairy tale: 'For the Amusement of All Those Little Masters and Misses Who, by Duty to Their Parents, and Obedience to Their Superiors, Aim at Becoming Great Lords and Ladies.' And in *The Fairing* the telling of the two fairy tales is followed by a short debate on their probity, concluding 'that Fairy Tales should never be read but on Fair Days, when People are inclined to have their Heads stuffed with Nonsense' (p.208).[28]

Another emerging genre with which Newbery's children's publications manifestly have close ties was the novel. The 'rise of the novel' (though a matter of much debate among literary critics) was essentially coeval with Newbery's development of the new children's literature: Samuel Richardson's *Pamela*, *Clarissa* and *Sir Charles Grandison* were published in 1740–1, 1748 and 1753 respectively, Henry Fielding's *Tom Jones* in 1749, Tobias Smollett's *Peregrine Pickle* in 1751, Charlotte Lennox's *The Female Quixote* in 1752, Laurence Sterne's *Tristram Shandy* from 1759 to 1767, Horace Walpole's *Castle of Otranto* in 1764 and Goldsmith's *Vicar of Wakefield* in 1766 (to name only a few of the major titles). Self-evidently, Newbery's *Goody Two-Shoes*, one of the first continuous prose narratives written for children, and tracing a strongly characterised individual's adventures through a harsh world, was an attempt to bring the novel form to children. It was an attempt that had, in fact, been made already in the *Lilliputian Magazine*. Several of the *Lilliputian*'s constituent stories read like miniature novels, notably the 'History of Florella' which many eighteenth-century readers would surely have recognised as a drastically condensed rendering of the first part of Richardson's *Pamela*, published ten years earlier but still the subject of widespread public debate. Indeed, it was a recognition archly pre-empted by the *Lilliputian*'s editor's note that the story was 'Sent by an Unknown

---

[28] For a summary of the debate, and the place of the Newbery firm in keeping the fairy tale in print in the second half of the eighteenth century, see M. O. Grenby, 'Tame Fairies Make Good Teachers: The Popularity of Early British Fairy Tales', *The Lion and the Unicorn*, 30 (2006), pp.1–24.

Hand, And may, for ought we know, have been published before' (p.13). There are some differences – Florella, unlike Pamela, is not a servant in her would-be seducer's house, and she is not the victim of an attempted rape, as is Pamela – but the similarities are more striking. Both narratives are developed through the letters of the protagonists and hinge on the seducer's interception of letters between the heroine and her parents, and in both the seducer is finally reformed by the heroine's chastity and financial probity, allowing the narrative to close with a happy marriage.

Another of the *Lilliputian*'s stories deals with equally adult themes: 'The Adventure of Master Tommy Trusty And his delivering Miss Biddy Johnson, From the Thieves who were going to murder her ' (p.10). Representing the abduction of a child and her attempted murder, this was surely more likely to induce childhood trauma than any of the fairy tales against which critics were warning. Its terror is amplified by the text's geographical specificity, and it seems possible that, as was the case with other elements of Newbery's publications, this was a story taken from real life.[29] On the other hand, Tommy's cunning trick of making a hullabaloo to persuade the villains that he is approaching with a numerous posse, allowing him to rescue a girl in distress seems distinctly novelistic. A possible source is an episode in Fielding's *Tom Jones*, published two years before, in which the hero charges into a remote wood to rescue a woman who has been abducted there and is about to be murdered.[30]

---

[29] A possible inspiration for the story of Biddy Johnson, as recorded in *The Proceedings of the Old Bailey*, is the case of Ann Brooks, tried for robbery on 6 September 1749. She 'was indicted for that she, in a certain necessary house, on Jane Randolph, spinster, did make an assault, her in corporal fear and danger of her life did put, taking from her person one linen cap, val[ue]. 4d. one silk knot, val[ue]. 1 d. one camblet skirt, one coat, one flannel peticoat, val[ue]. 6d . one pair of shoes, val[ue]. 6d. the goods of the said Jane Randolph , July 8. | The child was found in its shift only, after it had been seen in the prisoner's hand leading it, the prisoner had carry'd the cloaths to her house, where she and the clothes were found.' Brooks was found guilty of the lesser crime of felony and sentenced to transportation. *Old Bailey Proceedings Online* (www.oldbaileyonline.org, version 7.0, accessed 7 September 2012; t17490906–86).

[30] Henry Fielding, *The History of Tom Jones, a Foundling* (London: A. Millar, 1749), bk.9, vol.2, p.293.

In Fielding's novel, Tom cannot restrain himself from glancing at the half-naked woman he has rescued, and proceeds to sleep with her, and we might think that this kind of highly sexualised fiction, intended for adults, would have been a world away from children's literature. But the *Lilliputian Magazine* is not prudish in the way that children's books would become. Its retelling of a bible story unabashedly explains that Joseph was 'a very comely youth' and that 'his mistress was so charmed with his person, that she used all the arts of fond persuasion to lure him to her bed' (p.35). And how, one wonders, would a parent explain Polly Meanwell's gratitude for being rescued from a pirate who 'made several attempts on her virtue' or that she 'would not comply with his wicked desires' (p.71)? Or her plea that her rescuer should not 'for a sensual gratification, a momentary pleasure, make me miserable for ever?' (p.71; see also pp.15 and 128) The explicit moralising that periodically rears up in the narratives only adds to the generic confusion. Biddy Johnson, it is carefully explained, was only abducted as a result of her vanity about her appearance and her filial disobedience. Whoever wrote the story evidently knew that such moral lessons ought to form the proper content of a children's book, but chose a curious medium for transmitting them. The impression we get from many of Newbery's early publications is that the authors were feeling their way, and had only a dim sense of what was and was not a 'fit' subject or tone for children's books. At this early date, the proprieties of children's literature had not yet reified.

Besides the novelistic content, the *Lilliputian Magazine* mélange also featured fables, poetry, jests, bible narratives, hymns, recipes, riddles, country dances, letters debating current events (against the cruel sport of cock-throwing, for example, on the occasion of its prohibition in London: p.22) and an eccentric assortment of illustrations. Perhaps the most remarkable sections are the four separate accounts of children's voyages to fantastical regions, as susceptible to satirical and allegorical readings as Swift's *Gulliver's Travels* which they openly emulated. As for *The Fairing*, alongside its fairy tales, stories familiar from standard editions of classical history ('Cincinnatus', p.173) jostle side by side with comic sketches ('Neighbour Tumble-turf, and Neighbour Chopstick', p.183), and moral fables ('The history of Honesty and Knavery',

'Miss Pride and Miss Prudence', pp.169 and 171) with exposés of magic tricks (p.189) and original verse (such as 'Drunken Will', p.178, a poem that Brian Alderson calls 'on the brink of being a limerick'[31]). In and of itself, the book also contributed to, and perhaps revived, a distinct literary genre: the 'fairing', a present traditionally given or bought as a souvenir of a fair. As with his other 'occasion books', including *The Easter Gift*, *Whitsuntide Gift* and *Valentine's Gift* which featured alongside *The Fairing* in the 1764 advertisement, Newbery thus ensured that there was a readymade market for his book. He was by no means the first to do so, books designed for adults to give children as mementoes of the fair having been in print since at least 1589 when the preacher John Stockwood published his *Bartholomew Fairing for Parentes, to bestow upon their Sonnes and Daughters*.

Newbery's *Fairing* went further though. Andrea Immel notes the accuracy of its description and suggests that the book may have been inspired in part by William Hogarth's famous engraving of 'Southwark Fair' (1733–4) or as a memorial to Southwark Fair and its well-known acts (the fair had been closed down for good in 1763, just before *The Fairing's* publication).[32] But the book was designed not only to describe the specific attractions, topography and feel of the fair (in both text and illustrations), but also actually to resemble a fair in its organisation, tone and what Alderson calls 'the almost random whirl of events'.[33] Thus, as the author puts it in a preface, to succeed, the book must be 'written without either Rule or Method, or Rhyme, or Reason … it must be one entire Whole, but a whole Heap of Confusion' (p.162). As such, the book now seems a perfect expression of the *carnivalesque*, the term Mikhail Bakhtin used for those chaotic, rumbustious,

---

[31] Brian Alderson, 'Preface' to *The History of Little Goody Two-Shoes* and *The Fairing* (New York and London: Garland Publishing, 1977), pp.iii–x (p.v). The Limerick form is usually said to have first appeared in print in *The History of Sixteen Wonderful Old Women* (1820) and to have achieved a permanent place in literature with Edward Lear's *Book of Nonsense* (1846).

[32] Andrea Immel, 'The Didacticism That Laughs: John Newbery's Entertaining Little Books and William Hogarth's Pictured Morals', *The Lion and the Unicorn*, 33 (2009), pp.146–66 (p.157).

[33] Alderson, 'Preface', p.vii.

humorous and grotesque texts that either represent actual carnivals or embody their spirit – both of which might be said of *The Fairing*. An allusion in *The Fairing*'s preface to François Rabelais' *Gargantua and Pantagruel* (1532–64), Bakhtin's key example of the carnivalesque, reinforces the point (p.162).[34] Yet for Bakhtin, the carnivalesque is strongly connected with the attempt to destabilise prevailing power structures, even if only temporarily. On the face of it, this is not the case with *The Fairing*. Instead, the book can seem to offer a picture of disorder only as vehicle for the imposition of a series of conventional moral lessons. This reading supports the post-Bakhtinian view that carnival's licensed transgression, by providing a sort of safety valve, ensures that nothing fundamental ever actually changes, and thus that the carnivalesque is, in its effects, ultimately more conservative than radical. Certainly, while it celebrates the carnival, *The Fairing* is circumspect, or even critical, of its ethos: 'A Fair…may be compared to a Journey through Life, where Mankind are always busy, but too frequently in Schemes that are idle and ridiculous'. And, closing the main part of the book: 'You now seem tired of the Fair; and are sensible, I hope…that there is no real Pleasure, but in living a virtuous, peaceable and good Life.' (p.213)

In fact, what we see in *The Fairing* is an attempt to drive a wedge between children and popular culture. Peter Burke writes that before the eighteenth century, 'popular culture was everyone's culture; a second culture for the educated, and the only culture for everyone else', but that by the end of the 1700s, 'the clergy, nobility, the merchants, the professional men – and their wives – had abandoned popular culture to the lower classes, from whom they were now separated, as never before, by profound differences in world view.'[35] The same, thanks to Newbery and those who followed him, was becoming true for children. Before the mid-eighteenth century, their education and their literary pleasures had necessarily been either oral (lessons, sermons, the nursemaid's

---

[34] Bakhtin, *Rabelais and His World*, trans. Helene Iswolsky (Cambridge, MA: MIT Press, 1968). See also Terry Castle *Masquerade and Civilization: The Carnivalesque in Eighteenth-Century English Culture and Fiction* (Stanford: Stanford University Press, 1986).

[35] Burke, *Popular Culture in Early Modern Europe* (New York: New York University Press, 1978), p.270.

tales reviled by Locke) or obtained from religious books (the bible, the psalter, the prayer book) and popular literature (ballads, chap-books, romances). It was the ambition of Newbery's publications to remove children from this vulgar, plebeian culture and to offer them instead something more refined, edifying, bourgeois, and specific to their perceived needs. In *The Fairing*, we see this manoeuvre underway. Although the book lured children in with an offer of the fair, it was intended to replace the need for an actual visit. As its title-page specifies, in the book children 'may see all the fun of the fair | And at home be as happy as if they were there.' (p.159) Fairings were souvenirs of a trip to the fair; this *Fairing* was intended as a souvenir of the whole history of the fair, for its intended readers were supposed to derive their pleasures at home, reading and partaking in polite society, not out among the 'mobbing' masses (p.165).

Indeed, we should think of Newbery's publication as an attempt to bring children into the culture of politeness that had developed during the early eighteenth century. Lawrence Klein writes that this eighteenth-century idea of politeness 'referred…to the pro-tocols of conversation [and] also to its outcomes, the edification and refinement that, it was hoped, would eventuate from polite conversation'. Like other cultural historians, he links it with the civil and to an extent democratic sociability of the new coffee houses, locations where (at least in theory) men of many differ-ent backgrounds could meet for pleasant and mutually instructive discussion, could learn what was taking place in their vicinities and the wider world, and where their manners would inevita-bly be refined as they conversed.[36] Joseph Addison and Richard Steele were its most celebrated proponents, using their periodicals *The Tatler, The Spectator* and *The Guardian* (appearing in succes-sion from 1709–14) simultaneously to distil into print the polite conversation of the coffee house, and to encourage the spread of the coffee houses' polite and inclusive ethos among their readers. The *Lilliputian*, and Newbery's publications in general, evidently shared a similar ambition (though, unlike the coffee houses, they

---

[36] Lawrence E. Klein, 'Coffeehouse Civility, 1660–1714: An Aspect of Post-Courtly Culture in England', *Huntington Library Quarterly*, 59 (1996), pp.30–51 (pp.47–8).

were notably willing to invite female readers to participate in this culture). Some of the statements of intent in the *Lilliputian*'s preface might have come straight from the *Spectator*. Dialogues have been introduced, we are told, to make children 'more dexterous in their conversation', and 'There is nothing more certain and obvious, than that children form their style, as well as their manners, from those they converse with; and next to that of keeping polite company, I don't known any thing so likely to polish their style, as the reading of polite dialogues' (p.3). Addison, in the *Spectator*, said he would 'endeavour to enliven Morality with Wit, and to temper Wit with Morality'.[37] The Newbery publications patently subscribed to this same programme.

Politics and ideology

Rather than focussing on their participation in, and propagation of, a culture of politeness, most recent attempts to root Newbery's publications in their eighteenth-century context have focussed on the ideological work they perform. Typically, *Goody Two-Shoes* has been seen as a product, and propagator, of 'radical bourgeois ideology', to use Isaac Kramnick's term. Its heroine, Kramnick argues, personifies the middle-class values of industry, self-reliance, thrift, honesty and individuality. According to this reading, Margery's story offers a subversively egalitarian challenge to older forms of social hierarchy in which power and status were inherited, by showing how it was possible to earn one's own socio-economic elevation, and moreover, to do it by practicing simple virtues and not through the intervention of the supernatural, as in fairy tales, for instance.[38]

---

[37] Addison, *The Spectator*, 10 (12 March 1711).

[38] Isaac Kramnick, 'Children's Literature and Bourgeois Ideology: Observations on Culture and Industrial Capitalism in the Later Eighteenth Century', in *Culture and Politics from Puritanism to the Enlightenment*, ed. Perez Zagorin (Berkeley: University of California Press, 1980), pp.203–40. For caveats, see Alan Richardson, *Literature, Education, and Romanticism: Reading as Social Practice*, 1780–1832 (Cambridge: Cambridge University Press, 1994), pp.109–12 and Ronald Paulson, *The Beautiful, Novel, and Strange: Aesthetics and Heterodoxy* (Baltimore, MD: Johns Hopkins Press, 1996). Paulson argues that Margery, unlike other protagonists of later

It is difficult to quarrel with the broad thrust of this reading. Margery herself is emphatic about the principles she practises and preaches. 'See what Honesty and Industry will do for us', she tells the children in her school: 'Half the great Men in *London*, I am told, have made themselves by this Means, and who would but be honest and industrious, when it is so much our Interest and our Duty.' (p.124) Master Tommy Thoroughgood in the *Lilliputian Magazine* is just such a man, who from being as a boy 'very diligent and honest, as well as good' (his commercial virtues considered separately from his moral qualities, we note) 'had, by his own industry, and from a small fortune, gained one considerably better' (p.51). Newbery's books were all steeped in a culture of commerce. Many of their inset tales revolve around overseas ventures, the fluctuations of international trade, the rewards of fair dealing and wise investment, and it is no surprise that 'Dick Whittington', the story of a boy who gains his wealth through a shrewd, if fortunate, commercial speculation, is pronounced the favourite fairy tale in *The Fairing* (though it is not strictly speaking a *fairy* tale at all). Indeed, in Newbery's world, the chief danger to society, besides sloth, greed, vanity and other decadent vices, seem to be those arch-enemies of mercantilism, the pirates, who in his books are often lying in wait to intercept trading vessels issuing from the Port of London (pp.71 and 125). It is telling that, even in the *Lilliputian*'s retelling of a bible story, Joseph advises Pharaoh 'to fill all his store-houses with corn during the first seven years; by which means he might gain immense sums of money by selling it again to his people at the approach of the famine', whereas in the Authorised Version, Joseph counsels only that the laid-up food 'shall be for store to the land against the seven years of famine... that the land perish not through the famine.' (p.36)

Reading *Goody Two-Shoes* as a manifesto of the new bourgeoisie helps to explain its remarkable 'Introduction'. The attack on Sir Timothy Gripe and Farmer Graspall, representing the land-owning classes, is uncompromising, specifically of 'the unaccountable

---

eighteenth-century children's books, 'does not succeed or grow rich as a consequence of her industry' but remains 'an outsider, liable to be charged with being a witch' until plucked from humble life by a rich suitor (p.195).

and diabolical Scheme which many Gentlemen now give into, of laying a Number of Farms into one, and very often of a whole Parish into one Farm' (p.93). In powerful language we are told that this process, called enclosure, whereby smaller tenants (like Margery's parents) were evicted from their farms and common grazing and mowing rights ended, 'must reduce the common People to a State of Vassalage, worse than that under the Barons of old, or of the Clans in *Scotland*' (p.93). As Sarah Trimmer, an early critic of children's literature, pointed out in 1802, this was the rhetoric of class war (not, of course, her term) and had, she said, no place in a children's book.[39] Yet this attack on the socio-economic elite permeates *Goody* and Newbery's other works. Patricia Crain's reading of Lady Ducklington's funeral, as described in *Goody*, makes this clear, for instance. Lady Ducklington is made a representative of much that is wrong with the old elite: their profligacy, pride and ostentation, even in death. When Margery dispels the villagers' idea that Lady Ducklington's ghost is haunting the church, she symbolically exorcises the spirit of the aristocracy and exposes and explodes the illusion of social prestige that has kept the aristocracy reverenced and unchallenged for so long.[40]

Yet, within a paradigm that commended industry and deplored idleness, Newbery's publications urged compassion and charity too. The Introduction to *Goody* goes into some detail about the iniquities of the Poor Law as it then stood, and Margery, once she gains her fortune, becomes a 'Mother to the Poor...and a Friend to all who were in Distress', giving freely without enquiry about individual circumstances (p.146). The rendition of 'Dick Whittington' in *The Fairing* similarly includes several warnings against reproaching those who beg on the streets with being work-shy (notably Sir William Thompson's interpolated story: p.193). Parts of the *Lilliputian Magazine* are far more extreme in their attack on inequality. The Angelicans, a fantastical race Jemmy Gadabout meets on his ill-fated voyage, believe '*that no*

---

[39] Trimmer, *The Guardian of Education*, 1 (1802), pp.430–1.

[40] Patricia Crain, 'Spectral Literacy: The Case of Goody Two-Shoes', in *Seen and Heard: The Place of the Child in Early Modern Europe 1550–1800*, eds. Andrea Immel and Michael Witmore (New York: Routledge, 2005), pp.213–42 (especially p.229).

man should secure to himself more of any thing than he has occasion for, and especially if he knows it will be serviceable to another'. Thus, in the ideal society of Angelica, 'there is no such thing as a beggar to be found in their streets.' (p.43) In the Mercolian state, as it was established by the messianic boy-king Turvolo in another of the *Lilliputian*'s voyage narratives, an even fuller kind of equality was apparently endorsed. Here, 'worth and honour are confined to no particular class of people' and status cannot be inherited but must be earned (p.47). Moreover, since, prior to the renewal of the state, 'the ill use of money had corrupted the morals of the people', in the reformed nation King Turvolo 'obliged all the inhabitants every four years to bring their money into the public treasury, from which an equal distribution was again made, to each person his share'. Those who had grown rich began each four-year cycle as equals, receiving nothing save 'the thanks of the community, and some marks of royal favour from the king' (p.48).[41] These were contributions to an eighteenth-century tradition of utopian writing, and were distinctly Swiftian too. As such they might be read as satirising contemporary British society more than advancing a genuine political, social and economic programme.[42] Yet the radicalism of this writing is extraordinary: it is unusual to find such extreme political opinions in any mid eighteenth-century writing, let alone writing for children. Like some of the novelistic and sexual content of Newbery's books, this kind of political material would soon be largely purged from children's literature.

Readership, influence and legacy

The print runs of Newbery's books tended to be between 2000 and 4000 copies: larger than for many other kinds of eighteenth-

---

[41] For further discussion of the apparently republican content of the *Lilliputian Magazine*, see M. O. Grenby, ' "Very Naughty Doctrines": Children, Children's Literature, Politics and the French Revolution Crisis', in *The French Revolution and the British Novel in the Romantic Period*, eds. A. D. Cousins, Dani Napton and Stephanie Russo (New York: Peter Lang, 2011), pp.15–35.

[42] See Gregory Claeys, *Utopias of the British Enlightenment* (Cambridge: Cambridge University Press, 1994).

century publications but, even taking frequent reprints into consideration, reaching only a fraction of the country's juvenile population. Children's literature was a new product, after all, and would take several decades to become an indispensable accessory of even middle- and upper-class childhoods. But Newbery's books were consumed by a wide range of people, socially, geographically and demographically. The list of subscribers appended to the *Lilliputian Magazine* can be interrogated to reveal the gender, location and sometime class of its consumers. Most subscribers were female. Perhaps less surprisingly, most were also from London, particularly from near Newbery's premises in the city, probably reflecting the personal contacts by which subscribers were obtained.[43] That Newbery expected nationwide sales (though the standard retail channels, rather than by advance subscription) is evidenced by the advertisements appearing for the *Lilliputian* in, for example, the *Scots Magazine* (4 January 1752) and the *Newcastle Courant* (2 March 1751). *Goody Two-Shoes*, a few years later, was advertised even more widely in the regional press. The *Lilliputian's* subscription list also reveals a sizeable market in the colony of Maryland. Until the War of Independence, American newspapers routinely carried advertisements for Newbery publications.[44]

In the pricing of his books, Newbery undercut most of his few rivals and it seems that he was attempting to capture quite lowly readers as well as the sort of affluent children who generally feature as protagonists in his books. The 'Author' prophesies the success of the *Lilliputian* because 'there are gentlemen and ladies enough, who will encourage the undertaking, by purchasing the numbers as they come out, either for their own children, or their poor neighbours' (p.4). Jan Fergus, drawing on the surviving order books of a Midlands bookseller in the mid-eighteenth century, notes that a servant, Samuel Hitchins, ordered six copies of *The Fairing*. At the top end of the social spectrum, Fergus has also shown that boys at the high-status Rugby School were large-scale

---

[43] For fuller analysis of the subscription list see M. O. Grenby, *The Child Reader 1700–1840* (Cambridge: Cambridge University Press, 2011), pp.58 and 61–2.

[44] See d'Alté Welch, *A Bibliography of American Children's Books Printed Prior to 1821* (American Antiquarian Society and Barre Publishers, 1972), p. xxvi.

consumers of Newbery publications.[45] Perhaps most readers of Newbery's books were aged between four and twelve, but there is anecdotal evidence that adults relished them too. One witness recounted discovering the grown-up Samuel Johnson 'reading eagerly the last pages of this little book' – given as 'The Village Schoolmistress', but presumably *Goody Two-Shoes*: 'Tears were rolling plentifully down his face. As I entered, he threw the book from him and cried out: 'Psha...but they need not have killed the poor old woman at last.'[46]

Johnson's tears are apocryphal but there can be no doubt that Newbery's publications made a substantial impression. They had their enemies, at least by the 1780s when a new generation of writers could see them as violent and vulgar. For instance, Lady Ellinor Fenn, author of the successful primer *Cobwebs to Catch Flies* (1783), writes in one of her prefaces of her dissatisfaction with a book depicting 'children riding in a *Merry-go-round* – boys and girls tossed up and down; and a great many pretty things' – surely *The Fairing* – adding that because she 'did not like the story at all' she jettisoned the text but cut out the pictures to paste in to a book of her own. But by and large, Newbery's books remained popular – and profitable – as demonstrated not only by the Newbery firm's successive editions but also by the many piracies. Either the whole text or one or more miscellaneous extracts could be purloined, or new material might be presented under a Newbery-like title, or as 'Compiled for the use of all her pupils, by Mrs. Margery Two-Shoes, Governess of A, B, C College'.[47] By the nineteenth century,

---

[45] Fergus, 'Provincial servants' reading in the late eighteenth century' in *The Practice and Representation of Reading in England*, eds. James Raven, Helen Small and Naomi Tadmor (Cambridge: Cambridge University Press, 1996), pp.202–25 (p.205), and *Provincial Readers in Eighteenth-Century England* (Oxford: Oxford University Press, 2007), chapter 3.

[46] From the memoir of Maria Dundas, later Lady Callcott, quoted in the *Children's Books History Society Newsletter*, 40 (April 1990), p.8.

[47] This was the sub-title of a compilation, partly of new material, partly taken from Newbery, given the familiar-sounding title *The Sugar-Plumb; or, Golden Fairing* (York: E. Peck, no date but c.1800?). Perhaps the strangest appropriation of Newbery material was the unacknowledged (and hitherto unrecognised) reuse of the 'History of the Progress of Learning in Lilliput' and 'The History of the Mercolians' from the *Lilliputian Magazine*, and 'An Account of what passed on a journey with old Zigzag'

Goody Two-Shoes had been updated, had been given sequels, had been turned into a popular pantomime, and had spawned such miscellaneous titles as *Little Goody Two Shoes' Quadrilles, Waltzes, & Polkas* (1854) and *Scenes From the Life of Goody Two-Shoes: A Little Play for Little Actors* (1882).[48] As the author of one reworking put it, writing less than 40 years after *Goody*'s first publication, 'so renowned did this little girl become, that her life has been written by more than one author, and her story has been told differently by different writers.'[49]

It is striking just how quickly *Goody Two-Shoes* came to be thought of as one of 'old classics of the nursery' (as Charles Lamb called it), and even as a traditional tale that seemed to have been in circulation from time immemorial.[50] One early nineteenth-century critic professed himself angry that a new generation of modern, instructional books for children had 'superseded Goody two Shoes [*sic*] and Jack the Giant-Killer.' Another tried to argue for the antiquity of 'Dick Whittington' by saying that, in English folklore, it 'holds a rank scarcely inferior to Goody Two-Shoes, to Jack the Giant-Killer, or even to Tom Thumb himself'.[51] Yet another, writing in 1826, was even more incensed that revisers were now tampering with *Goody* than he had been about their modernising of Shakespeare: 'so deeply is the image of the affecting heroine graven in our hearts,' he wrote, 'that even the casual

---

from Newbery's *Valentine's Gift* (1765), in *A Supplement to the History of Robinson Crusoe, Being the History of Crusonia, or Robinson Crusoe's Island, Down to the Present Time* (Newcastle: T. Saint, 1782), a piece of agitprop by the notorious radical Thomas Spence.

[48] Mary Elliott, née Belson, was responsible for a notable new version, *The Modern Goody Two-Shoes; Exemplifying the Good Consequences of Early Attention to Learning and Virtue* (London: William Darton, 1819), and full-length sequel, *The Adventures of Thomas Two-Shoes* (London: W. Darton, 1818).

[49] *The History of Goody Two-Shoes, and the Adventures of Tommy Two-Shoes. With Three Copperplates. A New Edition* (London: Tabart and Co., 1804), p.3. The author may have been William Godwin or his wife Mary Jane Godwin.

[50] Lamb to Samuel Taylor Coleridge, 23 October 1802, *The Letters of Charles and Mary Anne Lamb*, ed. Edwin W. Marrs Jr (3 vols. Ithaca: Cornell University Press, 1976), vol. ii, pp.81–2.

[51] Review of Andrew St. John's *Tales of Former Times* in *The Annual Review*, 7 (1808), 607; *The Imperial magazine*, 7 (1825), 1141.

mention of her name, will at times produce the most powerful emotions.' He added that 'surely there cannot be...any writing that has so magical an effect upon us as Goody Two Shoes.'[52] For the Romantics and Victorians *Goody* was a totem of an older, more innocent era, and, in the age before *Alice*, was widely regarded as the perfect children's book. Reading Newbery's books today we notice their didacticism, and find them thoroughly dated, but these fond memories of *Goody* are reminders of their capacity to charm and delight. By any measure, these are classics of children's literature. What is surprising is how quickly they became so.

---

[52] G. H., 'Thoughts on the purification of Gibbon, Shakespeare, &c. and on the Improvement of Goody Two-Shoes', *Monthly Magazine, or British Register*, n.s., 2 (July 1826), 63–4.

Note on the Texts

The text and illustrations of John Newbery's publications were often revised from one edition to the next. Most changes were minor, but substantial additions, or cuts, could be made, especially when pirated editions of his titles began to appear. The principle for this edition has been to use the earliest obtainable texts, but, for reasons of availability and convenience of reproduction, the illustrations have been taken from subsequent editions.

The Lilliputian Magazine was first published as a periodical, in three parts, in 1751–2, but no copies are known to be extant. The text reproduced here has been taken from a compilation of those three parts 'Published by T. Carnan at Mr. Newbery's' (but actually by John Newbery himself), probably in 1752. The images reproduced here have (with one exception: see p.25) been taken from a later edition, 'Printed for T. Carnan and F. Newbery' in 1772.

The History of Little Goody Two-Shoes was first published in 1764–5, but the text used here is from the 'third edition' published by John Newbery in 1766, which contains some substantial additions. The illustrations have been taken from an edition published by 'T. Carnan, Successor to Mr. J. Newbery' in 1783.

The Fairing: or, A Golden Toy for Children was probably first published in 1764–5, although no edition earlier than 1767 survives. The text and illustrations reproduced here are taken from an edition 'Printed for T. Carnan and F. Newbery' in 1777.

See the Introduction for more details of the publication dates of these titles and the relationship between John Newbery and his successors Thomas Carnan (his step-son), Francis Newbery (his son), and Francis Newbery (his nephew).

Throughout this edition, unusual and archaic spellings, capitalisation and punctuation have been retained, but obvious typographical errors have been silently corrected, including the addition of material (apostrophes, quotation marks, occasionally whole words) evidently missing from the copy-text. The 'long s' (ʃ) has not been kept, except where it features in Goody Two-Shoes' alphabets. The original layout of text and illustrations has been followed where possible, although page breaks in the original texts have not always been retained.

Further Reading

Buck, John Dawson Carl. 'The Motives of Puffing: John Newbery's Advertisements, 1742–1767', *Studies in Bibliography*, 30 (1977), 196–210.

Crain, Patricia. 'Spectral Literacy: The Case of Goody Two-Shoes', in *Seen and Heard: The Place of the Child in Early Modern Europe 1550–1800*, eds. Andrea Immel and Michael Witmore. New York: Routledge, 2005, 213–42

Fergus, Jan. *Provincial Readers in Eighteenth-Century England*. Oxford: Oxford University Press, 2007 (chapters three and four).

Grenby, M. O. 'The Origins of Children's Literature', in *The Cambridge Companion to Children's Literature*, eds. M. O. Grenby and Andrea Immel. Cambridge: Cambridge University Press, 2009, 3–18.

Grenby, M. O. *The Child Reader 1700–1840*. Cambridge: Cambridge University Press, 2011.

Grey, Jill. 'The Lilliputian Magazine a Pioneering Periodical?', *Journal of Librarianship*, 2 (1970), 107–15.

Immel, Andrea. 'Children's Books and School-Books', in *The Cambridge History of the Book in Britain*, vol.5: 1695–1830, eds. Michael F. Suarez S.J. and Michael L. Turner. Cambridge: Cambridge University Press, 2009, 736–49.

Immel, Andrea. 'The Didacticism That Laughs: John Newbery's Entertaining Little Books and William Hogarth's Pictured Morals', *The Lion and the Unicorn*, 33 (2009), 146–66.

Kramnick, Isaac. 'Children's Literature and Bourgeois Ideology: Observations on Culture and Industrial Capitalism in the Later Eighteenth Century', in *Culture and Politics from Puritanism to the Enlightenment*, ed. Perez Zagorin. Berkeley: University of California Press, 1980, 203–40.

Lerer, Seth, *Children's Literature. A Reader's History from Aesop to Harry Potter*. Chicago: University of Chicago Press, 2008 (chapter five).

O'Malley, Andrew. *The Making of the Modern Child: Children's Literature and Childhood in the Late Eighteenth Century* . New York: Routledge, 2003.

Paulson, Ronald. *The Beautiful, Novel, and Strange: Aesthetics and Heterodoxy*. Baltimore, MD: Johns Hopkins Press, 1996 (chapter seven).

Plumb, J. H. 'The New World of Children in Eighteenth-Century England', *Past & Present*, 67 (1975), 64–95.

Richardson, Alan. *Literature, Education, and Romanticism: Reading as Social Practice*, 1780–1832. Cambridge: Cambridge University Press, 1994.

Townsend, John Rowe. *John Newbery and His Books: Trade and Plumb-Cake for Ever, Huzza!* Cambridge: Colt Books; Metuchen, NJ: Scarecrow Press, 1994.

The
Lilliputian Magazine:

or the

Young Gentleman & Lady's
Golden Library

being

An Attempt to mend the World, to

render the Society of Man more

Amiable & to establish the Plainness,

Simplicity, Virtue & Wisdom of the

Golden Age

So much Celebrated by the

Poets and Historians.

Man in that Age no Rule but Reason knew,

And with a native bent did Good pursue: –

Unforc'd by Punishment, unaw'd by Fear, –

His Words were Simple & his Soul sincere.

LONDON.

Printed for the Society and Published by

T. Carnan at Mr. Newbery's, the Bible and Sun

in St. Paul's Church yard.[1]

Freeman

THE
Lilliputian Magazine:

OR, THE

Young GENTLEMAN and LADY's

GOLDEN LIBRARY.

BEING

An Attempt to mend the World, to render
the Society of Man more amiable; and
to establish the Plainness, Simplicity,
Virtue, and Wisdom

OF THE

GOLDEN AGE,

So much celebrated by the POETS and
HISTORIANS.

Man in that Age no Rule but Reason knew,
And with a native Bent did Good pursue;
Unforc'd by Punishment, unaw'd by Fear,
His Words were simple, and his Soul sincere.

LONDON:

Printed for *T. Carnan* and *F. Newbery*, jun. No. 65,
in St. Paul's Church-Yard : but not for *F. Newbery*,
at the Corner of Ludgate-Street, who has no Share in
the late Mr. *John Newbery*'s Books for Children.

M.DCC.LXXII.

[Price One Shilling.]

THE
PREFACE.

IN most of our modern books, a preface has been introduced in conformity to custom; but here 'twill be found necessary to explain the work.

The authors concerned in this little book, have plann'd out a method of education, very different from what has hitherto been offered to the publick; and more agreeable, and better adapted to the tender capacities of children than anything I have seen. The extream novelty of their design, the diminutive size, and the dress in which it appears, may, perhaps, make some people look on it with an eye of contempt; but, I think, merit in every garb should be countenanced, and wisdom be cherished in whatever form it may present itself. Had nobody deviated from the beaten path, we should have had no improvements in the sciences, nor even in the common business of life; and have enjoyed our forefathers ignorance and bigotry, without their simplicity and innocence.

There is no part of the work perhaps more liable to exception, than that of introducing persons of distinction in the dialogues, which may seem above the comprehension of children; but this also has its use; for, by means of this imaginary conversation, children are taught to address their superiors by their proper titles, and according to their different degrees of quality and distinction; and I don't perceive, that those terms are harder to pronounce, than any other in the *English* language.

What the authors propose by it is, to remove that rusticity and aukwardness, which appears in the common people when talking to their superiors, and to make them more dexterous in their conversation. There is nothing more certain and obvious, than that children form their style, as well as their manners, from those they converse with; and next to that of keeping polite company, I don't known any thing so likely to polish their style, as the reading of polite dialogues.

More had been said by way of preface, but the authors, by the following dialogue, have rendered it unnecessary.

✳   ✳   ✳

A
DIALOGUE
BETWEEN
A GENTLEMAN and the AUTHOR.[2]

Gentleman. I Have seen, sir, an advertisement in the papers, of the Lilliputian Magazine, to be published at Three pence a Month: pray what is the design of it?

Author. Why, sir, it is intended for the use of children, as you may perceive by the advertisement, and my design is by way of *history* and *fable*, to sow in their minds the seeds of polite literature, and to teach them the *great grammar of the universe*; I mean, the *knowledge of men and things*.

Gent. But pray, how is that to be done in so small a compass? for you can afford but very little at that price, after you have paid the necessary expences of paper, print, and advertisements.

Auth. Your observation, sir, is very just and rational. But as my principal view is to promote learning, I shall not be afraid of a little expence. In fine, I shall give my young pupils, as much for three pence one month, as I apprehend they will be able to learn before the beginning of another; and if I am so happy as to succeed for the first six months (in which time, the most dry and trifling part of my work will be over) I don't in the least doubt, but there are gentlemen and ladies enough, who will encourage the undertaking, by purchasing the numbers as they come out, either for their own children, or their poor neighbours.

Gent. Why, sir, do you think such a trifling affair will ever engage the attention of people of consequence?

Auth. A trifling affair, sir, do you call it! If education is a trifling affair; I profess to you I don't know what is momentous; and was

I not assured by my friends, that there was some merit in the design, and even in the execution, I should not be so impertinent as to obtrude myself upon the public.

Gent. Your pardon, sir, I do not speak this of your performance, for that I like very well, and will promote it as much as possible, all my children shall have it I assure you: but what I call a trifling affair, is, the price of your book, and for your own sake I wish it had been double.

Auth. You'll please to consider, sir, that the largest book is not always the best, and that books of this sort are to be made as cheap as possible; for there are a great many poor people in his majesty's dominions, who would not be able to purchase it at a larger price, and yet these are the king's subjects, and in their station, as much to be regarded as the rest.

Gent. Sir, I am perfectly satisfied, I like your scheme, and I heartily wish you success in the publication.

Auth. Thank you, good sir, but before we part, pray let me tell you a story, which I think is applicable to the conversation we have had.

"There was in the land of *Lilliput* one Mr. *Mano*, who had a fine house and garden, and adjoining to them a wood in which he took care to nourish a great number of birds, and among the rest he had abundance of eagles and crows: Now it came to pass in spring-time, when birds lay their eggs, that two boys got into this wood of Mr. *Mano*'s, and robbed the nests of one of the eagles and of a crow; but as they were bearing off their prize, who should they meet but Mr. *Mano* himself, who obliged them to carry the eggs back to the nests again. In the midst of their fright and confusion, they accidently put the crow's eggs into the eagle's nest, and the eagle's eggs into the nest of the crow: now in process of time, the young birds were hatched, and grew flush, and the crows observing their supposed mother soar aloft, mounted after her, and out-braved all the birds; while the young eagles that were hatch'd under the crow, insensible of their superior faculties, sat groveling on the ground, and never attempted to mount hither than their inauspicious nurse the crow."

By this excellent emblem[3] is evidently shewn the surprising force and benefit of education. The young eagles, who were by accident hatch'd under a crow, grovel on the ground, and look no higher than their supposed mother; while the young crows, who had the advantage of being nurtured under the eagle, soar aloft, and over-look their fellow-creatures.

As education, therefore is a matter of such vast importance, that our happiness and misery (and in some measure) the welfare of the kingdom and government must rest upon it, what care ought not to be taken, to unloose the minds of children, from the fetters of habit and custom, to enlarge their ideas, enoble their senti-ments, and fix them firmly in the principles of virtue and good manners; for as the celebrated Mr. *Pope* observes,

'Tis *education* forms the tender mind;
Just as the *twig* is bent, the *tree's* inclin'd.[4]

* * *

SOME
ACCOUNT
OF THIS
SOCIETY.

ON the 26th of *December*, 1750, little master *Meanwell* (who had by reading a great many books, and observing every thing his tutor said to him, acquired a great deal of wisdom) perfected his scheme of raising a society of young gentlemen and ladies; and there were then assembled a young PRINCE, several of the young nobility, and a great many little gentlemen and ladies. After they were all seated, master *Meanwell,* by order of the prince, stood up, and made a very pretty speech on the *usefulness* of *learning, and the benefit of being good*; for which he received the thanks of the whole house: and being again seated, they proceeded to chuse proper officers for the management of the society. The PRINCE was elected perpetual president; master *Meanwell*, on account of his great learning was chosen speaker; and the honourable master *Prime* principal secretary, because he could write better than any of the rest; and *R. Goodwill,* Esq; his under secretary or assistant. Master *Meanwell* arose off his seat, and thanked the society for the honour they intended him, but begged to be excused, as there were so many gentlemen of superior birth, fortune and merit, who would better become that elevated place; but the PRINCE replied, Mr. Meanwell, *we are not met here to distinguish ourselves by birth and title, but for our mutual improvement, and to publish what we apprehend may be of use to the world in all the valuable branches of learning. We have already had sufficient instances of your modesty and good manners; but we are all too sensible of your merit and learning to suffer you to decline the chair; therefore, as our moments may be better employed, pray let no more time be lost in fruitless ceremony.* Upon this, Mr. *Meanwell* bowed to the PRINCE, and to the whole society, and then ascended the chair; where being seated, the pieces sent to the several members of the society were read by the secretary, and the following ordered for publication.

* * *

THE
HISTORY
OF
LEO the Great LION;
And of his GRATITUDE.

Communicated by Mr. MALO of
TREBON in AFRICA.

As Master *Billora* and three other little boys were going to school on a fine spring morning, the other three would go out of their way to find a bird's nest. Master *Billora* objected to this, for he was wiser than them, and very unwilling to go; 'tis late, says he, and we ought to make haste to school to learn our books and not loiter thus by the way. But the others intended to draw him in to play truant, for they were very naughty boys. Just as they came to the side of a large wood, and were looking for a parrot's nest, they heard a great lion roar, and saw him coming towards them. They were all terribly frighted, and the other three attempted to run away; but Master *Billora* bid them get up a high tree, that was just by; for, says he, if we run away the lion will certainly overtake us and tear us in pieces, but if we get up this tree he cannot come at us. So they all climbed up the tree, and just as they were got to the first bough, up came the lion. He had been there much sooner, but he was lame. When he came under the tree he looked up at them, and instead of roaring, as lions usually do, he there laid himself down, held up his fore leg and wined. This was a sad situation for four little boys to be in, and, which made it worse, they had left their satchels at the bottom of the tree, and the lion devoured all their victuals; so that they could expect nothing but to be starved or torn in pieces by the lion. When night came on, the other boys cried sadly, and wished they had been at school, and not played truant and run a bird's nesting. Master *Billora* knew that crying would make their case no better, he therefore spoke to them as follows: You now see the consequence of being wicked, and running to play when we should have been at church, or at school; and I hope, if you live to get out of the paws of this lion, you will never be naughty any more. Crying will do us no service, and therefore I beg you would be comforted; we will stay in this tree all night, and perhaps it may please God Almighty to send the lion away before the morning. What gives me great uneasiness is to think what pain our parents will be in for us, and how my poor dear father and mother will bemoan my absence; however, let us say our prayers, and depend upon God Almighty, for he only can deliver us out of the paws of this creature. Don't you remember how *Daniel* was delivered from a whole den of lions? Why then should we despair? 'Tis true, indeed, we are wicked, but let us repent and determine to be good for the future and the Lord will forgive us. This said, they composed themselves in the best manner they could, but it was a dismal night and very dark. About twelve o'clock it thundered and lightened dreadfully, and their fears were continually awakened by the howling of the lions, tygers, wolves, and other wild beasts in the wood. Now they wished for morning, but when morning came how were they surprised and confounded to see their old enemy the lion at the bottom of the tree? Nothing was expected but death, for they were almost perished with hunger, and upon this occasion Master *Billora* addressed himself to them in the following manner:

My dear school-fellows,

We have by our folly, idleness and disobedience, here drawn ourselves into a snare, from which nothing can deliver us but the immediate hand of Providence? you are already so weak for want of sleep and sustenance, that you are scarce able to sit on the tree, and behold our deadly enemy is at the bottom; however, I am not without hopes, for this lion doth not rage and roar as is usual, but whineth as if he was in extreme pain: I will descend the tree, perhaps I may be able to get clear of him as he is lame, and may call somebody to your assistance: but if he should catch me and carry me to his den, you may get off with safety, and 'tis better for one to die than all of us to perish. If I fail in the attempt and am destroyed, commend me to my friends, and the Lord protect you.

This said, he descended the tree on that side opposite the lion, but that creature turned himself with surprising agility, and laid hold on him with one paw before he was well got to the bottom of the tree; and what greatly and agreeably surprised *Billora*, instead of offering him any violence, he only reached out one of his fore paws in which was a great thorn festered. This our young hero extracted, and the grateful beast leaped round him, licked his feet, and behaved in such a friendly manner as induced the other three to come off the tree. The lion ran before them leaping and playing like a spaniel till they came near the town, and after licking *Billora*'s feet again he left them. Now what I am going to tell you may perhaps surprise every body, but it shews the gratitude of the lion, and evidently proves that some beasts have better hearts than some men, which, by the way, is, I think, a scandal to the human species. *Billora* was some years after this, hunting in the same wood, and one of the ladies unfortunately fell off her horse and was very much hurt. *Billora* dismounted immediately to assist her, when out sprung from one thicket of bushes a large tyger, and from another a lion. Both ran towards *Billora* and the lady as if they intended to make them their joint prey. The lion, which was *Billora's* old friend, happened to be fore-most, and immediately upon seeing him, turn'd short, attacked the tyger, and demolished him in a few minutes, and after that ran to *Billora,* and behaved to him in the same submissive manner as before, which agreeably surprised the lady, who apprehended herself in the utmost danger.

Master *Malo,* the young gentleman who sent this account to the society, has now a fine young lion of this breed, which is in all respects as friendly as old *Leo,* and is to him extremely useful; for he carries his satchel to school every day, and waits for him at the school-door to bring him home safe at night. Then he is very quiet, for he never makes any noise but when any of the children tell lies, or are naughty, and then he growls very much and seems angry.

* * *

AN
ADVENTURE
OF
Master TOMMY TRUSTY
And his delivering
Miss BIDDY JOHNSON,
From the THIEVES who were going
to murder her.
Communicated by her Governess.

MISS *Biddy Johnson* was a pretty girl, and learned her book very well, but she was too fond of herself. Her beauty made her proud and disobedient to her parents, and by not taking their advice, and doing as they bid her, she had almost lost her life.

As she was their only child, her papa and mamma were remark-ably fond of her, and thought nothing too good for her either to eat, or drink, or wear. She was always dress'd as fine as a little lady, but her papa and mamma ordered her never to go out but in their company, or with their consent; however, she did not mind what they said, but whenever she had any thing new on, away she run to shew it her play-mates. Pride makes us do many silly things. One day when her new coat and stays[5] were brought home, she got her maid, who was a silly girl, to put her bobs in her ears,[6] and away she ran forsooth without any body with her to see miss *Fanny Tinsel*. Miss *Fanny* was as proud a little girl as any in *London*, she hated every body that was finer than herself, and because miss *Biddy* was dress'd out so, she would not play with her: upon which miss *Biddy* huffed, and left her. As she was going home, she miss'd her way, and, travelling over *London-bridge,* she got as far as St. *George's* church,[7] and there sat down upon a step and cry'd. A woman who was just by came up to her and gave her an orange, and ask'd her whose little girl she was. I am, answered she, miss *Biddy Johnson,* and I have lost my way. Oh, says the woman, you are Mr. *Johnson's* little girl, are you? My husband is looking after you, to carry you home to your papa and mamma; and here, says she, (beckoning to a man that stood by) do you carry this little miss home and I will go along with you; so they took her up, and miss *Biddy* did not cry because she thought they came from her papa and mamma. When they got her out of town, she knew that was not the way home, and began to cry, but the man stuffed a nasty rag into her mouth, and tied a black crape hat-band over that, to prevent her making a noise, and then gave her to the woman, who carried her under her cloak. They conveyed her in this manner over the fields to *Norwood,*[8] and there stript her of her cloaths, and was going to kill her. Master *Tommy Trusty,* as it was a holiday, happened to be in the wood a nutting, and hearing a child cry, made up towards the noise, and looking thro' a bush, he saw miss *Biddy* and the man with a large knife in his hand, just going to murder her. Master *Trusty* was a little boy of very good sense, and great courage, and of a good natured merciful disposition. He was willing to save miss *Biddy, but* how to do it was the question: *I am alone says he,* (reasoning with himself) *but they don't know it. I have innocency and God Almighty on my side, and these wretches have only the devil and guilt on theirs, which will naturally make them afraid; for their consciences will fly in their faces. I'll make a noise,* says he; so just as the villain was about to murder miss *Biddy,* he called out, *Here they are! here they are! and going to kill her.* He then popt a whip he had in his hand, which made the thieves conclude that they were pursued by men on horseback, and they ran away as fast as possible, leaving miss *Biddy*'s cloaths behind them. Master *Trusty* watch'd them out of the wood, and then returned to miss *Biddy,* whom he found with her hands ty'd and crying sadly: but as soon as she saw him she jump'd for joy. Master *Tommy* unty'd her hands, and putting on her cloaths he found that one of her ear-rings and bobs were wanting; but she did not mind that, for, says she, I will never be proud any more, but go home to my papa and mamma, and do every thing they bid me, and be a very good girl. Master *Tommy* went with her. 'Twas night when they came home, and her papa and mamma thinking she was lost, were ready to devour her with kisses. They presented to master *Trusty* a fine library of books and a pretty little horse, as a reward for his courage, and the care he had taken of their daughter; and he has now the satisfaction of having preserved the life of one of his play-fellows, and of being caress'd and esteem'd by Mr. *Johnson*, and all who have heard this story. Miss *Biddy* from being a proud naughty girl is become exceeding dutiful to her parents, obliging to all her play-mates, and charitable to the poor: she now despises fine cloaths, and says, *that virtue and good nature are the best ornaments a young lady can wear.*

* * *

THE
HISTORY
OF
FLORELLA.

Sent by an UNKNOWN HAND,

And may, for ought we know, have been published before.[9]

AN eminent citizen who had lived in good fashion and credit, was by a train of accidents, and by an unavoidable perplexity in his affairs, reduced to low condition. There is a modesty usually attending faultless poverty, which made him rather chuse to reduce his manner of living to his present circumstances, than solicit his friends in order to support the shew of an estate when the substance was gone. His wife, who was a woman of sense and virtue, behaved herself on this occasion with uncommon decency, and never appeared so amiable in his eyes as now. Instead of upbraiding him with the ample fortune she had brought him, or

the many great offers she had refused for his sake, she redoubled all the instances of her affection, while her husband was continually pouring out his heart to her in complaints, that he had ruined the best woman in the world. He sometimes came home at a time when she did not expect him, and surprised her in tears, which she endeavoured to conceal, and always put on an air of chearfulness to receive him. To lessen their expense their eldest daughter, whom I shall call *Florella*, was sent into the country, to the house of an honest farmer, who had married a servant of the family. This young woman was apprehensive of the ruin which was approaching, and had privately engaged a friend in the neighbourhood to give her an account of what passed from time to time in her father's affairs. *Florella* was in the bloom of her youth and beauty, when the lord of the manor, who often called in at the farmer's house as he followed his country sports, fell passionately in love with her. He was a man of great generosity, but from a loose education had contracted a hearty aversion to marriage. He therefore entertained a design upon *Florella's* virtue, which at present he thought fit to keep private. The innocent creature, who never suspected his intentions, was pleased with his person; and having observed his growing passion for her, hoped by so advantageous a match she might quickly be in a capacity of supporting her impoverish'd relations. One day as he called to see her, he found her in tears over a letter she had just received from her friend, which gave an account that her father had lately been stript of every thing by an execution.[10] The lover, who with difficulty found out the cause of her grief, took this occasion to make her a proposal. It is impossible to express *Florella's* confusion when she found his pretensions were not honourable. She was divested of all her hopes, and had no power to speak: but rushing from him in the utmost disturbance, lock'd herself up in her chamber. He immediately dispatch'd a messenger to her father with the following letter.

SIR,
I HAVE heard of your misfortune, and have offer'd your daughter, if she will live with me, to settle on her four hundred pounds a year, and to lay down the sum for which you are now distressed. I will be so ingenuous as to tell you I do not intend marriage; but if you are wise, you will use your authority with her not to be too nice when she has an opportunity of saving you and your family, and of making herself happy. I am, &c.

This letter came to the hand of *Florella's* mother, she opened and read it with great surprise and concern; she did not think it proper to explain herself to the messenger, but desiring him to call again the next morning. She wrote to her daughter as follows:

Dear Child,

YOUR father and I have just now received a letter from a gentleman who pretends to love you; with a proposal that insults our misfortunes, and would throw us to a lower degree of misery, than any thing that is come upon us.

How could the barbarous man think, that the tenderest of parents would be tempted to supply their want, by giving up the best of children to infamy and ruin: It is a mean and cruel artifice, to make this proposal, at a time, when he thinks our necessities must compel us to any thing. But we will not eat the bread of shame, and therefore we charge thee not to think of us, but to avoid the snare which is laid for thy virtue; beware of pitying us, it is not so bad perhaps as you have been told, all things will yet be well, and I shall write my child better news.

I have been interrupted I know not how, I was moved to say things would mend; as I was going on, I was startled by a noise of one that knocked at the door, and hath brought us an unexpected supply of a debt which hath long been owing. Oh! I will now tell thee all: it is some days I have lived without support, having conveyed what little money I could raise to your poor father – Thou wilt weep to think where he is, yet be assured he will soon be at liberty. That cruel letter would have broke his heart, but I have concealed it from him, I have no companion at present besides little *Fanny,* who stands watching my looks as I write, and is crying for her sister; she says, she is sure you are not well, having discovered that my present trouble is about you. But do not think I would thus repeat my sorrows to grieve thee: no, it is to entreat thee, not to make them insupportable by adding what would be worse than all. Let us bear cheerfully an affliction which we have not brought on ourselves; and remember, that there is a power who can better deliver us out of it, than by the loss of thy innocence: heaven preserve my dear child!

Thy affectionate mother,

* * *

The messenger, notwithstanding he promised to deliver the letter to *Florella*, carried it to his master; whom, he imagined, would be glad to have an opportunity of giving it into her hands himself. His master was impatient to know the success of his proposal, and therefore broke open the letter privately to see the contents. He was not a little moved at so true a picture of virtue in distress: but at the same time was infinitely surprised to find his offers rejected. However, he resolved not to suppress the letter; but carefully sealed it up again, and carried it to *Florella*. All his endeavours to see her were vain, till she was assured he brought a letter from her mother. He would not part with it, but upon condition, she should read it without leaving the room. While she was perusing it, he fixed his eyes on her face with the deepest attention. Her concern gave a new softness to her beauty, and when she burst into tears, he could no longer refrain from bearing a part in her sorrow, and telling her too that he had read the letter, and was resolved to make reparation for having been the occasion of it. My reader will not be displeased to see the second epistle which he now wrote to *Florella's* mother.

Madam,

I AM full of shame, and will never forgive myself, if I have not your pardon for what lately I wrote. It was far from my intention to add trouble to the afflicted; nor could any thing but my being a stranger to you, have betrayed me into a fault, for which, if I live, I shall endeavour to make you amends as a son. You cannot be unhappy while *Florella* is alive, nor shall be, if any thing can prevent it that is in the power of,

Madam,

Your most obedient humble servant.

    This letter he sent by his steward, and soon after went up to town himself, to compleat the generous act he had now resolved on. By his friendship and assistance, *Florella's* father was quickly in a condition of retrieving his perplexed affairs. To conclude, he married *Florella*, and enjoyed the double satisfaction of having restored a worthy family to their former prosperity and making himself happy by an alliance to their virtues.

* * *

AN
HISTORY
OF THE
RISE and PROGRESS of LEARNING
IN
LILLIPUT.[11]

Brought over in the Ship SWALLOW by Master RAMBLE.

N. B. *Before we read the following account of these people, 'twill be proper to observe, that, though the vulgar tongue, or common language of* Lilliput, *was a branch of the* Etrolan; *yet that used at court, and among people of the best taste, was the* English; *which the king, out of the great esteem he has had for these people, ever since his acquaintance with Mr.* Gulliver, *has endeavoured to introduce and establish throughout his dominions.*

BILLY HIRON, was born at *Savo* in *Lilliput*. His father was a gentleman of great integrity and honour, and on that account much admired by all degrees of people. It is said of him, that he never told a lie in his life, never injured any body, nor desired any thing that was not his own. He was a compleat master of his passions, possessed a great share of contentment, and was for that very reason exceeding happy. That a *contented mind is a continual feast,* was one of his maxims, and without it, he said, it was impossible to live with any degree of satisfaction. To illustrate and inforce this maxim, be would often mention *Alexander,* who, although he had conquered all the world, and made even kings his slaves, was not satisfied; but cryed like a naughty school-boy, because he had no more business for his ambition.[12] When the great ones in the state were quarrelling about wealth he would laugh at them. *Riches and titles,* says he, *are like bubbles on a running stream, liable to be blown away by the first breeze, or jostled into nothing by the next wave. Why all this anxiety, this longing after riches? You can eat no more, drink no more, sleep no more,*

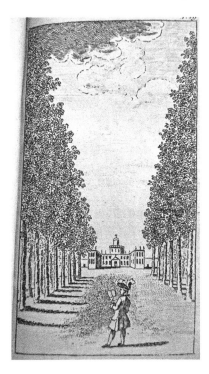

than you do now. Believe me, friends, a woollen coat is as warm as a silken one, and there is as much comfort in a cap as in a crown. Exercise was his chief physick, and tho' a gentleman, he earned his bread before he eat it, that he might eat it with the greater pleasure.

His mother was one of those sort of ladies, who took delight in houshold affairs, and the management of her children. She saw no one she could have liked so well as her husband, or that she thought half so wise. Her principal study was to please him, and, if possible to render him and his family more happy. And by this means, old Mr. *Hiron* and his lady lived a long and peaceful life, though all the rest of the state were continually in arms.

Master *Billy*'s father gave him what learning *Lilliput* at that time of ignorance afforded, which was very little; however, he had good natural parts, and the small assistance he had from his tutor, served to set the machinery of his genius at work. When he was but ten years old, he formed a scheme for the cultivation of learning, but it was rejected by king *Abiho;* this king died however soon after, and left his son *Miram* to reign over the people of *Lilliput. Abiho* was a morose, ill-natured, illiterate prince. He was universally hated for his cruel and inhuman disposition, and his pride and ambition led him into continual wars with the neighbouring nations and domestic quarrels with his own subjects. So that his whole reign was a continued series of perplexity and sorrow.

Miram was a very little boy when he ascended the throne, but he had by reading the best books he could procure, by conversing with master *Hiron,* and by keeping company with those only, who were admired for their virtue and wisdom; acquired the understanding, penetration and prudence of a man. Then he was of a sweet disposition; affable, mild and generous; capable of the strictest friendship, and so great a patron and encourager of truth, that the telling a lie was in his reign deemed a capital crime, and punished with death. *Miram* saw the rock on which *Abiho* split, and avoided it. After the decent interment of his father, whom he loved extremely, he sent for his principal subjects to court, and in a polite and princely harangue, told them, that it should be his study to make his reign agreeable to them. That he bore to them the affection of a father, and he hoped, in return, they would consider themselves as his children, and endeavour to live with each other, as brothers ought to do, in peace and love; otherwise his designs, which were intended to promote their glory and happiness would be frustrated. The assembled applauded the young prince, thanked him for his gracious speech, and then dispersed themselves with hearts full of joy, and minds big with expectation.

King *Miram* having thus dissolved all animosities at home, bent his thoughts towards accommodating matters abroad, with the nations with whom his father was at war. But before he sent ambassadors for that purpose, he issued out orders for a mighty preparation of warlike stores; lest the neighbouring princes, should think his propositions were the effect rather of timidity or fear, than any pious disposition for peace and good neighbourhood.

All the ministers that met at the appointed congress were alarmed at the intelligence they received of these mighty preparations; but king *Miram* assured them by his ambassadors, that though he was in all respects provided to avenge his father's quarrel, yet he should always prefer peace to war, provided he found the same friendly disposition in his neighbours. In fine, by the prudence of the prince, and the vigilance of his ministers, but especially of master *Hiron,* a solid and lasting peace was concluded; which left king *Miram* at full liberty to reform some vices in the state; and to encourage virtue, learning and commerce.

Now liberty sprung up and displayed itself, like the tree of life in paradise; the dews of heaven came upon it, and the earth offered all her nourishment; its trunk was reared in strength and beauty, its branches spread over the land, its root was deep in virtue, on its leaves were the sciences written, the people were happy who dwelled under its shade, and the fruit of glory dropped upon them. King *Miram* took no step without the advice of master *Hiron;* and as he studied the interest and peace both of the prince and the people, the whole Community was exceedingly happy.

How master Hiron *improved the arts and sciences in* Lilliput, *and taught even little children to become polite gentlemen and ladies, will be shewn in the future part of this work; which all our society are desired to learn, for by learning of that account perfectly, they will also learn the arts and sciences.*[13]

* * *

A
LETTER
FROM
Master *LOWTHER*,
TO THE
SPEAKER of the SOCIETY,

In Behalf of honest *Robin*, Mr. *Littlewit's* Dunghill Cock, dated from BARNET,[14] *Feb*. 16, 1750.

Mr. SPEAKER,

I Have often addressed your honour in favour of my own species, and have hitherto been heard with complacency and good-nature; you have always promised me redress, and what is more, you have ever performed your promises to a tittle,[15] and generally been before-hand with my expectation, which is exceedingly meritorious in a gentleman of your high station, and emboldens me to address you again without fear or ceremony; for while my theme is humanity, I know my letters can never offend you.

What I now presume to trouble you with, is the case of honest *Robin*, the dunghill cock of Mr. *Littlewit* of *Barnet*, in the county of *Hertford*. *Robin* was six years a faithful servant to his master, had the principal care of his poultry, and warded off both the hawk and the buzard; he took care likewise to provide his master with eggs for custards, puddings and pancakes; and as the *Littlewits* were ever a lazy family, and apt to lie long in bed, to the great prejudice of their health, and neglect of their business; *Robin*, ever watchful of his master's interest, made it his business to call him every morning. Besides these, he did him other signal services, all out of pure honest love, and hearty friendship, without any gratuity or reward; for he never so much as asked him, either for meat, drink or cloaths; but supported himself, like a good member of society, by his own industry. Yet, notwithstanding this, his ungrateful master Mr. *Littlewit,* hath cruelly, barbarously, and inhumanly twice tied him to a stake, and for *Twopence three throws,* suffered him to be bandied about by all his relations, who are very numerous;[16] for the family of the *Littlewits* is a large family: his head and body were sadly bruis'd, one of his wings and both his legs were broken, and yet his cruel master (who by the way calls himself a Christian) intends next *Tuesday* to prop him up with sticks, that his brother *Littlewits* may murder him by inches, and then feast on fritters,[17] and rejoice over his mangled body.

Cruelty to animals is a crime so great, that in scripture we are frequently admonished to use them tenderly.

There is a passage in the book of *Jonas,* when God declares his unwillingness to destroy *Nineveh,* where methinks that compassion of the Creator, which extends to the meanest rank of his creatures, is expressed with wonderful tenderness — *Should I not spare* Nineveh *the great city, wherein are more than six score thousand persons – and also much cattle?*[18] And we have in *Deuteronomy* a precept of great good nature of this sort, with a blessing in form annexed to it in these words; *If thou shalt find a bird's nest in the way, thou shalt not take the dam with the young, but thou shalt in any wise let the dam go; that it may be well with thee, and that thou may'st prolong thy days.*[19] To conclude; there is certainly a degree of gratitude owing to those animals that serve us; as for such as are mortal and noxious, we have a right to destroy them; but for those that are neither of advantage or prejudice to us, the common enjoyment of life is what I cannot think we ought to deprive them of; and I hope you will admit none into your society, who are guilty of any of those inhuman practices. I am, Sir,

Your most obedient humble servant,
T. LOWTHER.

ORDERS of the SOCIETY in consequence of this LETTER.

Notwithstanding it is the opinion of this wise nation, that the cocks of the present time had a hand in the persecution carried on by the *Danes* seven hundred years ago; yet this society has acquitted them of that fact, and declared them innocent.[20]

'Tis the resolution also of this house, that a committee be appointed to return their thanks to the right honourable the Lord-mayor and the magistrates of this city, for abolishing that inhuman practice of throwing at cocks within their jurisdiction.[21] They have likewise resolved to petition the right reverend, and the reverend clergy to draw up a bill to be laid before the parliament, utterly to abolish the same throughout the kingdom; and to order, that none of their church-yards, which are dedicated to solemnity and peace, shall for the future be stained with the blood of any innocent animal.

N.B. Six little masters of this society, are discharged from the register for being concerned in throwing at cocks last Shrove-Tuesday, *and notice is given them of it by our secretary; so that they are to expect no more books.*

* * *

JESTS.

A Gentleman in company complaining that he was very subject to catch cold in his feet; another, not overloaded with sense, told him, that might easily be prevented, if he would follow his directions: I always get (said he) a thin piece of lead out of an *India* chest, and fit it to my shoe for that purpose. *Then,* sir, (says the *former) you are like a rope-dancer's pole, you have lead at both ends.*

A country farmer was observed never to be in a good humour when he was hungry; which caused his wife to watch carefully the time of his coming home, and always to have dinner on the table. One day he surprised her, and she had only time to set a mess of broth ready for him. He, according to custom, began to open his pipes and maunder over it,[22] forgetting what he was about, and burnt his mouth to some purpose. His wife seeing him in that condition, comforts him in the following manner: *See how it is now; had you kept your breath to cool your pottage, you had not burnt your mouth,* John.

It was an usual saying of king *Charles* II that sailors get their money like horses, and spend it like asses; and the following story, I think, is an instance of it. One sailor coming to another on a pay-day, desired to borrow twenty shillings of him. The money'd man fell to telling out the sum in shillings, but a half crown thrusting its head in, put him out, and he began to tell again, when an impertinent crown piece was as officious as his half-brother had been, and interrupted the tale: so taking up a hand-ful of silver, he cried, *Here* Jack, *give me a handful when your ship is paid, what signifies counting it.*

A taylor sent his bill to a lawyer for money; the lawyer bid the boy tell his master that he was not running away, but very busy at that time. The boy comes again, and tells him he must needs have the money. *Didst tell thy master, said the lawyer, that I was not running away,* yes, sir, says the boy, but he bid me tell you, *that he was.*

One told another, who was not used to be cloathed often, that his new coat was too short for him; *that's true*, said he, *but it will be long enough before I get another.*

Henry IV of *France*, reading the following ostentatious inscrip-tion on the monument of a *Spanish* officer. *Here lies the body of Don,* &c. &c. *who never knew what fear was,* Then, says the King, he never snuffed a candle with his fingers.

The standers-by, to comfort a poor man who lay on his death bed, told him, he should be carried to church by four lusty proper fellows. *I thank you,* said he, *but I had much rather go myself.*

* * *

The STUDENT.[23]

A New

Country-Dance,

Composed
By Master WILLIE DUFF of *Edinburgh*.

Foot it to your partner, and cast off one couple; then foot it and cast up again –

Cross over two couple, and lead up to the top, and then foot it and cast off.

* * *

THE
HAPPY NIGHTINGALE.
A SONG.

BY POLLY NEWBERY.[24]

(45)

I.

THE Nightingale, in dead of night,
On some green hawthorn, hid from sight,
    Her wond'rous art displays;
While all the feather'd choir's at rest,
Nor fowler's snares her joys molest.
    She sings melodious lays.

II.

The groves her warbling notes repeat,
The silence makes her music sweet,
    And heightens every note.
Benighted travellers admire
To hear her thus exert her fire,
    And swell her little throat.

III.

No fear of phantoms, frightful noise,
Nor hideous form her bliss destroys;
    Darkness no terror brings;

But each returning shade of night
Affords the songster new delight;
　　Unaw'd she sits and sings.

IV.

So children who are good and wise,
Hobgoblin stories will despise,
　　And all such idle tales;
Virtue can fortitude instil,
And ward off-all impending ill,
　　Which over vice prevails.

✶　✶　✶

A Receipt to make MINCE-PIES, of such Materials as are cheap,
agreeable to every Palate, and will not offend the Stomach.
Communicated by Miss TASTE.

TAke golden pippins par'd, two pound,[25]
　　Two pounds of well shred good beef suet,
Two pounds of raisins chop'd and ston'd,
　　And put two pounds of currants to it;
Half ounce of cinnamon well beat,
　　Of sugar three fourths of a pound,
And one green lemon peel shred neat,
　　So that it can't with ease be found;
Add sack or brandy, spoonfuls, three,[26]
　　And one large *Seville* orange squeeze;
Of sweat-meats a small quantity,
　　And you'll the nicest palate please.

✶　✶　✶

NEW RIDDLES.

By MEMBERS of the SOCIETY.
To be answered in our Next.[27]

RIDDLE I. Sent by Miss *Bloom*.

THE first hour I was born, to full stature I rose,
And ne'er in a cradle once sought for repose,
But yet there's no mortal on earth ever had,
So many good children, or so many bad.

RIDDLE II. By Miss *Scott*.

Tho' a cook I'm so lean,
        As my ribs may be seen,
But I care not a farthing for that,
        'Cause when vict'als I dress
        All about me confess,
They are cover'd all over with fat.

RIDDLE III. By Miss *Young*.

'Tis true I have both face and hands,
        And move before your eye,
Yet when I go my body stands,
        And when I stand I lie.

RIDDLE IV. By Master *Hunter*.[28]

Like W____TON,[29] in different dress,
        I either sex can ape,
And like her, all mankind confess,
        Have comeliness and shape:
Had she the innocence of me,
        And I her air and parts,
She would a perfect goddess be,
And I should gain more hearts.

* * *

NEW EPIGRAMS.

By MEMBERS of the SOCIETY.

An EPIGRAM, *on seeing two pretty misses dancing a minuet. By Master* Long.

> WHILE now you trace the number of your years,
> Bright innocence in ev'ry step appears:
> Oh ! may you when that number doubles, be
> From every reigning vice and dang'rous passion free.

An EPIGRAM *on a little miss's pricking her finger in gathering a rose. By Master* Grove.

> Cease, JENNY, cease, to pine and grieve,
> The trifling wound you now receive,
>   Admits of present cure;
> Think rather of that cruel smart
> You'll one day cause in DAMON'S heart,
>   Which he may long endure.

An EPIGRAM *on a drowsy dull boy, who was often whipped for not learning his lesson. By Miss* Peggy Smart.[30]

> HOMER, 'tis said, wou'd sometimes nod,
> *Humphry* no certain *Vigil* keeps;
> But like his top defies the rod;
> The more he's whipp'd the more he sleeps.

✳   ✳   ✳

A
PASTORAL HYMN.

By a GENTLEMAN.[31]

I.

How chearful along the gay mead,
  The dasies and cowslips appear,
The flocks as they carelessly feed,
  Rejoice in the spring of the year.
The myrtles, that shade the gay bow'rs,
  The herbage that springs from the sod,
Trees, plants, cooling fruits, and sweet flow'rs,
  All rise to the praise of my God.

II.

Shall man the great master of all,
  The only insensible prove?
Forbid it fair gratitude's call,
  Forbid it devotion and love.
The Lord who such wonders could raise,
  And still can destroy with a nod,
My lips shall incessantly praise,
  My soul shall be wrapt in my God.

✳   ✳   ✳

THE
ADVENTURES
Of
Little TOMMY TRIP.
AND HIS
DOG *JOULER*.

TOMMY *Trip* was but a little tiny fellow; not much bigger than *Tom Thumb*, but a great deal better; for he was a good scholar, and whenever you see him, you will always find him with a book in his hand, and his faithful dog *Jouler* by his side. *Jouler* serves him for a horse as well as a dog, and *Tommy*, when he has a mind to ride, pulls a little bridle out of his pocket, whips it upon honest *Jouler,* and away he gallops, tantwivy.[32] As he rides thro' the town, he frequently stops at the doors, to know how the little children do within; and if they are good and learn their books? and then leaves an apple, an orange, or a plumb-cake at the door, and away he gallops, again, tantwivy, tantwivy, tantwivy.

You have heard how he beat *Woglog* the great giant, I suppose, Have you not?[33] But lest you should not, I will tell you. – As *Tommy* was walking thro' a meadow on a moon-light night, he heard a little boy cry, upon which he called to *Jouler,* bridled him, and galloped away to the place; when he came there, he found *Woglog* with a little boy under his arm, whom he was going to throw into the water. Little boys should never loiter about in the fields, nor even in the streets after it is dark. However, as he had been a good boy in other respects, little *Trip* was determined the giant should not hurt him; and therefore he called to him. "Here you great giant, you *Woglog!* set down the little boy, or I'll make you dance like a pea on a tobacco-pipe! Are not you ashamed to set your wit to a child?" *Woglog* turned round, attempted to seize little *Trip* between his finger and thumb, and thought to have cracked him as one does a walnut; but just as his hand came to him, *Jouler* snapped at it, and bit a piece of his thumb, which put

the giant in so much pain, that he let fall the little boy, who ran away. Little *Trip* then up with his whip and lashed *Woglog* till he lay down, and roared like a town-bull,[34] and promised never to meddle with any little boys and girls again. After he had thus beat the giant, *Trip* put the little boy upon *Jouler,* and carried him home to his father and mother; but upon the road he charged him to be a good boy, and to say his prayers, and learn his book, and do as his papa and mamma bid him, which this little boy has done ever since; and so must all other little boys and girls, or no body will love them.

✳   ✳   ✳

JOSEPH and his BRETHREN.

A SCRIPTURE HISTORY.[35]

THE patriarch *Jacob* had twelve sons; but *Joseph* and *Benjamin* were his peculiar favourites. The former having always the ear of his indulgent father, and telling him several officious stories (which in all probability were too true) to the disadvantage of his brothers, became the object of their scorn and mortal hatred: but what was still a higher aggravation, he openly (and perhaps with a secret pride too) related to them two particular dreams of his own, which portended his future advancement, and their bowing the knee before him.

Upon this, in the height of their resentment, they determined to destroy him. But when *Ruben,* one of his brothers, heard it, he delivered him out of their hands, and that he might carry him again to his father, said, shed no blood, but cast him into the pit. They then stript him of his coat of many colours, and cast him into the pit, and sat down to eat bread. As they were thus regaling themselves, and triumphing over their poor brother's misfortunes, a company of merchants advanced towards them, and they ran instantly to the pit, drew up *Joseph*, and sold him for twenty pieces of silver. When *Ruben*, who had left them, returned unto the pit and saw that *Joseph* was not there, he rent his cloaths, and returned unto his brethren and said, the child is not, and I, whither shall I go?

As the merchants were going from *Gilead* to *Egypt*, they carried *Joseph* with them directly to court; where they soon disposed of him, at an advanced price, to *Potiphar*, a captain of *Pharaoh's* guards.

No sooner was the lad out of sight, but his brethren formed a scheme to conceal their guilt, and delude their poor aged father. Accordingly, they killed a kid, and having dipped *Joseph's* coat into the blood, they carried it directly home to *Jacob,* insinuating, with hypocritical tears in their eyes, that some wild beast had devoured his little darling, and left only his bloody garment.

Jacob, upon this melancholy sight, not suspecting any fallacy, but concluding that *Joseph* was torn to pieces, burst into a flood of tears, and would not be comforted.

In the mean time, *Potiphar,* observing that the lad whom he had purchased was industrious to the last degree, and that all things prospered which he took in hand, made him steward over all his houshold.

Now *Joseph* being a very comely youth, his mistress was so charmed with his person, that she used all the arts of fond persuasion to lure him to her bed; but he turned a deaf ear to her amorous intreaties. Upon this unexpected coldness, her love soon turned to hatred, and she warmly accused him before her husband of insolently attempting to rob her of her honour. *Potiphar*, being too easy and credulous, resented the indignity, and without farther enquiry cast his slave into the king's prison.

Joseph had not been long confined there, before he gave such undeniable evidences of his virtue and wisdom, that the keeper proved as indulgent to him, as *Potiphar* had been before. He had a peculiar talent at interpreting dreams; and it came to pass in process of time, that *Pharaoh* himself had two that were very remarkable, and gave him no small uneasiness: the one, that seven fat kine came out of the river, and grazed in an adjacent meadow, and seven lean kine followed and immediately devoured them; the other, that seven full ears of corn shot out upon one stem, and seven thin ears that very instant sprang up and destroyed them.

Now, tho' *Pharaoh* sent for all his learned magicians to interpret these perplexing dreams, no one was found capable of giving him the least satisfaction, till *Joseph* was brought out of prison.

No sooner was the dream repeated, but *Joseph*, without the least hesitation, assured *Pharaoh* that the seven fat kine, and the seven full ears of corn, denoted seven years of plenty; and the seven lean kine, and the seven thin ears, in like manner, signified seven years of famine: and thereupon he advised the king to fill all his store-houses with corn during the first seven years; by which means he might gain immense sums of money by selling it again to his people at the approach of the famine.

This scheme was highly approved of, and put into execution accordingly: and as every thing came to pass as *Joseph* had fore-told, he was made steward immediately of all the king's houshold, and chief manager under the king over all the land of *Egypt*.

And it came to pass, that the famine extended as far as the land of *Canaan* where *Jacob* lived; who wanting the common necessaries of life, sent all his sons (except *Benjamin*) down to *Egypt* to buy corn for his subsistence. Now *Joseph* saw his brethren and knew them, but made himself strange; and speaking roughly to them, said, Whence came ye? And they said, From the land of *Canaan* to buy food. But *Joseph* accused them of being spies, and told them, that they were come to see the nakedness of the land. And they answered, We are no spies; but thy servants are twelve brethren, the sons of one man in the land of *Canaan*; and behold the youngest is this day with our father, and the other is not. 'Tis well, said *Joseph,* and hereby ye shall be proved; for, by the life of *Pharaoh*, ye shall not go hence unless your younger brother come unto me. Send one of you, and let him fetch your brother, and ye shall be kept in prison, that your words may be proved. And he shut them up for three days; and on the third day, he said unto them, This do and live, for I fear God. If you be true men, let one of your brethren be bound in the house of your prison; and go ye, carry corn to your father; but bring your brother to me that your words may be verified, and ye shall not die. In this distress, they reflected on their ill treatment of *Joseph*, and said, Surely for his sake is this evil come upon us. And *Reuben* upbraided them, saying, "I spoke to you not to hurt the child, and ye would not hear me: and now behold his blood is come upon us." All this was spoken in the presence of *Joseph*; but they knew not that he understood them, for he conversed with them by an interpreter. *Joseph* turned from them, and wept; and returning again took *Simeon,* and bound him before their eyes. Then he commanded their sacks to be filled with corn, and gave secret orders to put each man's money in his sack. Now, when they were departed, one of them opening his sack to give his ass provender, espied the money, and shewed it to his brethren; and they were sore afraid, and said one to another, Why has this evil happened to us? And they came to *Jacob,* and told him all that had befallen them; and that the lord of the country had demanded their brother *Benjamin.* And *Jacob,* their father, was sorrowful, and said, Me have ye bereft of my children; *Joseph* is not, and *Simeon* is not, and ye will take *Benjamin* also. And *Ruben* and *Judah* comforted their father, and promised to restore *Benjamin*, if committed to their care. So *Jacob* dismissed them with a present to the lord of the country, and double money in their sacks. Now, when *Joseph* saw *Benjamin,* he said to the ruler of his house, bring these men home, slay, and make ready, for they shall dine with me at noon. And his brethren were afraid, because they were brought into the house. Howbeit, *Simeon* their brother was brought out unto them, and they were kindly received. As soon as *Joseph* came in, they brought him their presents, and made obeisance to him. When *Joseph* however saw his brother *Benjamin*, he could not contain himself, but retired and wept. Howbeit, at dinner he washed his face, and returned to them again. And he took and set messes before each of them, but *Benjamin's* mess was five times as big as the rest.[36] And he commanded his steward to fill their sacks with corn, and put each man's money into his sack, and his silver cup into the sack belonging to *Benjamin.* Now when they were got out of the city, he sent a messenger after them, who accus'd them with stealing the cup. But they said, "We have neither taken gold nor silver from thy lord. Search each man's sack, and with whom it is found let him die, and we will be bondsmen for ever." And the cup was found in *Benjamin's* sack. And they rent their cloaths, and returned to the city. And *Judah* and his brethren came to *Joseph's* house, and fell before him to the ground. And *Joseph* said, What deed is this that ye have done? Did not ye know that I could divine? And *Judah* said, "What shall we say unto my Lord, or how shall we clear ourselves? God has found out the iniquity of thy servants, and we are thy bond-slaves." But *Joseph* answered, God forbid! The man with whom the cup is found shall be secured, but get ye up in peace to your father. And *Judah,* came near, and said, "O my Lord, let thy servants I pray thee, speak a word in my Lord's ears, and be not angry; for thou art even as *Pharaoh.* When thou didst command thy servants to bring this our brother down, we could not prevail with our father to part with him; for he said, My son *Joseph* is torn in pieces already, and *Benjamin* will perish also. If ye take him from me, and mischief should befal him, ye will bring down my grey hairs with sorrow to the grave. Now, therefore when I come to my father, and the lad is not with me, he will surely die. Thy servant become a surety for the lad, saying, If I bring him not unto thee again then will I bear the blame for ever. So I pray thee let thy servant be a bondsman instead of the lad, and send him up with his brethren; for how can I go up to my father, and see the evil that will befal him?" At this *Joseph* could no longer refrain, but ordered every man to go out of the room, before he made himself known to his brethren. And he wept aloud, and said, I am *Joseph* your brother. Doth my father yet live? And his brethren could not answer him, for they were troubled at his presence. And he said unto them, Come near I pray you; and they came near. And he said, "I am *Joseph* your brother, whom ye sold into *Egypt.* Now therefore be not grieved, nor angry with yourselves, that ye sold me hither; for God did send me before you to preserve life: So 'twas not ye that sent me but the Almighty. Haste ye, and go my father, and say unto him, Thus saith thy son *Joseph,* God hath made me lord of all *Egypt.* Come down unto me, tarry not: And thou shalt dwell in the land of *Goshen,* and there will I nourish thee, lest thou and thy houshould come to poverty; for there will yet be five years famine. Behold your eyes see, and the eyes of my brother *Benjamin*, that 'tis my mouth that speaketh unto you. Tell my father all my glory in *Egypt*, and of all that ye have seen; and ye shall haste, and bring down my father hither." And he fell upon his brother *Benjamin's* neck and wept, and *Benjamin* wept upon his neck. Moreover, he kiss'd all his brethren, and wept upon them, and after that his brethren talk'd with him freely.

This pathetic interview came to the ears of *Pharaoh*, who ordered *Joseph* to send waggons out of the land of *Egypt* to bring down his father, and *Joseph* did so, and gave them provisions for the way. And to each man he gave also changes of raiment; but to *Benjamin* he gave 300 pieces of silver, and five changes of raiment. And he sent his father twenty asses laden with the good things of the land. But when they came to their father, and told him, saying, *Joseph* is yet alive, and is governor over all the land of *Egypt, Jacob's* heart fainted, For he believed them not, and when they told him the words of *Joseph,* and he saw the waggons that were sent to carry him down, the spirit of Jacob revived, and he said, it is enough, *Joseph* my son is yet alive; I will go and see him before I die. So *Jacob* made ready to go down into *Egypt,* and *Joseph* prepared his chariot to meet him, and presented himself to his father; and he fell on his neck, and wept greatly; and *Israel* said unto *Joseph*, now let me die; since I have seen thy face, and thou art yet alive, O my son.

* * *

A
Narrative of a VOYAGE to the Island of ANGELICA:
By Master JEMMY GADABOUT.

MASTER *Jemmy Gadabout,* the only son of an eminent merchant in the city, was an extraordinary fine boy, and very good; but was often brought into difficulties, by a share of curiosity, seldom

to be found in persons of his age, which was now about ten. He spent all his pocket-money in going to see wild beasts and strange fish, and had more joy in viewing an *Indian* prince, than another would have had in eating a ginger-bread king.[37] He possessed a great portion of personal bravery; he was the cock of his seat in the school; neither would he have refused, upon a proper occasion, to have encounter'd *Jack* the *Giant-killer* himself.

About the year 1741, Mr. *Jonathan Gadabout,* his father, was preparing to make a voyage in person to the *West-Indies*; he having some affairs to settle in *Jamaica,* which could not be managed without his presence. The day before his departure, Master JEMMY, as was his constant custom both morning and evening, came to ask his Papa's blessing, which he did with more than usual earnestness; and when he had obtained it, he remained still on his knees, urging that he had still another favour to ask. "Name it, my

child, says his father." *Why, it is*, replied he, *that I may accompany you to the* West-Indies. Nothing could have surprised Mr. *Jonathan Gadabout* so much, as a request of this nature, from a child so young! He was however determined not to comply with it; but being a very tender parent, he condescended to give him some reasons for his refusal. He remonstrated to him, that he was by no means able to bear the fatigues of the ocean, or the change of the climates. He observed to him, that such a scheme would be taking him from his books, and teachers, and be squandering that time, which, at his age, was particularly precious.

These things, and many more he urged, to dissuade our sanguine young hero; who, nevertheless, still remained on his knees. He declared he was not at all alarmed at any danger, which he must share in common with the best of parents, whom, he desired to recollect, that he never could be terrified with nonsensical stories of witches and hobgoblins, as naughty boys were. As for his books, they might be sent on board with him: And with regard to his master, he could have none abler, or better, than his dear papa. In short, with tears, intreaties and embraces, he at length so wrought on Mr. *Jonathan*, that he consented; and they went on board the *Charming Nancy*, Captain *Flipsop* commander, on the 11th of *June O. S.* 1741, and the 12th they set sail with a fair wind.[38]

Every thing went on prosperously for some days; Master JEMMY was not in the least sea-sick, and clamber'd up the ropes with the activity of a squirrel. But after their passing the channel about a day's voyage, on the great *Atlantic*, they spied a vessel of an enormous size, and of a form so singular, that they could at no rate guess to what country she belonged; and, to say the truth, they must have been conjurors at least to have found them out; for they were a crew of the *Angelicans*, those sagacious people, whom nature has not only furnished with two eyes in their foreheads, but with a supernumerary one on the tip of the right-hand middle finger. By making a proper use of this eye, as Master JEMMY afterwards discovered, they can see into the hearts of men, which if they appear the least polluted, render them incapable of being subjects to the monarch of *Angelica*.

When they came up with *the Charming Nancy*, they hoisted an artificial Olive-branch, form'd entirely of emeralds, and white wands composed of the purest pearl, upon which Captain *Flipsop* very rightly concluded they intended no violence. They boarded the ship, however, and upon so near a view, appeared to be no more than a gigantic sort of *Lilliputians*, about the size of the fairies in Mr. *Garrick's Queen Mab.*[39]

The commanding officer ordered all the *Charming Nancy's* crew upon deck, and put the middle finger of his right hand down the throats of every man, one after another, but shook his head terribly, till he came to Master JEMMY, who was the last he examined; and then he cried out with a voice of transport, *Pegill pogosi,* which we have since learnt signifies, *he is spotless and will do.* – Upon which they took JEMMY aboard their own vessel from the arms of his weeping father, whom we must leave, at present, to accompany his son to *Cherubinium,* the capital city of the kingdom of *Angelica,* an island in the Golden Ocean.

This city is built on the summit of a hill, which overlooks the sea. As the country round it abounds with the finest marble, gold, diamonds, rubies, and other precious stones, 'tis no wonder the buildings should be more superb and grand than any thing the gentle reader can conceive. The streets are spacious; their public structures, and indeed all their houses are lofty, and nobly designed; and as the outer walls are marble and jasper, the window frames studded with diamonds, and the roofs, instead of tiling, overlaid with sheets of pure gold, the city, when the sun shines, makes a glorious appearance, and when you are at sea, has a most surprising effect. *Cherubinium* is surrounded with orange and citron groves, overtop'd by several rows of stately pines at a distance; and to render the place more romantic and amazing, nature has formed two large cataracts, one on each side of the city, which pour their crystal streams down the hill with great rapidity; and the noise of those water-falls, when echoed back by the distant woods, is more entertaining than the most harmonious music.

Between these cataracts, and just opposite the south gate of the city, is a large bason, made for their shipping, with a good key,[40] on which master *Jemmy* was landed. No sooner was our young traveller ashore, but he was surrounded by a croud of spectators, who all behaved to him with great politeness, and seemed highly delighted with the figure he made, having never seen such a creature before. I forgot to inform my reader, that Mr. *Jonathan Gadabout*, before he parted from his son, took care to fill both his fob-pockets with money to secure him from want; which piece of paternal affection had almost cost poor *Jemmy* his life. 'Tis a maxim with the *Angelicans, that no man should secure to himself more of any thing than he has occasion for, and especially if he knows it will be serviceable to another:* For they say a man's carrying more money than he wants, is as absurd as a man's wearing two great coats. By means of this maxim which is carried into execution by a law, the *Angelicans* have all necessaries in common, and there is no such thing as a beggar to be found in their streets. Now when master *Jemmy* came to be examined and searched, as the custom is in that country, and money being found in both his pockets, he was suspected of having a bad heart, and this question was put to him, *viz. Whether there were not several persons of his own country on board his ship that had none? Jemmy* answered in the affirmative, and all the people cried out, *Cog ma Gootha! Cog ma Gootha!* that is in *English*, let him suffer! let him suffer! upon which master *Jemmy* was thrown into a prison, where he endured innumerable hardships; for the gaolers there are not like those in *England*; they would not accept of any bribe to lessen his confinement, or to remove his chains, but behaved to him in all respects as their law directed.

Master *Gadabout*, after being confined about a month, was taken very ill, which being made known to the magistrates by the gaolers, who are in that country mighty honest good people; a physician was ordered to attend him. The physicians of *Angelica* don't affect an unintelligible jargon of unmeaning syllables to give a high opinion of their knowledge, as is customary in some other countries; nor do they ever destroy their patients by an inundation of physic; what they principally regard is the nature of the disorder, and the constitution of the patient; and towards a true investigation of both these, the eye at the end of the middle finger doth not a little contribute, as the reader will see in our next volume.

As soon as the doctor had thrust his eye-finger down *Jemmy's* throat, he turned to the magistrates, and delivered himself in the following manner.

"This patient has heretofore used a great deal of exercise, and since his confinement here has been in a state of indolence, by which means the tubes and glands, or pipes and strainers, whereof the body is composed, being deprived of their usual activity or motion, are as it were rusted over, like the wheels of a jack[41] for want of use; you must therefore *calbolade* him; but give him no other physic."

Master *Jemmy* was very earnest to know what physic they would prepare for him, and often made signs to the nurse for his medicines; but instead of *Pills, Potions, Bolusses, Draughts, Lotions,* and *Liniments,* he was surprised to see four of the strongest *Angelicans* enter the next morning with a blanket; however, amazed as he was, they threw him in, and carrying him up to the sunny side of the hill, there first swung him, and after that tossed him gently, till he was in a profuse sweat, and then being wrapped up in the blanket, he was again conveyed home to his own bed.

Jemmy the next morning complained that he was cold, which the doctor being informed of, ordered so large a parcel of billet-wood into his apartment, that you would have thought he had intended to burn down the whole house, and on that score *Jemmy* was in some pain; but when signs were made for him to carry this wood up stairs, and lay it in the room above, his fears dispersed, and finding himself sufficiently warmed, and much better for the exercise, he every day during his confinement, carried the same wood up stairs and down, till he was both warmed and weary, and by that means soon recovered both his health and strength. And this method of getting well without physic, and keeping himself warm without the expence of fire, *Jemmy* has desired us to publish for the benefit of the *British* nation.

N. B. Here it unfortunately happens that we are obliged to break off, and that abruptly, which may seem somewhat like a disappointment to our readers. However, as Mr. Jonathan Gadabout *has unhappily lost, or mislaid, the papers that came from his son, we must beg of our readers to suspend their curiosity till these valuable materials can be obtained, for the recovery of which a reward is hereby offered of* twenty thousand pounds.

* * *

THE
HISTORY
OF THE
MERCOLIANS.

Communicated by
Master BROLIO of LILLIPUT.

The Road to the Temple of FAME *is through the Temple of* VIRTUE.

THE MERCOLIANS, a people who possessed an island in the *Lilliputian* seas, had by their industry, trade, and commerce, acquired immense riches. By their shipping they made the product of all nations their own, and the inhabitants of the neighbouring isles, and on the continent, were their slaves and dependants. Nothing, however, is so difficult to manage as too much wealth; and a state may be crushed under the weight of its own power, which was the fate of the MERCOLIANS. They grew proud, insolent and idle. The only use they made of their riches was to purchase them new invented pleasures. They sunk in down-beds, and grew effeminate; exercise, which strings the nerves and preserves health, was a stranger to them; they turned day into night, and night into day, and wasted their most valuable and precious time, in routs, drums, and riotous assemblies: but see at once the force of human folly, and the end of human grandeur! They made a law to naturalize the slaves and refuse of other nations; they took counsel of strangers; they chose their generals and officers from a foreign people, and were at last plundered and dispossessed of their property by their own dependants. Such was the fate of the MERCOLIANS; and may this be a warning to all future states.

In this confusion some of the best families left MERCOLIA, and took possession of an island uninhabited in the same seas, but were followed by their enemies, who drew up in battle array to destroy them. At this instant of time, when no prospect of safety remained, and every man expected his fate, Master TURVOLO, a lad of about fourteen years, arose, and thus addressed himself to the MERCOLIANS. *"Brethren and you men of* MERCOLIA! *let not fear drive you to madness! you have lives, you have families, you have effects worth preserving, and the means is in your hands to do it. Let every man deliver to me his money, the only source and cause of his misfortune, and I will deliver you from these people, who from being your slaves and dependants, are now become your lords and dictators."* He then took a large heap of money which he divided into three hundred bags; untied, and distributed those bags to the same number of men; to each man his bag; and placed them behind those of his friends who were armed; and when the pursuers came upon them, those men as they were directed, scattered the money upon the ground, which diverted the soldiers from their duty, and set them to fighting among themselves; and the MERCOLIANS stood at a distance and beheld them destroying one another, till such time as their forces were sufficiently weakened, and then they turned upon them, and overthrew them with a great slaughter. After this Master TURVOLO was placed at the head of the people, and made their king; and in order to establish in them virtuous and good principles, he erected two temples, one whereof was called the temple of FAME, and built on the top of a high hill, fortified round with a strong wall and deep ditch; and the other was placed in the middle of the road, leading to that on the hill; so that there was no coming through it; and this was called the temple of VIRTUE. The first portal of this temple was dignified with this inscription, namely,

The Road to the Temple of FAME *is through the Temple of* VIRTUE.

And after passing through a spacious court, a beautiful portico presented itself, on which was written in azure and gold the following letters, *Thou shalt love the* LORD *thy* GOD *with all thy heart, with all thy soul, and with all thy strength, and thy neighbour as thyself.*[42]

In the temple of FAME were registered the names of all those who were good men, whether ploughmen, tradesmen, or whatever else; (for worth and honour are confined to no particular class of people) and seals were given them at the public expence, as a testimony of their esteem;[43] but to those who were lazy, indolent, and did nothing for the service of the community, no seals were given, nor were they suffered to enter the temple. And if at any time those who had procured that honour degenerated, that mark of esteem was taken from them, and a badge of infamy placed on their backs, which they were obliged to wear, or abandon their

friends and country. Nor did either honour or infamy descend from the father to the son, for every man was to win his own laurels, and be accountable for his own actions *only.*—Besides this, as the ill use of money had corrupted the morals of the people, rendered them effeminate, and overthrew them before; he obliged all the inhabitants every four years to bring their money into the public treasury, from which an equal distribution was again made, to each person his share; and those who had multiplied their stock by honest means, had the thanks of the community, and some marks of royal favour from the king.

Thus did little king Turvolo raise a ruined state, and make a miserable people happy; for, in a few years, peace reigned in every breast, and plenty smiled in every valley: They had no ambition but of excelling in virtue, and no contentions, but who should be most religious and most just. Locks, bolts, and bars, they had no occasion for, since thieves there were none, nor did they need any of the dreadful instruments of war: – *For every man loved the* Lord *his* God *with all his heart, with all his soul, and with all his strength, and his* Neighbour *as himself.*

* * *

THE
HISTORY
OF
Master TOMMY THOROUGHGOOD,
AND
Master FRANCIS FROWARD,
Two Apprentices to the same Master.

Inserted at the Request of several Gentlemen of the Common Council of the City of LONDON.[44]

MASTER *Thomas Thoroughgood*, the younger son of a country gentleman, was put out apprentice to an eminent tradesman in *Cheapside*.[45] The master finding his business increase, was obliged to take another about two years after, whose name was *Francis Froward*.

Thomas had behaved exceedingly well, was very diligent and honest, as well as good; he used to say his prayers constantly every morning and night; he never went to play when he should be at church or about his master's business; never was known to tell a lye, nor ever staid when he was sent on an errand. These rare qualifications had gained him the affections of his master and mistress, and made him a favourite in the family before *Francis* came to them. It was in a great measure owing to master Tommy's character in the Neighbourhood, that Mr. *Froward* was induced to comply with the master's demands, not doubting but his son, in such a happy situation, and with a companion of so sweet a disposition, would one day turn out to his satisfaction, and be a comfort to him in his old age.

Francis, in the first year of his apprenticeship, began to discover the natural bent of his inclination. He chose to associate himself with naughty boys in the streets, and seemed to place his whole delight in loose and idle diversions; he neglected the business of the shop when at home, and entirely forgot it when he was abroad. These, and many more indiscretions of the like nature, *Tommy Thoroughgood* concealed at first from his master, though not without some inward uneasiness.

In the fourth year's service, our young spark, who was an only child, and heir to a pretty fortune, gave farther proofs of his vicious turn of mind, and frequently launched out into follies and debaucheries of a more heinous nature; for now he made no scruple of absenting himself from church on the Lord's day; always staid out late when he knew his master was engaged in company, and at such times very rarely returned home sober; nay, he had sometimes the assurance to lie out of his master's house all night. In order to deter him from pursuing this wicked course of life, Mr. *Thoroughgood* threatened to inform his master of his scandalous behaviour, and to acquaint his parents of his misconduct. But alas! all these menaces prov'd ineffectual, and instead of working out his reformation, served only to heighten his resentment, and to raise daily squabbles and animosities between them. Hereupon Mr. *Thoroughgood* finding all his good offices hitherto thrown away, at length determined no more to meddle in the affair, or even to offer his brotherly advice; but to leave the unhappy youth to follow the dictates of his own perverse will; being resolved at the same time to take particular care that he should not, in any of his mischievous frolicks, defraud his master, and thereby cast an odium upon his fellow-prentice.

The master was chosen alderman of the ward,[46] and Mr. *Thoroughgood* was out of his time in the same year;[47] and from his faithful service, and unblameable conduct, had now the whole management of the trade, as well abroad as at home, committed to his care and inspection. This great charge oblig'd him to keep a stricter eye over *Francis's* behaviour, who was just entering into the last year of his apprenticeship, and imagined his actions were above the cognizance of one, who, the other day was but his equal; and on this account would neither bear his reproof, nor hearken to his admonition; but continued to riot in all the follies and degeneracies of human nature, till his apprenticeship was expired. So true it is, that *the wicked hateth reproof, but the wise man lendeth his ear to instruction.*

Mr. *Francis* having been for a long while impatient of a servile life, was now become his own master, and seem'd eager of putting himself upon a level with his late companion. To effect this, he goes down to his father, and prevails upon him to set him up in the business, that he might trade for himself. The reins were no sooner laid on his neck,[48] than he gave a loose to his sensual appetites, and in little more than four years had a statute of bankruptcy taken out against him. The unexpected news of this fatal event instantly broke his mother's heart, nor did the old gentleman survive her long. Hereupon our heir was obliged to sell the personal and mortgage the real estate, to procure his liberty, and to satisfy the assignees. In this sinking situation, after the days of mourning were over, he lett the house his father lived in, and returned again to *London*, where he purchased a handsome equipage, commenced the fine gentleman, frequented the balls, masquerades, playhouses, routs, drums, &*c.* &*c.* and cut as good a figure as the best of them. But here let us leave him for a while, and turn our eyes to a worthier object.

In the same space of time which Mr. *Froward* took to squander away a good estate, Mr. *Thoroughgood* had, by his own industry, and from a small fortune, gained one considerably better, and was in a fair way of increasing it. The former made pleasure his business, but the latter made business his pleasure, and was rewarded accordingly. The alderman, who by his own application and Mr. *Thoroughgood's* assiduity, was grown very rich, had no child now living but a daughter, of whom both he and his lady were extremely fond; they had nothing so much at heart as to see her well settled in the world. She was the youngest, and just now turn'd of twenty. She had many suitors, but resolved to encourage none without the consent of her parents, who would often, when by themselves, tell her that it was their joint opinion she could not dispose of herself better than to Mr. *Thomas,* and would frequently ask how she liked him? for they would be unwilling to marry her against her own inclination. Her usual answer was, "Your choice shall be mine; my duty shall never be made subservient to any sensual passion." This reply was not so full and expressive as they expected; and as mothers are commonly very dexterous in finding out their daughters maladies, madam had good reason to believe from some observations she made on miss's behaviour, that her affections were already fixed, and that she was deeply in love with somebody else, which was the cause of her unusual anxiety. Hereupon, as she was sitting at work one evening in a melancholy posture, they call'd her, and desired to be inform'd whether the husband they proposed was disagreeable to her, if so, she should chuse for herself.

The young lady (after some hesitation) with blushes confessed her regard for Mr. *Thoroughgood;* which gave infinite satisfaction to the alderman and his lady, who were overjoyed at the prospect they had of marrying their daughter to a person of such prudence, integrity and honour.

The next day, as soon as dinner was over, the alderman and his lady withdrew, and left the two lovers together all the evening; from this interview they became sensible of each other's approaching happiness, and about a month after were joined together, to the great satisfaction of all parties concerned. From this day the bridegroom was taken into partnership, and transacted the whole business himself. In process of time his father-in-law died, and left him in possession of all his substance. He succeeded him also in his dignity, and after having served the office of sheriff, was in a few years called to the chair.[49]

Mr. *Froward*, whom we left a while ago pursuing his pleasures and wicked inclinations, had long before this time been reduced to poverty, and like many other thoughtless wretches, betook himself to the highway[50] and the gaming-table in hopes of recovering a lost fortune. He had followed this destructive trade with some success, and, without being discovered, above three years; but was at length taken near *Endfield*,[51] and brought to his trial at the *Old-Bailey*,[52] during his fellow-prentice's mayoralty, and cast for his life.[53] When he was brought to the bar to receive sentence, his lordship recollecting Mr. *Froward's* name, examined who he was, and asked if he was not the same person that served his time with Mr. Alderman ***, in *Cheapside*. This he positively denied; but notwithstanding he used all possible means to disguise himself, his person and speech betrayed him. My lord, animated with the principles of compassion and benevolence, and imagining that his design of concealing himself in this wretched situation

might very probably proceed from shame or despair, took no farther notice of it in court, but forgetting his present disgrace, as
well as his former arrogance and indiscretion, privately procured
his sentence to be changed into transportation for life.

The ship in which Mr. *Froward* embarked, by stress of weather
drove into a certain port in *Jamaica*, where he, in less than ten
days, was sold to a noted planter, and doom'd to perpetual slavery.
You may imagine how shocking this prospect must appear to a
gentleman, who had just before squandered away a good estate in
indolence and pleasure, who never knew what it was to work, nor
had ever given himself time to think upon the nature of industry.
However, he no sooner began to reflect upon his present wretched
situation, and his late providential deliverance from death, than
he also began to repent of his former transgressions; and finding himself in a strange country, unknown to any person about
him, he patiently submitted his neck to the yoke, and endured his
servility with an uncommon fortitude of mind. In the first place,
he determined during all the time of his labour, to offer up continual thanksgivings to Almighty God for his manifold mercies
bestowed on so unworthy a creature, and to devote all his leisure
hours to the duty of repentance. His next resolution was to obey
his master's commands, to serve him faithfully, and to perform
whatever business was imposed on him, so far and so long, as his
health and strength would permit; not doubting but the same
God, who had preserved him hitherto, in such a wonderful manner, would accept the oblations of a contrite heart, and enable
him to go thro' it with courage and chearfulness.

The first month's service, as he himself told me, went very hard
with him. His hands blistered, his feet grew sore and raw, and the
heat of the climate was almost insupportable; but as custom makes
every station familiar, before three months were expired, all these
grievances were at an end; and he, naturally endued with a spirit
of emulation, would not suffer himself to be outdone by any of his
fellow slaves. The superintendent observing his extraordinary assiduity, could not help taking notice of him, and would frequently
give him encouragement either by calling him off to go on a trivial
errand, or by thrusting some money into his hand. He behaved
in this manner near two years, when his master was informed
of his good disposition, and removed him from that laborious

employment to an easier, where he had more frequent opportuni-
ties of paying adoration to that Almighty Being, who supported
him under all his afflictions. In these intervals, he was generally
found with a book in his hand, or on his knees, from which practice he received great consolation, as he often assured me.

At the expiration of three years, Sir *Tho. Thoroughgood*, who
made previous inquiry after his fellow-prentice's behaviour
abroad, sent orders to his agent in *Jamaica*, to purchase Mr.
Froward's freedom, and to advance him 100*l*.[54] that he might be
enabled to get his own livelihood; but at the same time gave strict
orders to his friend, not to let Mr. *Froward* know who was his benefactor, and to lay his master under the like injunction. In a short
time after, Mr. *Froward* was discharged from slavery; but did not
express so much joy on the occasion, as might have been reason-
ably expected. From the good usage he met with in servitude, and
the unusual favours he received from the superintendant, as well
as the planter, he had conceived a great liking for the latter, and
seemed to part with him not without some inward reluctance,

though with apparent surprize; which was much heightened by the additional favour of a note for a hundred pounds payable upon sight to Mr. *Francis Froward* or order, delivered to him by the same hand, soon after he received the discharge before-mentioned. During this confusion, the gentleman, who really had a value for his late servant, told him, he was welcome to be at his house till he was settled, and that he would do all the good offices in his power, to promote his future welfare. Mr. *Froward* replied, "Sir, you cannot do me greater service than to let me know who is my generous benefactor; because it is incumbent upon me to make some acknowledgment." The master positively refused to do this, and turned off the discourse, by asking how he intended to dispose of himself and money. "Sir," says he, "I am not unacquainted with the nature of trade, and labour is now become habitual to me, and as I am well skilled in the cultivation of the sugar-cane, I would willingly rent a small plantation of that kind, and work upon it for myself." The planter approved of this design, and promised him assistance.

In about a month after, Mr. *Froward* met with a bargain, agreeable to his substance, and worked upon it as hard as if he had been a real slave, with this difference only, that he could now spare more time in the service of his all powerful redeemer. In the interim, his late master procured him a wife with a handsome fortune, who had a sugar-work[55] of her own, and some negroes: he purchased more, and by his industry thrived amain,[56] and in a few years laid up 100*l.* in specie.

In this comfortable state, nothing gave him uneasiness, but that he could not come to the knowledge of his kind benefactor; never was man more anxious to shew his gratitude, or more sollicitous to find out his friend! One day, as he was at his devotions, a strange gentleman came to his habitation, and desired to see him. He was no sooner admitted, than he accosted him in the following manner: "Mr. *Froward,* I am commander of the *Dove* frigate, whose principal owner is Sir *Tho. Thoroughgood,* and am just arrived from *England*: By Sir *Thomas's* orders I am to inform you that his *Jamaica* agent is dead, and he has made choice of you to succeed him here in that station. I have a commission from him, for you, in my pocket, to dispose of my cargo, and to freight me again for my voyage home. He never would own it, but I am well assured, he is the person who saved your life, who redeemed you from bondage, and was the sole instrument of your present prosperity." Nothing could have given Mr. *Froward* so great pleasure and satisfaction as this last piece of intelligence; he knew not how to make the captain welcome enough, he kept him all night, and in the morning made him a present of a hogshead of rum.[57] He made all the possible dispatch in disposing of his cargo, and freighted him out with the utmost expedition. With the rest of the goods, he sent Sir *Thomas* ten hogsheads of sugar, and as many of rum, for a present, with the following letter.

"Honoured Sir,

Transported with joy, and drowned in tears, I send this testimony of my esteem, of which I humbly hope your acceptance, as well as of these small tokens of my gratitude, with which it is accompanied. Next under God, 'tis to you, dear Sir, that I owe my life, my liberty, and my all. Happy me, had I listened to your advice in my nonage! happy still, as by your means, I have been directed to the paths of virtue. 'Tis to you I am indebted for my present comfortable situation, and the dawning prospect of future happiness: The bills of lading, &c. are sent by Mr.✴✴✴✴✴, and all your business here, with which I am entrusted, shall executed with the utmost diligence and fidelity. I have only to add my prayers for the continuation of your life and health, who have been so beneficial to many, but more particularly to,

Honoured Sir, *Your most humble, most obliged, though most unworthy, servant,*

FRANCIS FROWARD."

Sir *Thomas* was highly pleased with the purport of his letter, though he rallied the captain for letting him know to whom he was obliged for his freedom. The same ship was sent the next season on the same voyage, when the captain was ordered to pay Mr. *Froward* the full price for the rum and sugar he had sent to the knight, and to deliver him the following letter.

Mr. Froward,

"Sir,

I thank you for the acknowledgment you made for the good offices I did you, and shall ever esteem the present as it was intended; but have neither power nor inclination to rob you of any thing you have acquired by dint of merit. My design is, to add to your acquisitions, and not to diminish them, as you will experience: only persevere in your present course of life, and you will make me ample amends for all I have, or can do for you.

> I am, Sir, your real friend,
> T. THOROUGHGOOD."

Mr. *Froward,* who was uneasy that his friend refused his present, continued in a thriving condition several years. And now his wife died without issue; he grown very rich, and advanced in years, disposed of the sugar-work, and left off all manner of business, except that of Sir *Tho. Thoroughgood*'s. At length he himself was seized with a pestilential fever, and carried off in a few days. He bore the torture of his distemper with exemplary patience, and met his approaching destiny with an intrepidity of soul scarce to be parallelled. That you may the better judge of his sentiments of gratitude, I have herewith sent a copy of his last will.

In the name of God, Amen. I *Francis Froward* of ——, in *Jamaica*, being of sound mind and memory, do hereby make my last will and testament, in form and manner following, that is to say:

Imprimis.[58] I bequeath my soul to Almighty God that gave it, hoping, and fully trusting, that I shall be saved and made eternally happy by the merits of my dear redeemer *Jesus Christ*, who suffered for me and all mankind.

Item, As the poor convicts in prison, where I had once the misfortune to be confined, are not attended, and instructed as they ought to be, by persons who seek their eternal salvation; I do give and bequeath fifty pounds a year, to purchase for their use such books as the archbishop of *Canterbury,* the bishop of *London,* and the sheriffs of *London* and *Middlesex* shall think proper to put into their hands.

Item, As the laws of *England,* however wisely constructed, have made no provision for poor people born in distant parts, and become miserable there, but left them to perish in the streets, lanes, and publick places; I do give and bequeath five hundred pounds a year, to be laid out for their relief, in such a manner as shall seem most agreeable to the lord-mayor of *London,* for the time being, and to the trustees that shall be nominated by my executors.

Item, And as many poor tradesmen and labourers are artfully seduced and persuaded to enter themselves on board merchant ships for this and other colonies in his majesty's dominions; and are afterwards at sea unwarily drawn in to indent themselves servants to the owners of the vessel, and from that moment commence slaves, and as such are sold in the publick markets of the colonies, and generally ill- treated;[59] I do give and bequeath five hundred pounds a year for the redemption of such unhappy people and for the prosecution of those who have been the abettors and contrivers of their ruin.

Item, As gratitude is of all oblations the greatest and most acceptable, I do give and bequeath to my dear friend Mr. *Thomas Thoroughgood*, merchant in *London,* who saved me from an ignominious death, and redeemed me from slavery, all the rest and residue of my real and personal estate; and I do nominate and appoint him, and his heirs and executors, my heirs and executors forever. In witness whereof I have hereunto set my hand and seal, this third day of *May*, 1680.

Witness   *Francis Froward.*
Thomas Williams,
John Wilson,
Richard Jones.

* * *

THE
HISTORY
OF
Miss SALLY SILENCE:
Communicated by Lady BETTY LIVELY.

MISS SALLY SILENCE was to be sure the best little girl in the world: She did every thing her papa and mamma bid her: Nay, more – she endeavoured to avoid giving them that trouble; for, if she knew of any thing they wanted, away she ran for it in an instant, and agreeably surprised them with what they had occasion for, before they had time even to ask for it. This to be sure made every body admire her; but what rendered her still more amiable was her great love of truth, and her vast dislike to noise and nonsense. When other girls were hollowing, quarrelling, and disturbing the whole neighbourhood, she was demure and silent. Now, there lived in that country a certain duke, who valued his peace and quiet above every earthly blessing; he made his addresses to several ladies, but found they were proud, conceited, and too much given to prattle; at last, being informed of Miss SALLY's good sense, virtue, and prudent behaviour, he made her several visits, and was so charmed with her chearfulness and sweet disposition, that he married her, though she had not a farthing to her fortune, and made her the great golden dutchess of *Downright*. Soon after his grace was married, he bought her a fine gilt coach, on which were painted two doves with an olive-branch, to represent their peace and conjugal affection, and she was drawn by six milk-white horses, as an emblem of her virtue and innocence. She lived with my lord duke in a state of happiness for many years, and when she died, he ordered this inscription to be wrote on her tomb, as a lesson to all little girls,

Here lie the Remains of the Dutchess of
DOWNRIGHT,
who, when a maiden, was no other
than SARAH JONES,
a poor Farmer's Daughter;
From her Attachment to GOODNESS she
became GREAT:
Her Virtue raised her from a mean
State to an high degree of Honour,
And
Her INNOCENCE procured her peace in her
last Moments.
She smiled, even in agony,
And embraced death, as a friendly pilot
who was to steer her
To a more exalted state of Bliss.
LITTLE READER

Whoever thou art, observe these her Rules,
and become Thyself
A copy of this bright EXAMPLE.

Be chearful, but be innocent. – Be obliging to all, though familiar with none but the good – hear what all men say, but take counsel only of the wise – Never be tempted to tell a lie, nor do any thing whereby your virtue and your honesty may be called in question; for among all your grandeur, all your riches and equipage, those are your brightest and most valuable gems. – Be peaceable, and be happy – love your friends, love your neighbours, love your enemies; but above all, love, honour and adore that ALMIGHTY BEING who gave you being; observe his laws which are written in the Holy Scriptures; and in the midst of your misfortunes, if you meet with any, rely entirely on his protection; who *is a father to the fatherless, who putteth down the wicked from their seat, and exalteth the humble and meek.*

* * *

A
MORNING HYMN,
FOR
All Little good BOYS and GIRLS:

Which is also proper for People of riper Years.

By a Young Gentleman.[60]

1.
O Thou! who lately clos'd my eyes,
And calm'd my soul to rest,
Now the dull blank of darkness flies,
Be thank'd, be prais'd, and blest.

2.

And as thou sav'st me in the night
　From anguish and dismay,
Lead through the labours of the light,
　And dangers of the day.

3.

Tho' from thy laws I daily swerve,
　Yet still thy mercy grant;
Shield me from all that I deserve,
　And grant me all I want.

4.

Howe'er she's tempted to descend,
　Keep reason on her throne;
From all men's passions me defend,
　But chiefly from my own.

5.

Give me a heart t'assist the poor,
　Ev'n as thy hand bestows;
For thee and man a love most pure,
　And friendship for my foes.

6.

This, thro' the merits, death and birth
　Of our bless'd Lord be giv'n;
So shall I compass peace on earth,
　And endless bliss in heav'n.

The PEACOCK.[61]

THE Peacock, of his gaudy train
And tread majestic idly vain,
Each simple gazer views with joy,
And dotes upon the feather'd toy;
But when he screams with hideous cry,
The ear is plagu'd to please the eye.

MORAL.

By this allusion justly stung,
Each tinsel'd fop should hold his tongue.

✳   ✳   ✳

AN
HISTORY
OF THE
RISE and PROGRESS
OF
LEARNING
IN
LILLIPUT.

MASTER HIRON, the young gentleman of whom we gave you some account in page 18, observing, that the language of the *Lilliputians* was irregular, and difficult to be understood, established the following alphabet of letters, and regulated their sounds, when blended and intermixed with each other, in this manner.

The alphabet consisted of the following twenty-six letters;

A b c d e f g h i j k l m n o p q r ſ t u v w x y z.

And these letters, at the request of master *Hiron,* and by authority of the king, were to bear the following sounds.

a, bee, cee, dee, e, eff, gee, aytch, i, ja, ka, el, em, en, o, pee, qu, ar, eſs, tee, yu, vee, double *yu, eks, wi, zed.*

Now out of these twenty-six letters, you will observe, there are five that express a sound of themselves, without the aid or assistance of any other letter; for which reason those are called vowels; and without one of these vowels, that is to say, without the assistance either of an *a,* or an *e,* or an *i,* or an *o,* or an *u,* no word can be form'd. Besides these five vowels the *w* and *y* are sometimes considered as such, and are very often made use of; the former instead of *u,* and the latter instead of *i;* and when used in this manner, they convey the sound, and have the power of those two vowels. You are likewise desired to observe, that sometimes two of those vowels, when joined together, make but one sound; as in the words, *Boy, too, Day, Lee, Tea,* and then they are called *Dipthongs.* And sometimes three vowels are also joined in one sound, as in the words *beau, lieu, view,* and these are called *Tripthongs.*

All those letters in the alphabet above mentioned, which cannot be sounded without being joined to one or more of the vowels, are called *Consonants.* And by these twenty-six letters, all the words in the world may be expressed and wrote down; which is amazing, and what one would never suppose such a little boy could have discovered. Pray consider how wonderful it is, that twenty-six letters should be found out, by which alone the *Lilliputians,* the *Mercolians,* the *English,* the *French,* the *Spaniards,* the *Italians,* the *Dutch,* and in short, the people of all other nations upon the earth, can express all the words that ever have been, or ever will be invented by any of them: and then tell me if you don't think *Billy Hiron* was a charming little boy! And from hence it is plain, my dear, that little boys and girls can do very surprizing things, and learn a great deal in a very little time, if they please; and as we all know, that learning is the road to preferment, to riches, to honour, and even wisdom itself, I hope we shall have no dunce amongst the members of our society; if there be, we shall serve him as the bees do a drone in the hive, send him packing to some other place.[62]

After this alphabet had been some time in use, master *Hiron* found it was necessary in many cases, that the letters should be made in a different manner; he therefore procured an order from the king for them to be made thus:

A B C D E F G H I J K L M N O P Q R S T U V W X Y Z.

And these he called *Capitals*, because the use he put them to was to distinguish any word that required more than ordinary notice. He likewise ordered, that every line in poetry, the name of every person and thing, and the first letter in every discourse after a period or full point, should begin with a *Capital*.

* * *

NEW EPIGRAMS.

By MEMBERS of the SOCIETY.

On seeing two beautiful Sisters at a Farmhouse, by Master HOOKE.

> WHY did I into danger run?
> I came, I saw, and am undone!
> No more can fix my love;
> Their beauteous forms distract my mind!
> This VENUS is for MARS design'd!
> That SEMELE for JOVE![63]

EPIGRAM II.

On reading the OLD WOMAN'S MAGAZINE.[64] *By Master* BRIDGES *of* BATH.

> THE dull and stupid we old women call;
> But this old woman contradicts us all!
> To the polite, she wit and humour gives,
> And to instruct the many writes and lives:
> O! may she never – never barren grow;
> But every month some useful birth bestow.

RIDDLE I.

When Cæsar did this isle invade,
I first experienced royal aid;
Nay, now to Majesty belong,
Tho' subject to the vulgar throng,
Who with uncivil usage treat,
And trample me beneath their feet;
With heavy burdens me oppress,
And money gain by my distress;
Yet all their insults I endure,
While they my given bruises cure.
I am in every country found,
And traverse all the kingdom round:
Say what my name is, so well known:
That I'm a common proverb grown.

RIDDLE II.

In courts and cottages we may be found,
Our skirts with fringe of colours bound;
And as we were by providence design'd,
To guard from harm a fav'rite apple join'd,
For this cause we ne'er far asunder stray,
But meet and part a thousand times a day.
When dark, like loving couples we unite,
And cuddle close together every night.

RIDDLE III.

I was before the world began,
    And shall for ever last,
'Ere *Adam* was form'd into a man,
    And out of *Eden* cast.
Your mirthful moments I attend;
    And mitigate your grief,

Th' industrious peasant I befriend,
  To pris'ners give relief.
Make much of me if you are wise,
  And use me while you may;
For you will leave me in a trice,
  And I for no man stay.[65]

* * *

That's My Honey.
A
New Country Dance.

By *Miss Alice* ****

CLAP three, and cast off and turn — Second couple do the same —
Foot it to your partner, cast off, and right and left.

* * *

JESTS.

A *Gascon* officer who served under *Henry* IV king of *France*, not having received any pay for a considerable time, came to the king, and confidently said to him, Sir, three words with your majesty, *Money or Discharge*. Four with you, answered the king, *neither one nor t'other*.

A young student shewing the *Musæum* at *Oxon* to gentlemen and ladies, among other things produced a rusty sword:[66] This, says the student, is the sword with which *Balaam* was going to kill his ass.[67] Upon which one of the company replied, that he thought *Balaam* had no sword, but only wished for one. You are right, says the student, and this is the very sword he wished for.

It has been often observ'd, and with too much truth, that *English* gentlemen reap no benefit by travelling. *Tom Smart* made a pretty use of this, when he told a prating coxcomb just returned from *Italy, that the* English *went out figures and returned cyphers.*

✳   ✳   ✳

The Last
ÆNIGMAS
ANSWER'D.

By Master SAMMY SYDROPHEL.[68]

IF a young *Lilliputian* your riddles find out,
You will give him a book for his trouble no doubt.
The first then is ADAM – for no male beside
E'er so young did encounter a beautiful bride.
The second's a GRIDIRON, whose ribs, when meat's on,
Drop fat in the fire, altho' they have none.
The third is – but hold – for mistaken I may be,
A fine painted DOLL, or a *Gingerbread-Baby.*

An HYMN *from the* 37th *Psalm.*

By a LADY.[69]

I.

As by the streams of *Babylon*,
   Far from our native soil we sat,
Sweet *Zion*! thee we thought upon,
   And every thought a tear begat.

II.

Aloft the willows waving there
   Our silent harps we pensive hung.
Said they, who captiv'd us, let's hear
   Some song which ye in *Zion* sung.

III.

How shall we tune our voice to sing,
   Or touch our harps with skilful hands,
Can hymns of Joy to God our King,
   Be sung by slaves in foreign lands?

IV.

O *Salem!* our once happy seat,
   If I of thee forgetful prove,
Let then my trembling hand forget
   The speaking string and art to move.

V.

If I to moan o'er thee forbear,
   Eternal silence seize my tongue;
Or if I sing one chearful air
   'Till thy deliverance is my song.

✳ ✳ ✳

THE
HISTORY
OF LITTLE
POLLY MEANWELL.

Who was afterwards the Queen of

PETULA.

Polly Meanwell's father and mother died when she was very young, and left her to the care of an uncle, who was an old rich batchellor, covetous to the last degree, and one who cared for nobody but himself. He put her to school a little after her parents' death,

but finding that by a flaw in some writings, he had the power of taking every thing to himself, he did so, and deprived poor *Polly* of what her father and mother left for her subsistance, and turned her out of doors.

Polly was at first very uneasy at losing all her fine cloaths, and at being obliged to go to hard work, which Mr. *Williams* the parson of the parish observing, that good man came to her one day, and comforted her in this manner. "Don't be cast down, *Polly*, at your fine cloaths being gone, those ragged ones will keep you warm, and that is the only use of cloaths; for people are not a bit the better for wearing fine garments. 'Tis true, you can't have your tea and your coffee, your tarts and your cheesecakes, your custards and syllabubs as usual, but what does that signify? You can by your labour get other victuals: then your working for it makes it go down the sweeter, and at the same time keeps you in health; the bed you lie upon seems as soft, after a hard day's work, as your down beds, I suppose, used to be; why then should you be uneasy? Be a good girl, say your prayers, and put your trust in God Almighty; and he will give you what his all knowing wisdom sees you want." *Polly* was so pleased with this speech, that she dropt Mr. *Williams* a courtesy,[70] and for the future, resolved to mind nothing but her duty, and not repine at Providence.

As she went to church constantly, and was very devout there, every body took notice of her, and one merchant's wife in particular, sent to the sexton to know what little ragged girl that was that came to church so constantly, and behaved so well there. The Sexton answered, that 'twas *Polly Meanwell*; and, "Madam," said he, "though *Polly* is so poor and so ragged, she is the best girl in the parish." "Is she so?" says the lady, "then pray give her this new bible, and this piece of money;" and put into his hand a crown for her. Some time afterwards, this lady, who was very rich, dropped as she was stepping into her coach, a green purse full of guineas, and a fine diamond ring, which *Polly* had the good fortune to pick up. Now some naughty girls would have kept all this money, and not have carried it to the lady; and indeed one of her neighbours advised her to do so. But *Polly* was angry with her, and told her, she was a wicked woman to put such naughty things into a little girl's head. "How can I go to church and say my prayers to God Almighty, says she, and at the same time be guilty of such a dishonest thing; and what good do you think this money will do me? why none; 'twill only corrupt what little I get by my labour, and make God Almighty angry with me." So she got a paper wrote, and nailed it up at the church-door, to let every body know that *Polly Meanwell,* the little ragged girl, had found a large sum of money, and a fine diamond ring, and that the owner might have it on describing the purse and ring.

The lady hearing of this, sent for *Polly* and described the purse and the ring, which *Polly* returned to her, who gave her ten guineas. "And now *Polly*, says she, as I know you are a very honest, religious, and good girl, I will provide for you. Go into the next room, and strip off those ragged cloaths, and put on those new ones you'll find on the great chair, and you shall wait on my daughter to the *East-Indies*; where, if you behave in the same manner you have hitherto done, you will become a great woman; for God Almighty will certainly bless you."

Some years after this, and when *Polly* was grown a woman, the lady set off for the *East-Indies,* and *Polly* with her. But in their passage, they were taken by *Angria* the pirate;[71] and poor *Polly* being a beautiful girl, was again reduced to great distress; for *Angria* made several attempts on her virtue, and because she would not comply with his wicked desires, he put her into a dark prison, and would not suffer her mistress to see her. Now this happened at a time when *Kolan-mi Dolan*, a very rich king in *India*, came to visit his dominions; for part of which, *Angria* the pirate paid him a tribute; and being informed how this poor captive had been punished on account of her virtue, he procured her freedom of *Angria*, and took her with him to his palace of *Ilstohan.*

King *Kolan-mi Dolan* intended to make her one of his concubines; but *Polly* was determined not to be guilty of any thing so wicked, she therefore fell on her knees to him, and said, "O king! you have done a glorious action in delivering me from that wicked man *Angria*, for which I hope God Almighty will amply reward you; for he hath promised to be a friend to those who defend the innocent, and support the helpless. Do not, therefore, O king, lose the blessing of the Almighty, and sully your own honour, by depriving me of my virtue, which I hold more dear than life itself. Ah! why should you, for a sensual gratification, a momentary pleasure, make me miserable for ever? Consider, I beseech you, before whom you stand: God Almighty takes notice of your actions as well as mine, nor can these things be hid from his sight; for the darkness is no darkness with him; but the night is as clear as the day. You and all your hosts are but as nothing with respect to him. Look in the charnel-houses of your fathers, where is now their power, their pomp, their grandeur? they are now but dust, and mingled with the dross of mankind. Why then should pride tempt you to provoke God, or wickedness prompt you to commit a sin, which perhaps may be your overthrow? Kill me you may, but you shall never deprive me of my virtue and honour."

Kolan-mi Dolan was so surprised at this heroic answer, that for a considerable time he could make no reply: he was dumb with amazement, and fixing his eyes on the beloved object, he revolved in his soul the instability of human grandeur, the majesty of the deity, the dignity of virtue, and the power and persuasive force of

kneeling artless innocence. He then raised *Polly* from the ground, and addressed himself to her in these words: "O my divine creature! thou art marked out by Providence, to read me the lecture I most wanted, to teach me to turn my thoughts to their proper centre, and to search the bottom of my heart. Ambition, pride, luxury, and revenge had planted themselves there; but thou hast by thy prudence and angelic virtue, banished them thence. I now see myself, and admire and adore thy superior sense and virtue. Be my companion for life, and I will this moment discharge all my concubines, the creators of my luxury and folly, and make myself for ever happy with thee only." He then married miss *Polly* in the most solemn manner, according to the ceremonies of her religion, and built for her a palace of jasper, the front of which was overlaid with pure gold, the floor paved with pearls and emeralds, the walls bedecked with the brightest diamonds, and the cielings adorned with the most curious paintings of sacred history. She had a large garden richly decorated with the finest grottos, groves, mazey walks, fountains, and purling streams. The turf in it bears a continual verdure, the most delicious fruits bow down the labouring branches, to salute the enchanted eye, and the never fading flowers pay an eternal tribute to her piety and virtue. Here she every evening recreates herself with those ladies of her court who are most distinguished for their virtue and good sense; but her mornings are always spent in hearing the complaints of her people, and promoting their happiness. Virtues or vices fly from the court, and disperse themselves through a country, in the same manner as the fashions and garbs of dress; what is worn by the great will be affected by the meaner sort. Hence it followed, that the morality and good principles cultivated at court, by miss *Polly* the queen, were soon spread throughout all the kingdom, and it became fashionable for people to be virtuous and honest. And what was at first introduced through fashion, is now maintained through prudence; for as it became unfashionable to be wicked, the murders, adulteries, robberies, thefts, &c. with which the nation was continually plagued before, were now not so much as heard of, and the people found, that in consequence of being Virtuous they became Happy.

So ends the History of little Polly Meanwell, the Queen of *Petula.*

✳   ✳   ✳

THE
HISTORY
OF
Master PETER PRIMROSE,
Sent to the SOCIETY

BY

Master TOMMY TRUSTY.

MASTER *Peter Primrose* was a boy of such uncommon abilities, that he was admired by every body. When he was but seven years old, he could say all his catechism perfectly, and repeat the greatest part of his Prayer-book and Testament by heart; then he could answer any question in the Bible, and by reading the *Circle of the Sciences*, he had also obtained some knowledge of men and things; for all these books you are to observe had been translated into the language of the country where he lived.[72] Master *Peter's* fame was sounded through the whole kingdom, and though his father was only a shepherd, and he bred up among the flocks, the king sent for him to court, and placed him among the wise men of the nation. Here he lived in great splendor for some time; for the king gave him a little prancing horse, cloathed with purple and gold, and caused him to ride out every day in company with his only son. How uncertain are riches and honours, and indeed how frail is all human felicity! Master *Peter* had not been at court above two years, before the good old king and his son were expelled the kingdom, by an unaccountable faction that arose in the state. Duty and gratitude obliged this young gentleman to take the part of his king and his prince; for which he was persecuted by the opposite party with great fury, and one day, forced into the woods to shield himself from their hatred. Here he lay securely all day, but in the evening, his fears were continually alarmed by the roaring of lions, tygers, wolves, and other beasts of prey, and his compassion excited by the groans and cries of the tender part of the animal creation, who not being endowed by nature with strength and fierceness to oppose their enemies easily became victims, and were devoured. This called up in his mind, the cruelties which had been exercised on his poor master's family and himself, the thoughts of which so robbed him of his resolution, that he grew heedless of his safety, and sitting down on the green turf, resigned himself to the mercy of the beasts; *Ah! why should these creatures*, says he, *fill me with horror, who are more merciful than men? These spare their own, and slay only those of another species, but men, more savage men, are bent against each other, and seek their own destruction. Let me fall then by the lion, the tyger, or other animals less cruel, and that act consistently with the dictates of nature.* As this was delivered with great emotion; he was overheard by a hermit, whose cave was concealed under the thicket, by which he lay. The good old man startled at the sound of the human voice, which he had not heard before for years, and supposing it came from one in distress, kindled a brand, for fear of the wild beasts, and ran to his assistance. He found master *Primrose* stretched on the ground, and by sorrow rendered insensible of any danger. The old man reproached him for despairing of God's providence and mercy. *Is it for this,* says he, *that man is endowed with superior reason, and so highly favoured of the Almighty? Shall the dove, shall the lamb, and other creatures fly for refuge, and seek their own safety, and shall man basely and ungratefully disregard and throw away the life that has been given him? Arise and shake off this shameful sloth, nor longer despair of God's protection. Do your duty, and you will always meet with the favour of Heaven.*

The young man, sensible of the justness of this reproof, arose and bowed respectfully, and was led by the hermit into his cave, and refreshed with a simple repast the good old man had provided for him, and then reposed himself till the morning on a couch of flocks,[73] that here seemed more soft than the down-bed he had been so long used to.

In the morning, when he awoke, he related to the old man the history of his life; and the hermit, after giving him such things as were necessary to support him in his journey, dispatched him with this advice. *You see, my son, what mischiefs attend the ambitious. The love of riches and of power drew you from a state of innocence, from a delightful place, where your paths were paved with violets and primroses, to a court where your road was planted with thistles and thorns. True greatness consists in being good, in promoting the happiness of mankind and not in wealth and power, as is vainly imagined; for he that hoards up treasure, hoards up trouble, and he that aspires to the highest office of state makes himself a public mark for the multitude to throw their envious arrows at. Retire, my son, to thy former peaceful abode, there worship thy God, comfort thy neighbours, and tend thy innocent flock, and leave the affairs of state to those who have less virtue and more experience.* Contentment is the only ingredient that can render life happy, and that is seldom to be found in the palaces of princes.

* * *

THE LAST
ÆNIGMAS
ANSWERED.

In a Letter from Master *Tommy Trueman.*

Ladies and Gentlemen,

As I have no talents for poetry, you will excuse my answering your last Ænigmas in prose; the first then I take to be the *Highway,* or *Public Road;* the second is the *Eye-lids,* and the last is *Old Time,* to the end of whose reign, I hope your LILLIPUTIAN SOCIETY will subsist.

I am,
Ladies and Gentlemen,
Your truly affectionate friend, and very humble Servant,
PEKIN, in *China,*
JULY 19, 1751.   TOM. TRUEMAN.

* * *

Be MERRY and WISE:

A NEW

COUNTRY DANCE.

By Miss *Polly Prudence*.

FIRST Couple cross over and turn, 2d Coup. the same – Man hay with the 3d Coup. Woman with the 2d Coup. — Lead down, up again and cast off.[74]

* * *

Friendship Displayed; or,

A poor Man's last

WILL AND TESTAMENT.

A Poor indigent beggarly creature, weak in body, but sound in sense, sent for an attorney to draw his will, which was as follows:

There are two persons, says he, naming them, men of quality and estate, who have ever shew'd themselves my generous friends, and I shall be much to blame not to leave them some token of my love for a remembrance, before I depart this life.

This formal speech, delivered with great gravity, set every body a longing to hear the legacies; for they all knew the man was not worth a groat.[75]

"I do bequeath, says he, my aged mother to the care of Aretæus, my particular friend, to be by him provided for and maintained, out of respect to my memory, when I am dead and gone. And to Philoxenus I bequeath my only daughter to be by him disposed of in marriage with as fair a fortune as he can well spare."[76]

This testament look'd more like romance than matter of fact; 'till the two friends appeared and undertook the trust. Philoxenus died in five days after, and upon his death Aretæus took the whole charge upon himself, and having a daughter of his own, he disposed of her and his friend's daughter both in one day, and gave them two thousands pounds a piece for their portions.

APPLICATION.

'Tis often out of a man's power to do what he would for himself and family, which renders it extremely necessary for him to make choice of a faithful friend, who is, as the wise son of *Sirach* observes, *The Medicine of Life.*[77]

✻ ✻ ✻

WE whose names are hereunto subscribed, members of the *Lilliputian Society*, and proprietors in this magazine, do promise, covenant and agree with each other;

FIRST, To say our prayers every morning and evening, to frequent the public service of the church to which we belong, and to keep holy the *Sabbath-day*; to love the *Lord* our *God* with all our hearts, with all our souls, and with all our strength; to worship him, to give him thanks, to put our whole trust in him, to honour his holy name and his word, and to serve him truly all the days of our lives.

SECONDLY, We do promise and agree to love and honour our fathers and mothers, brothers and sisters, relations and friends; to submit ourselves to all our governors and teachers, and to behave reverently to all our elders and betters; but more especially to all pious and good men.

THIRDLY, We do agree to live in the strictest friendship, to promote each others interest and happiness, and the interest and happiness of all mankind; but especially of those who are poor and distressed. We do also promise, to love our neighbours as ourselves, and to do unto all men as we would they should do unto us; to hurt nobody by word or deed, to be true and just in all our dealings; to bear no malice nor hatred in our hearts, to keep our hands from picking and stealing, and our tongues from evil speaking, lying and slandering; to shun the company of all those who use wicked words; to keep our bodies in temperance, sobriety and chastity, and that we will not covet other men's goods, but be contented with what it hath pleased God to give us; for we are well assured, that a contented mind is a continual feast.

Witness our hands, *July* 3, 1752.

Master George Aduace, Austin-fryars
Miss Hannah Arnold, Newgate-street
Master Allen
Master James Adams
Miss Sarah Adams
Miss Elizabeth Susannah Ambrose, Hungerford Park, Berks
Master George Angel, Clerkenwell
Miss Rebecca Andrews, Walbrook
Miss Molly Andrews, Cheltenham

Master Robert Ashley, St. Paul's Churchyard
Master George Arnold
Master Charles Apsey, Cambridge
Master Avis, Houndsditch
Master Jeremiah Beal, Maryland
Master Samuel Brown in West-Smithfield
Miss Ann Berry, Gutter-lane
Master John Beardsworth, without Bishopsgate
Miss Benford, Houndsditch
Miss Hannah Boult, Cheapside
Master Harry Belchier, Grays-inn-lane
Miss Elizabeth Burton
Miss Suky Burton, Red-lion-street, Holborn
Miss Catherine Briggs, Thomas-street
Miss Jane Ann Bever, Oxendon-street, Piccadilly
Master John Berens
Master Joseph Berens, Throgmorton-street
Miss Byne Beale, Red-Lion-street, Holborn
Master Thomas Beale
Master James Bowey, Whitechapel
Miss Baugh, Great-Turnstile, Holborn
Miss Peggy Brown, Prescot-street, Goodman's-fields
Miss Nancy Blakiston, Hatton-Garden
Master John Buxton, Bishopsgate-street
Master Jacky Newman Beech
Miss Betsy Beech, Little Queen-street, Holborn
Miss Mary Bownin, Duke's-Court, Drury-lane
Miss Betsy Bagghett, at Hulet on the Hill
Miss Betsy Benfield, Cheltenham
Miss Suky Bird, Whitegate-street
Master John Boulton, Edmonton
Master Thomas Boulton
Master John Boulton, Finchley
Master Richard Bernard
Miss Sally Bernard, Cornhill
Miss Fanny Brooks, Strand
Master Charles Brown
Miss Anna Maria Barker
Miss Frances Mary Bilboa

Master John Blacard, St. Martin's-lane
Miss Bellamy, New North-street, Red-Lion-square
Miss Sarah Burn, Goodman's-fields
Master Isaac Hawkins Brown, Ormond-street
Master Thomas Birch
Master Francis Brown, Bloomsbury-square
Miss Nancy Brodhead, High-Holborn
Miss Nancy Barron, High-Holborn
Miss Elizabeth Bellar, Doctors-Commons
Miss Ann Banyer, Aldermanbury
Miss Charlotte Buckingham, Devonshire-street, Red-Lion-square
Master Joey Bird, Cockhill, Ratcliff
Miss Betsy Bailey
Master George Bailey, Stratford, Essex
Miss Dorothy Backhurst
Miss Dorothy Bathurst
Master Robert Butty, Cheapside
Master William Powell Bilstone, Oxford
Master Thomas Bliss, Oxford
Master Dicky Baily
Master Billy Bennett
Miss Sally Brooks
Master Bruckshawe
Miss Blacow
Master Onslow Selvin Beaver
Miss Polly Barnston
Miss Jane Barnston
Master Barnston
Master William Caws, in Coleman-street
Master Carreck
Miss Mary Cook, in the Strand
Miss Elizabeth Cook, Denham-yard
Miss Sally Cotton
Miss Crawford, Leadenhall-street
Master John Cock
Master James Cock, St. Katherine's-lane, Tower-hill
Miss Elizabeth Charlotte Cowper, Southampton-row
Master John Cornish
Miss Ann Cornish

Miss Elizabeth Cooke, Little Drury-lane
Master Jemmy Collinson, Gracechurch-street
Miss Cope
Miss Amy Cary, Watling-street
Master Cole, Holborn
Miss Polly Conner
Miss Peggy Conner, Chandois-street, Covent-Garden
Master William Collins
Master Nicholas Crisp, Bow-Church-yard
Master John Cooke, Camomile-street, without Bishopgate
Miss Cruise, New-Bond-street
Miss Sarah Collingwood, Prescot-street
Master Charles Collings, Strand
Miss Mary Calmur, Whitecross-street
Master William Cecill, Salisbury-Court
Master Hopkins George Carsan, Lambeth
Master Robert Collet, King-street, Covent-Garden
Miss Jane Clifton, Cary-street, Lincoln's-Inn;
Miss Polly Cox, Cheltenham
Miss Elizabeth Carpenter, Cheltenham
Miss Elizabeth Coapland, Cheltenham
Miss Betty Collings, Great James-street Bedford-row
Master Taylor Currie, Goodman's-fields
Master John Chapman, in Spittlefields
Miss Susannah Cooper, Goodman's-fields
Miss Alice Collet, St. James's-street, Golden-square
Miss Michael Calf, Nine-Elms, Battersea
Miss Nancy Crompton
Miss Polly Crutcher, King-street, Cheapside
Master James Crofts
Master Peter Crofts
Miss Polly Crofts, Great Queen-street, Lincoln's-Inn-fields
Miss Cox, at the Park near Cheltenham
Miss Polly Cator, Bankside, Southwark
Miss Clayton, Hatton-Garden
Miss Elizabeth Collyer
Master Joseph Collyer
Miss Betsy Cartwright
Master Dell, St. Paul's Church-yard
Master Harton Dann

Master Dorrien, Fenchurch-street
Miss Mary Dummer, Fore-street
Miss Betsy Baghot Detabor, Southam, Gloucestershire
Master John Davidson, Tower-hill
Master Thomas Darley, Wardour-Court, Holborn
Miss Polly Dickenson, Chick-lane, Smithfield
Master William Dess
Master Francis Dess, Hampstead
Miss Durour, Throgmorton-street
Master Thomas Entwisle, without Bishopsgate
Master James Elgy, Salisbury-Court, Fleet-street
Miss Elizabeth Elliot, Edmonton
Miss Earl, in Great Marlborough-street, St. James's
Miss Nancy Ellison
Master John Eyles, St. Paul's Church-yard
Miss Sally Eyres, Cockhill, Radcliff
Miss Englefield, Bloomsbury
Miss Ewers, Windfor
Miss Edwards, Garlick-hill
Miss Mary Fish, Aldergate-street
Miss Mary Forbes, Shadwell
Miss Mary Feline, King-street, Covent-Garden
Master Jemmy Fox
Miss Sukey Fox
Miss Judith Faden, Salisbury-court
Miss Jane Frici, Bishopsgate-street
Master John Fuller
Miss Polly Field
Master Tommy Field, Westham, Essex
Master Richard Fuller, Wood-street
Master Thomas Franklin, Chesham
Master Thomas Freeman
Master Joseph Freeman
Miss Marianne Falkiner
Master Philip Guibert, Southampton-street
Miss Mary Green, Fenchurch-street
Miss Ann Maria Gill, Fenchurch-street
Miss Polly Gardener, Cheltenham
Master Goadland
Miss Goadland, Mile-End

Miss Peggy Gisling
Miss Suky Gary
Miss Polly Gary, Watling-street
Miss Betty Grigson
Miss Ann Grigson, Ramsgate, Kent
Miss Patty Grindall, Chick-Lane, Smithfield
Miss Mary Gardener, Norwich
Master Joseph Groom
Master Billy Goodman
Master James Hatch, in St. Paul's Churchyard
Miss Ann Hopley, Leadenhall-street
Master Thomas Hopkins, St. Paul's-Churchyard
Miss Martha Hoppe, St. Paul's-Churchyard
Miss Ann Harris, St. Paul's-Church-yard
Master Joseph Humphries, Mason's-hill, Kent
Master Christopher Hunter
Master William Hunter, Ramsgate in Kent
Miss Mary Hill, Newgate-street
Miss Sarah Hurst, Blowbladder-street
Miss Sarah Hales, Shadthames, Southwark
Miss Margaret Hill, Basing-lane
Miss Harrison, Hampstead
Miss Mary Hare, Greenwich
Miss Allen Hammond, Fleet-market
Miss Francis Ann Hutchins, Little-Tower-street
Miss Kitty Harn in Devonshire
Master Thomas Hitt, Aldersgate-street
Miss Charlotte Harrison, Upminster
Miss Mary Harrison, Upminster
Mils Catherine Howard, London-Bridge
Master Joseph Hardy, Clement's-Inn-Passage

N. B. There are many Thousands of young Gentlemen and Ladies, who, by subscribing to this Work, are become Members of the Society, and have entered into the Agreement above specified, but as their Names are too numerous to be here inserted, we are obliged to omit them till the Publication of the next Volume.

JAMES TRUELOVE, *Sec.*

A LIST of Subscribers, from *Maryland*, which came too late to be inserted in the proper place

Master Tommy Addison of Prince George's County, Maryland
Master Harry Addison
Master Jacky Addison
Miss Nancy Addison
Miss Nelly Addison
Master Walter Beall, Frederick County
Master Tommy Beall
Master Brooke Beall
Master Jerry Beall
Master Sammy Beall
Master Isaac Beall
Miss Amelia Beall
Master Randolph Brandt, Charles County
Master Dicky Brandt
Master Dicky Brooke
Miss Sally Brooke, Prince George's County
Miss Jane Contee
Master Billy Cooke
Miss Rachael Cooke
Master Watty Dent
Master Dicky Dent
Miss Nancy Dobson
Master Dulany, in Annapolis
Master Lloyd Dulany
Miss Becky Dulany
Master Matthew Eversfield, Prince George's County
Master Charles Eversfield
Miss Debby Eversfield
Master Fitzchew, Calvert County
Master Tommy T. Greenfield, St. Mary's County
Miss Rachael T. Greenfield
Miss Gantt, Calvert County
Master Sammy Hepburn, Marlborough
Miss Nancy Hepburn
Master Tommy Hawkins, Prince George's County
Miss Betsy Hawkins

Miss Chloe Hanson, Charles County
Miss Jenny Hanson
Miss Fanny Jenning, Prince George's County
Master Tommy Lee
Miss Sally Lee
Master Dicky Lee, Charles County
Master Philly Lee
Miss Peggy Lawrence, Piscattaway
Master and Miss Mackall, Calvert County
Master and Miss Ogle, in Annapolis
Master Johnny Thomas, Ann Arundell County

FINIS.

THE
HISTORY
OF
Little GOODY TWO-SHOES;
Otherwise called,
Mrs. MARGERY TWO-SHOES.

WITH

The Means by which she acquired her Learning and Wisdom, and in consequence thereof her Estate; set forth at large for the Benefit of those,

Who from a State of Rags and Care,

And having Shoes but half a Pair;

Their Fortune and their Fame would fix,

And gallop in a Coach and Six.

See the Original Manuscript in the *Vatican* at *Rome*, and the Cuts by *Michael Angelo*.

Illustrated with the Comments of our great modern Critics.

The THIRD EDITION.

LONDON:

Printed for J. NEWBERY, at the *Bible* and *Sun* in St. *Paul's-Church-Yard*, 1766.
[Price Six-pence.]

Little Goody Two-Shoes.

TO ALL

Young Gentlemen and Ladies,

Who are good, or intend to be good,

This BOOK

Is inscribed by

Their old Friend

In St. Paul's Church-yard.

*   *   *

The Renowned
HISTORY
OF
Little GOODY TWO-SHOES;
Commonly called,
Old GOODY TWO-SHOES.

PART I.

INTRODUCTION. By the Editor.

ALL the World must allow, that *Two Shoes* was not her real Name. No; her Father's Name was *Meanwell*;[1] and he was for many Years a considerable Farmer in the Parish where *Margery* was born; but by the Misfortunes which he met with in Business, and the wicked Persecutions of Sir *Timothy Gripe*, and an over-grown Farmer called *Graspall*, he was effectually ruined.

The Case was thus. The Parish of *Mouldwell* where they lived, had for many Ages been let by the Lord of the Manor into twelve different Farms, in which the Tenants lived comfortably, brought up large Families, and carefully supported the poor People who laboured for them; until the Estate by Marriage and by Death came into the Hands of Sir *Timothy*.

This Gentleman, who loved himself better than all his Neighbours, thought it less Trouble to write one Receipt for his Rent than twelve, and Farmer *Graspall* offering to take all the Farms as the Leases expired, Sir *Timothy* agreed with him, and in Process of Time he was possessed of every Farm, but that occupied by little *Margery's* Father; which he also wanted; for as Mr. *Meanwell* was a charitable good Man, he stood up for the Poor at the Parish Meetings, and was unwilling to have them oppressed by Sir *Timothy*, and this avaricious Farmer. – Judge, oh kind, humane and courteous Reader, what a terrible Situation the Poor must be in, when this covetous Man was perpetual Overseer, and every Thing for their Maintenance was drawn from his hard Heart and cruel Hand.[2] But he was not only perpetual Overseer, but perpetual Church-warden;[3] and judge, oh ye Christians, what State the Church must be in, when supported by a Man without Religion or Virtue. He was also perpetual Surveyor of the Highways,[4] and what Sort of Roads he kept up for the Convenience of Travellers, those best know who have had the Misfortune to be obliged to pass thro' that Parish. – Complaints indeed were made, but to what Purpose are Complaints, when brought against a Man, who can hunt, drink, and smoke with the Lord of the Manor, who is also the Justice of Peace?[5]

The Opposition which little *Margery's* Father made to this Man's Tyranny, gave Offence to Sir *Timothy*, who endeavoured to force him out of his Farm; and to oblige him to throw up the Lease,[6] ordered both a Brick Kiln and a Dog-kennel to be erected in the Farmer's Orchard. This was contrary to Law, and a Suit was commenced, in which *Margery's* Father got the better. The same Offence was again

committed three different Times, and as many Actions brought, in all of which the Farmer had a Verdict and Costs paid him; but notwithstanding these Advantages, the Law was so expensive, that he was ruined in the Contest, and obliged to give up all he had to his Creditors; which effectually answered the Purpose of Sir *Timothy*, who erected those Nuisances in the Farmer's Orchard with that Intention only. Ah, my dear Reader, we brag of Liberty, and boast of our Laws: but the Blessings of the one, and the Protection of the other, seldom fall to the Lot of the Poor; and especially when a rich Man is their Adversary. How, in the Name of Goodness, can a poor Wretch obtain Redress, when thirty Pounds are insufficient to try his Cause? Where is he to find Money to see Council, or how can he plead his Cause himself (even if he was permitted) when our Laws are so obscure, and so multiplied, that an Abridgment of them cannot be contained in fifty Volumes in Folio?[7]

As soon as Mr. *Meanwell* had called together his Creditors, Sir *Timothy* seized for a Year's Rent,[8] and turned the Farmer, his Wife, little *Margery*, and her Brother out of Doors, without any of the Necessaries of Life to support them.

This elated the Heart of Mr. *Graspall*, this crowned his Hopes, and filled the Measure of his Iniquity; for besides gratifying his Revenge, this Man's Overthrow gave him the sole Dominion of the Poor, whom he depressed and abused in a Manner too horrible to mention.

Margery's Father flew into another Parish for Succour, and all those who were able to move left their Dwellings and sought Employment elsewhere, as they found it would be impossible to live under the Tyranny of two such People. The very old, the very lame and the blind were obliged to stay behind, and whether they were starved, or what became of them, History does not say; but the Character of the great Sir *Timothy*, and his avaricious Tenant, were so infamous, that nobody would work for them by the Day, and Servants were afraid to engage themselves by the Year, lest any unforeseen Accident should leave them Parishioners in a Place, where they knew they must perish miserably; so that great Part of the Land lay untilled for some Years, which was deemed a just Reward for such diabolical Proceedings.

But what, says the Reader, can occasion all this? Do you intend this for Children, Mr. NEWBERY? Why, do you suppose this is written by Mr. NEWBERY, Sir? This may come from another Hand. This is not the Book, Sir, mentioned in the Title, but the Introduction to that Book; and it is intended, Sir, not for those Sort of Children, but for Children of six Feet high, of which, as my Friend has justly observed, there are many Millions in the Kingdom; and these Reflections, Sir, have been rendered necessary, by the unaccountable and diabolical Scheme which many Gentlemen now give into, of laying a Number of Farms into one, and very often of a whole Parish into one Farm; which in the End must reduce the common People to a State of Vassalage, worse than that under the Barons of old, or of the Clans in *Scotland*; and will in Time depopulate the Kingdom. But as you are tired of the Subject, I shall take myself away, and you may visit *Little Margery.* So, Sir, your Servant,

The EDITOR.

* * *

CHAP. I.

How and about Little Margery *and her* Brother.

CARE and Discontent shortened the Days of Little *Margery's* Father.– He was forced from his Family, and seized with a violent Fever in a Place where Dr. *James's* Powder was not to be had, and where he died miserably.[9] *Margery's* poor Mother survived the Loss of her Husband but a few Days, and died of a broken Heart, leaving *Margery* and her little Brother to the wide World; but, poor Woman, it would have melted your Heart to have seen how frequently she heaved up her Head, while she lay speechless, to survey with languishing Looks her little Orphans, as much as to say, *Do Tommy, do Margery, come with me.* They cried, poor Things, and she sighed away her Soul; and I hope is happy.

It would both have excited your Pity, and have done your Heart good, to have seen how fond these two little ones were of each other, and how, Hand in Hand, they trotted about. Pray see them.

They were both very ragged, and *Tommy* had two Shoes, but *Margery* had but one. They had nothing, poor Things, to support them (not being in their own Parish[10]) but what they picked from the Hedges, or got from the poor People, and they lay every Night in a Barn. Their Relations took no Notice of them; no, they were rich, and ashamed to own such a poor little ragged Girl as *Margery*, and such a dirty little curl-pated Boy as *Tommy*.[11] Our Relations and Friends seldom take Notice of us when we are poor; but as we grow rich they grow fond. And this will always be the Case, while People love Money better than Virtue, or better than they do GOD Almighty. But such wicked Folks, who love nothing but Money, and are proud and despise the Poor, never come to any good in the End, as we shall see by and by.

* * *

CHAP. II.
How and about Mr. Smith.

MR. *Smith* was a very worthy Clergyman, who lived in the Parish where Little *Margery* and *Tommy* were born; and having a Relation come to see him, who was a charitable good Man, he sent for these Children to him. The Gentleman ordered Little *Margery* a new Pair of Shoes, gave Mr. *Smith* some Money to buy her Cloathes; and said, he would take *Tommy* and make him a little Sailor; and accordingly had a Jacket and Trowsers made for him, in which he now appears. Pray look at him.

After some Days the Gentleman intended to go to *London*, and take little *Tommy* with him, of whom you will know more by and by, for we shall at a proper Time present you with some Part of his History, his Travels and Adventures.

The Parting between these two little Children was very affecting, *Tommy* cried, and *Margery* cried, and they kissed each other an hundred Times. At last *Tommy* thus wiped off her Tears with the End of his Jacket, and bid her cry no more, for that he would come to her again, when he returned from Sea. However, as they were so very fond, the Gentleman would not suffer them to take Leave of each other; but told *Tommy* he should ride out with him, and come back at Night. When night came, Little *Margery* grew very uneasy about her Brother, and after sitting up as late as Mr. *Smith* would let her, she went crying to Bed.

* * *

CHAP. III.

How Little Margery *obtained the Name of* Goody Two-Shoes, *and what happened in the Parish.*

As soon as Little *Margery* got up in the Morning, which was very early, she ran all round the Village, crying for her Brother; and after some Time returned greatly distressed. However, at this Instant, the Shoemaker very opportunely came in with the new Shoes, for which she had been measured by the Gentleman's Order.

Nothing could have supported Little *Margery* under the Affliction she was in for the Loss of her Brother, but the Pleasure she took in her *two Shoes*. She ran out to Mrs. *Smith* as soon as they were put on, and stroking down her ragged Apron thus, cried out, *Two Shoes, Mame, see two Shoes*. And so she behaved to all the People she met, and by that Means obtained the Name of *Goody Two-Shoes*, though her Playmates called her *Old Goody Two-Shoes*.

Little *Margery* was very happy in being with Mr. and Mrs. *Smith*, who were very charitable and good to her, and had agreed to breed her up with their Family; but as soon as that Tyrant of the Parish, that *Graspall*, heard of her being there, he applied first to Mr. *Smith*, and threatened to reduce his Tythes if he kept her;[12] and after that he spoke to Sir *Timothy*, who sent Mr. *Smith* a peremptory Message by his Servant, that *he should send back* Meanwell's *Girl to be kept by her Relations, and not harbour her in the Parish.*[13] This so distressed Mr. *Smith* that he shed Tears, and cried, *Lord have Mercy on the Poor!*

The Prayers of the Righteous fly upwards, and reach unto the Throne of Heaven, as will be seen in the Sequel.[14]

Mrs. *Smith* was also greatly concerned at being thus obliged to discard poor Little *Margery*. She kissed her and cried; as also did Mr. *Smith*, but they were obliged to send her away; for the People who had ruined her Father could at any Time have ruined them.

*   *   *

CHAP. IV.

How Little Margery *learned to read, and by Degrees taught others.*

LITTLE *Margery* saw how good, and how wise Mr. *Smith* was, and concluded, that this was owing to his great Learning, therefore she wanted of all Things to learn to read. For this Purpose she used to meet the little Boys and Girls as they came from School, borrow their Books, and sit down and read till they returned;

By this Means she soon got more Learning than any of her Playmates, and laid the following Scheme for instructing those who were more ignorant than herself. She found, that only the following Letters were required to spell all the Words in the World; but as some of these Letters are large and some small, she

with her Knife cut out of several Pieces of Wood ten Setts of each of these:

a b c d e f g h i j k l m n o p q r ſ s t u v w x y z.[15]

And six Setts of these:

A B C D E F G H I K L M N O P Q R S T U V W X Y Z.

And having got an old Spelling-Book, she made her Companions set up all the Words they wanted to spell, and after that she taught them to compose Sentences. You know what a Sentence is, my Dear, *I will be good*, is a Sentence; and is made up, as you see, of several Words.

The usual Manner of Spelling, or carrying on the Game, as they called it, was this: Suppose the Word to be spelt was Plumb Pudding (and who can suppose a better) the Children were placed in a Circle, and the first brought the Letter *P*, the next *l*, the next *u*, the next *m*, and so on till the Whole was spelt; and if any one brought a wrong Letter, he was to pay a Fine, or play no more. This was at their Play; and every Morning she used to go round to teach the Children with these Rattle-traps in a Basket, as you see in the Print.

I once went her Rounds with her, and was highly diverted, as you may be, if you please to look into the next Chapter.

* * *

CHAP. V.

How Little Two-Shoes *became a trotting Tutoress and how she taught her young Pupils.*

IT was about seven o'Clock in the Morning when we set out on this important Business, and the first House we came to was Farmer *Wilson's*. See here it is.

Here *Margery* stopped, and ran up to the Door, *Tap, tap, tap.* Who's there? Only little goody *Two-Shoes*, answered *Margery*, come to teach *Billy*. Oh Little *Goody*, says Mrs. *Wilson*, with Pleasure in her Face, I am glad to see you, *Billy* wants you sadly, for he has learned all his Lesson. Then out came the little Boy. *How do doody Two-Shoes*, says he, not able to speak plain. Yet this little Boy had learned all his Letters; for she threw down this Alphabet mixed together thus:

b d f h k m o q s u w y z ʃ

a c e g i l n p r t v x j

and he picked them up, called them by their right Names, and put them all in order thus:

a b c d e f g h i j k l m n o
p q r ʃ s t u v w x y z.

She then threw down the Alphabet of Capital Letters in the Manner you here see them.

B D F H K M O Q S U W Y Z
A C E G I L N P R T V X J.

and he picked them all up, and having told their Names, placed them thus:

A B C D E F G H I J K L M
N O P Q R S T U V W X Y Z.

Now, pray little Reader, take this Bodkin,[16] and see if you can point out the Letters from these mixed Alphabets, and tell how they should be placed as well as little Boy *Billy*.

The next Place we came to was Farmer *Simpson's*, and here it is.

Bow wow, wow, says the Dog at the Door. Sirrah, says his Mistress, what do you bark at Little *Two-Shoes*. Come in *Madge*; here, *Sally* wants you sadly, she has learned all her Lesson. Then out came the little one: So *Madge!* say she; so *Sally!* answered the other, have you learned your Lesson? Yes, that's what I have, replied the little one in the Country Manner; and immediately taking the Letters she set up these Syllables:

> ba be bi bo bu, ca ce ci co cu
> da de di do du, fa fe fi fo fu.

and gave them their exact Sounds as she composed them; after which she set up the following:

> ac ec ic oc uc, ad ed id od ud
> af ef if of uf, ag eg ig og ug.

And pronounced them likewise. She then sung the Cuzz's Chorus, (which may be found in the *Little Pretty Play Thing*, published by Mr. NEWBERY) and to the same Tune to which it is there set.[17]

After this, Little *Two-Shoes* taught her to spell Words of one Syllable, and she soon set up Pear, Plumb, Top, Ball, Pin, Puss, Dog, Hog, Fawn, Buck, Doe, Lamb, Sheep, Ram, Cow, Bull, Cock, Hen, and many more.

The next Place we came to was *Gaffer Cook's* Cottage; there you see it before you.

Here a number of poor Children were met to learn; who all came round Little *Margery* at once; and, having pulled out her Letters, she asked the little Boy next her, what he had for Dinner? Who answered, *Bread.* (the poor Children in many Places live very hard) Well then, says she, set the first Letter. He put up the Letter B, to which the next added r, and the next e, the next a, the next d, and it stood thus, *Bread.*

And what had you *Polly Comb* for your Dinner? *Apple-pye* answered the little Girl: Upon which the next in Turn set up a great A, the two next a p each, and so on till the two Words Apple and Pye were united and stood thus, *Apple-pye.*

The next had *Potatoes*, the next *Beef and Turnips*, which were spelt with many others, till the Game of Spelling was finished. She then set them another Task, and we proceeded.

The next Place we came to was Farmer *Thompson's*, where there were a great many little ones waiting for her.

So little Mrs. *Goody Two-Shoes*, says one of them, where have you been so long? I have been teaching, says she, longer than I intended, and am afraid I am come too soon for you now. No, but indeed you are not, replied the other; for I have got my Lesson, and so has *Sally Dawson*, and so has *Harry Wilson*, and so we have all; and they capered about as if they were overjoyed to see her. Why then, says she, you are all very good, and GOD Almighty will love you; so let us begin our Lessons. They all huddled round her, and though at the other Place they were employed about Words and Syllables, here we had People of much greater Understanding who dealt only in Sentences.

The Letters being brought upon the Table, one of the little ones set up the following Sentence.

The Lord have Mercy upon me, and grant that I may be always good, and say my Prayers, and love the Lord my God with all my Heart, with all my Soul, and with all my Strength; and honour the King, and all good Men in Authority under him.

Then the next took the Letters, and composed this Sentence.

Lord have Mercy upon me, and grant that I may love my Neighbour as myself, and do unto all Men as I would have them do unto me, and tell no Lies; but be honest and just in all my Dealings.

The third composed the following Sentence.

The Lord have Mercy upon me, and grant that I may honour my Father and Mother, and love my Brothers and Sisters, Relations and

Friends, and all my Playmates, and every Body, and endeavour to make them happy.

The fourth composed the following.

I pray GOD *to bless this whole Company, and all our Friends, and all our Enemies.*[18]

To this last *Polly Sullen* objected, and said, truly, she did not know why she should pray for her Enemies? Not pray for your Enemies, says Little *Margery*; yes, you must, you are no Christian, if you don't forgive your Enemies, and do Good for Evil. *Polly* still pouted; upon which Little *Margery* said, though she was poor, and obliged to lie in a Barn, she would not keep Company with such a naughty, proud, perverse Girl as *Polly*; and was going away; however the Difference was made up, and she set them to compose the following

LESSONS

For the CONDUCT of LIFE.[19]

LESSON I.

He that will thrive,
Must rise by Five.
He that hath thriv'n,
May lie till Seven.
Truth may be blam'd,
But cannot be sham'd.
Tell me with whom you go;
And I'll tell what you do.
A Friend in your Need,
Is a Friend indeed.
They ne'er can be wise,
Who good Counsel despise.

LESSON II.

A wise Head makes a close Mouth.
Don't burn your Lips with another Man's Broth.

Wit is Folly, unless a wise Man hath the keeping of it.
Use soft Words and hard Arguments.
Honey catches more Flies than Vinegar.
To forget a Wrong is the best Revenge.
Patience is a Plaister for all Sores.[20]
Where Pride goes, Shame will follow.
When Vice enters the Room, Vengeance is near the Door.
Industry is Fortune's right Hand, and Frugality her left.
Make much of Three-pence, or you ne'er will be worth a Groat.[21]

Lesson III.

A Lie stands upon one Leg, but Truth upon two.
When a Man talks much, believe but half what he says.
Fair Words butter no Parsnips.
Bad Company poisons the Mind.
A covetous Man is never satisfied.
Abundance, like Want, ruins many.
Contentment is the best Fortune.
A contented Mind is a continual Feast.

A LESSON in Religion.

Love GOD, for he is good.
Fear GOD, for he is just.
Pray to GOD, for all good Things come from him.
Praise GOD, for great is his Mercy towards us, and wonderful are
    all his Works.
Those who strive to be good, have GOD on their Side.
Those who have GOD for their Friend, shall want nothing.
Confess your Sins to GOD, and if you repent he will forgive you.
Remember that all you do, is done in the Presence of GOD.
The Time will come, my Friends, when we must give
Account to GOD, how we on Earth did live.[22]

A Moral LESSON.

A good Boy will make a good Man.
Honour your Parents, and the World will honour you.

Love your Friends, and your Friends will love you.
He that swims in Sin, will sink in Sorrow.
Learn to live, as you would wish to die.

>As you expect all Men should deal by you:
>So deal by them, and give each Man his Due.

As we were returning Home, we saw a Gentleman, who was very ill, sitting under a shady Tree at the Corner of his Rookery. Though ill, he began to joke with Little *Margery*, and said, laughingly, so, *Goody Two-Shoes*, they tell me you are a cunning little Baggage;[23] pray, can you tell me what I shall do to get well? Yes, Sir, says she, go to Bed when your Rooks do. You see they are going to Rest already:

Do you so likewise, and get up with them in the morning; earn, as they do, every Day what you eat, and eat and drink no more than you earn; and you'll get Health and keep it. What should induce the Rooks to frequent Gentlemens Houses only, but to tell them how to lead a prudent Life? They never build over Cottages or Farm-houses, because they see, that these People know how to live without their Admonition.

Thus Health and Wit you may improve,
Taught by the Tenants of the Grove.

The Gentleman laughing gave *Margery* Sixpence; and told her she was a sensible Hussey.[24]

✳ ✳ ✳

CHAP. VI.

How the whole Parish was frighted.

WHO does not know Lady *Ducklington,* or who does not know that she was buried at this Parish Church?

Well, I never saw so grand a Funeral in all my Life; but the Money they squandered away, would have been better laid out in little Books for Children, or in Meat, Drink, and Cloaths for the Poor.

This is a fine Hearse indeed, and the nodding Plumes on the Horses look very grand; but what End does that answer, otherwise than to display the Pride of the Living, or the Vanity of the Dead.

Fie upon such Folly, say I, and Heaven grant that those who want more Sense may have it.

But all the Country round came to see the Burying, and it was late before the Corpse was interred. After which, in the Night, or rather about Four o'Clock in the Morning, the Bells were heard to jingle in the Steeple, which frightened the People prodigiously, who all thought it was Lady *Ducklington*'s Ghost dancing among the Bell-ropes. The People flocked to *Will Dobbins* the Clerk,[25] and wanted him to go and see what it was; but *William* said, he was sure it was a Ghost, and that he would not offer to open the Door. At length Mr. *Long* the Rector, hearing such an Uproar in the Village, went to the Clerk, to know why he did not go into the Church; and see who was there. I go, Sir, says *William*, why the Ghost would frighten me out of my Wits.– Mrs. *Dobbins* too cried, and laying hold of her Husband said, he should not be eat up by the Ghost. A Ghost, you Blockheads, says Mr. *Long* in a Pet,[26] did either of you ever see a Ghost, or know any Body that did? Yes, says the Clerk, my Father did once in the Shape of a Windmill, and it walked all round the Church in a white Sheet, with Jack Boots on, and had a Gun by its Side instead of a Sword. A fine Picture of a Ghost truly, says Mr. *Long*, give me the Key of the Church, you Monkey; for I tell you there is no such Thing now, whatever may have been formerly.[27] – Then taking the Key, he went to the Church, all the people following him. As soon as he had opened the Door, what Sort of a Ghost do ye think appeared? Why Little *Two-Shoes*, who being weary, had fallen asleep in one of the Pews during the Funeral Service, and was shut in all Night. She immediately asked Mr. *Long* 's Pardon for the Trouble she had given him, told him, she had been locked into the Church, and said, she should not have rung the Bells, but that she was very cold, and hearing Farmer *Boult's* Man go whistling by with his Horses, she was in Hopes he would have went to the Clerk for the Key to let her out.

* * *

CHAP. VII.

Containing an Account of all the Spirits, or Ghosts, she saw in the Church.

THE People were ashamed to ask Little *Madge* any Questions before Mr. *Long*, but as soon as he was gone, they all got round her to satisfy their Curiosity, and desired she would give them a particular Account of all that she had heard and seen.

Her TALE.

I went to the Church, said she, as most of you did last Night, to see the Burying, and being very weary, I sate me down in Mr. *Jones*'s Pew, and fell fast asleep. At Eleven of the Clock I awoke; which I believe was in some measure occasioned by the Clock's striking, for I heard it. I started up, and could not at first tell where I was; but after some Time I recollected the Funeral, and soon found that I was shut in the Church. It was dismal dark, and I could see nothing; but while I was standing in the Pew, something jumped up upon me behind, and laid, as I thought, its Hands over my Shoulders. – I own, I was a little afraid at first; however, I considered that I had always been constant at Prayers and at Church, and that I had done nobody any Harm, but had endeavoured to do what Good I could; and then, thought I, what have I to fear? yet I kneeled down to say my Prayers. As soon as I was on my Knees something very cold, as cold as Marble, ay, as cold as Ice, touched my Neck, which made me start; however, I continued my Prayers, and having begged Protection from Almighty GOD, I found my Spirits come, and I was sensible that I had nothing to fear; for GOD Almighty protects not only all those who are good, but also all those who endeavour to be good. – Nothing can withstand the Power, and exceed the Goodness of GOD Almighty. Armed with the Confidence of his Protection, I walked down the Church Isle,[28] when I heard something, pit pat, pit pat, pit pat, come after me, and something touched my Hand, which seemed as cold as a Marble Monument. I could not think what this was, yet I knew it could not hurt me, and therefore I made myself easy, but being very cold, and the Church being paved with Stone, which was very damp, I felt my Way as well as I could to the Pulpit, in doing which something brushed by me, and almost threw me down. However I was not frightened, for I knew, that GOD Almighty would suffer nothing to hurt me.

At last, I found out the Pulpit, and having shut too the Door, I laid me down on the Mat and Cushion to sleep; when something thrust and pulled the Door, as I thought for Admittance, which prevented my going to sleep. At last it cries, *Bow, wow, wow*; and I concluded it must be Mr. *Saunderson's* Dog, which had followed me from their House to Church, so I opened the Door, and called *Snip, Snip*, and the Dog jumped up upon me immediately. After this *Snip* and I lay down together, and had a most comfortable Nap; for when I awoke again it was almost light. I then walked up and down all the Isles of the Church to keep myself warm; and though I went into the Vault, and trod on Lady *Ducklington's* Coffin, I saw no Ghost, and I believe it was owing to the Reason Mr. *Long* has given you, namely, that there is no such Thing to be seen. As to my Part, I would as soon lie all Night in the Church as in any other Place; and I am sure that any little Boy or Girl, who is good, and loves GOD Almighty, and keeps his Commandments, may as safely lie in the Church, or the Church-yard, as any where else, if they take Care not to get Cold; for I am sure there are no Ghosts, either to hurt, or to frighten them; though any one possessed of Fear might have taken Neighbour *Saunderson* 's Dog with his cold Nose for a Ghost; and if they had not been undeceived, as I was, would never have thought otherwise. All the Company acknowledged the Justness of the Observation, and thanked Little *Two-Shoes* for her Advice.

REFLECTION.

After this, my dear Children, I hope you will not believe any foolish Stories that ignorant, weak, or designing People may tell you about *Ghosts*; for the Tales of *Ghosts*, *Witches*, and *Fairies*, are the Frolicks of a distempered Brain. No wise Man ever saw either of them. Little *Margery* you see was not afraid; no, she had *good Sense*, and a *good Conscience*, which is a Cure for all these imaginary Evils.

✳   ✳   ✳

CHAP. VIII.

Of something which happened to Little Two-Shoes *in a Barn, more dreadful than the Ghost in the Church; and how she returned Good for Evil to her Enemy Sir* Timothy.

SOME Days after this a more dreadful Accident befel Little *Madge*. She happened to be coming late from teaching, when it rained, thundered, and lightened, and therefore she took Shelter in a Farmer's Barn at a Distance from the Village. Soon after, the Tempest drove in four Thieves, who, not seeing such a little creep-mouse Girl as *Two-Shoes*,[29] lay down on the Hay next to her, and began to talk over their Exploits, and to settle Plans for future Robberies. Little *Margery* on hearing them, covered herself with Straw. To be sure she was sadly frighted, but her good Sense

taught her, that the only Security she had was in keeping herself concealed; therefore she laid very still, and breathed very softly. About Four o'Clock these wicked People came to a Resolution to break both Sir *William Dove's* House, and Sir *Timothy Gripe's*, and by Force of Arms to carry off all their Money, Plate and Jewels;[30] but as it was thought then too late, they agreed to defer it till the next Night. After laying this Scheme they all set out upon their Pranks, which greatly rejoiced *Margery*, as it would any other little Girl in her Situation. Early in the Morning she went to Sir *William*, and told him the whole of their Conversation. Upon which, he asked her Name, gave her Something, and bid her call at his House the Day following. She also went to Sir *Timothy*, notwithstanding he had used her so ill; for she knew it was her Duty to *do Good for Evil*.[31] As soon as he was informed who she was, he took no Notice of her; upon which she desired to speak to Lady *Gripe*; and having informed her Ladyship of the Affair, she went her Way. This Lady had more Sense than her Husband, which indeed is not a singular Case; for instead of despising Little *Margery* and her Information, she privately set People to guard the House. The Robbers divided themselves, and went about the Time mentioned to both Houses, and were surprized by the Guards, and taken. Upon examining these Wretches, one of which turned Evidence,[32] both Sir *William* and Sir *Timothy* found that they owed their Lives to the Discovery made by Little *Margery*, and the first took great Notice of her, and would no longer let her lie in a Barn; but Sir *Timothy* only said, that he was ashamed to owe his Life to the Daughter of one who was his Enemy; so true it is, *that a proud Man seldom forgives those he has injured.*

∗   ∗   ∗

CHAP. IX.

How Little Margery *was made Principal of a Country College.*

Mrs. *Williams*, of whom I have given a particular Account in my *New Year's Gift*,[33] and who kept a College for instructing little Gentlemen and Ladies in the Science of A, B, C, was at this Time very old and infirm, and wanted to decline that important Trust. This being told to Sir *William Dove*, who lived in the Parish, he sent for Mrs. *Williams*, and desired she would examine Little *Two-Shoes*, and see whether she was qualified for the Office. – This was done, and Mrs. *Williams* made the following Report in her Favour, namely, *that Little* Margery *was the best Scholar, and had the best Head, and the best Heart of any one she had examined.* All the Country had a great Opinion of Mrs. *Williams*, and this Character gave them also a great Opinion of Mrs. *Margery*; for so we must now call her.

This Mrs. *Margery* thought the happiest Period of her Life; but more Happiness was in Store for her. GOD Almighty heaps up Blessings for all those who love him, and though for a Time he may suffer them to be poor and distressed, and hide his good Purposes from human Sight, yet in the End they are generally crowned with Happiness here, and no one can doubt of their being so hereafter.

On this Occasion the following Hymn, or rather a Translation of the twenty-third Psalm, is said to have been written, and was soon after published in the *Spectator*.[34]

I.

> The Lord my Pasture shall prepare,
> And feed me with a Shepherd's Care:
> His Presence shall my Wants supply,
> And guard me with a watchful Eye;
> My Noon-day Walks he shall attend,
> And all my Midnight Hours defend.

II.

When in the sultry Glebe I faint,
Or on the thirsty Mountain pant;
To fertile Vales and dewy Meads,
My weary wand'ring Steps he leads;
Where peaceful Rivers, soft and slow,
Amid the verdant Landskip flow.[35]

III.

Tho' in the Paths of Death I tread,
With gloomy Horrors overspread,
My stedfast Heart shall fear no Ill,
For thou, O Lord, art with me still;
Thy friendly Crook shall give me Aid,
And guide me thro' the dreadful Shade.

IV.

Tho' in a bare and rugged Way,
Thro' devious lonely Wilds I stray,
Thy Bounty shall my Pains beguile:
The barren Wilderness shall smile,
With sudden Greens & herbage crown'd,
And Streams shall murmur all around.

Here ends the History of Little *Two-Shoes*. Those who would
know how she behaved after she came to be Mrs. *Margery Two-Shoes* must read the Second Part of this Work, in which an Account
of the Remainder of her Life, her Marriage, and Death are set forth
at large, according to Act of Parliament.

* * *

The Renowned
HISTORY
OF
Mrs. MARGERY TWO-SHOES.

PART II.

INTRODUCTION.

In the first Part of this Work, the young Student has read, and I hope with Pleasure and Improvement, the History of this Lady, while she was known and distinguished by the Name of *Little Two-Shoes*; we are now come to a Period of her Life when that Name was discarded, and a more eminent one bestowed upon her, I mean that of Mrs. *Margery Two-Shoes*: For as she was now President of the A, B, C College, it became necessary to exalt her in Title as well as in Place.

No sooner was she settled in this Office, but she laid every possible Scheme to promote the Welfare and Happiness of all her Neighbours, and especially of the Little Ones, in whom she took great Delight, and all those whose Parents could not afford to pay for their Education, she taught for nothing, but the Pleasure she had in their Company, for you are to observe, that they were very good, or were soon made so by her good Management.

✳ ✳ ✳

CHAP. I.

Of her School, her Ushers, or Assistants, and her Manner of Teaching.

WE have already informed the Reader, that the School where she taught, was that which was before kept by Mrs. *Williams*, whose Character you may find in my *New Year's Gift*. The Room was large, and as she knew, that Nature intended Children should be always in Action, she placed her different Letters, or Alphabets, all round the School, so that every one was obliged to get up to fetch a Letter, or to spell a Word, when it came to their Turn; which not only kept them in Health, but fixed the Letters and Points firmly in their Minds.

She had the following Assistants or Ushers to help her, and I will tell you how she came by them. Mrs. *Margery*, you must know, was very humane and compassionate; and her Tenderness extended not only to all Mankind, but even to all Animals that were not noxious; as your's ought to do, if you would be happy here, and go to Heaven hereafter. These are GOD Almighty's Creatures as well as we. He made both them and us; and for wise Purposes, best known to himself, placed them in this World to live among us; so that they are our fellow Tenants of the Globe. How then can People dare to torture and wantonly destroy GOD Almighty's Creatures? They as well as you are capable of feeling Pain, and of receiving Pleasure, and how can you, who want to be made happy yourself, delight in making your fellow Creatures miserable? Do you think the poor Birds, whose Nest and young ones that wicked Boy *Dick Wilson* ran away with Yesterday, do not feel as much Pain, as your Father and Mother would have felt, had any one pulled down their House and ran away with you? To be sure they do. Mrs. *Two-Shoes* used to speak of those Things, and of naughty Boys throwing at Cocks,[36] torturing Flies, and whipping Horses and Dogs, with Tears in her Eyes, and would never suffer any one to come to her School who did so.

One Day, as she was going through the next Village, she met with some wicked Boys who had got a young Raven, which they were going to throw at, she wanted to get the poor Creature out of their cruel Hands, and therefore gave them a Penny for him, and brought him home. She called his Name *Ralph*, and a fine Bird he is. Do look at him,

and remember what *Solomon* says, *The Eye that despiseth his Father, and regardeth not the Distress of his Mother, the Ravens of the Valley shall peck it out, and the young Eagles eat it.*[37] Now this Bird she taught to speak, to spell and to read; and as he was particularly fond of playing with the large Letters, the Children used to call this *Ralph's* Alphabet.

A B C D E F G H I J K L M N O P Q R S T U V W X Y Z.

He always sat at her Elbow, as you see in the first Picture, and when any of the Children were wrong, she used to call out, *Put them right Ralph.*

Some Days after she had met with the Raven, as she was walking in the Fields, she saw some naughty Boys, who had taken a Pidgeon, and tied a String to its Leg, in order to let it fly, and draw it back again when they pleased; and by this Means they tortured the poor Animal with the Hopes of Liberty and repeated Disappointment. This Pidgeon she also bought, and taught him how to spell and read, though not to talk, and he performed all those extraordinary Things which are recorded of the famous Bird, that was some Time since advertised in the *Haymarket*, and visited by most of the great People in the Kingdom.[38] This Pidgeon was a very pretty Fellow, and she called him *Tom*. See here he is.

And as the Raven *Ralph* was fond of the large Letters, *Tom* the Pidgeon took Care of the small ones, of which he composed this Alphabet.

a b c d e f g h i j k l m n o p q r s t u v w x y z.

The Neighbours knowing that Mrs. *Two Shoes* was very good, as to be sure nobody was better, made her a Present of a little Sky-lark, and a fine Bird he is.

Now as many People, even at that Time had learned to lie in Bed long in the Morning, she thought the Lark might be of Use to her and her Pupils, and tell them when to get up.

> *For he that is fond of his Bed, and lays 'till Noon, lives but half his Days, the rest being lost in Sleep, which is a Kind of Death.*[39]

Some Time after this a poor Lamb had lost its Dam,[40] and the Farmer being about to kill it, she bought it of him, and brought it home with her to play with the Children, and teach them when to go to Bed; for it was a Rule with the wise Men of that Age (and a very good one, let me tell you) to

> *Rise with the Lark, and lie down with the Lamb.*

This Lamb she called *Will*, and a pretty Fellow he is; do, look at him.

No sooner was *Tippy* the Lark and *Will* the Ba-lamb brought into the School, but that sensible Rogue *Ralph*, the Raven, composed the following Verse, which every little good Boy and Girl should get by Heart.

> *Early to Bed, and early to rise;*
> *Is the Way to be healthy, and wealthy, and wise.*[41]

A sly Rogue; but it is true enough; for those who do not go to Bed early cannot rise early; and those who do not rise early cannot do much Business. Pray, let this be told at the Court, and to People who have Routs and Rackets.[42]

Soon after this, a Present was made to Mrs. *Margery* of little Dog *Jumper*, and a pretty Dog he is. Pray, look at him.

Jumper, Jumper, Jumper! He is always in a good Humour, and playing and jumping about, and therefore he was called *Jumper*. The Place assigned for *Jumper* was that of keeping the Door, so that he may be called the Porter of the College, for he would let nobody go out, or any one come in, without the Leave of his Mistress. See how he sits, a saucy Rogue.

Billy the Ba-lamb was a chearful Fellow, and all the Children were fond of him, wherefore Mrs. *Two-Shoes* made it a Rule, that those who behaved best should have *Will* home with them at Night to carry their Satchel or Basket at his Back, and bring it in the Morning. See what a fine Fellow he is, and how he trudges along.

* * *

CHAP. II.

A Scene of Distress in the School.

IT happened one Day, when Mrs. *Two-Shoes* was diverting the Children after Dinner, as she usually did with some innocent Games, or entertaining and instructive Stories, that a Man arrived with the melancholy News of *Sally Jones's* Father being thrown from his Horse, and thought past all Recovery; nay, the Messenger said, that he was seemingly dying, when he came away. Poor *Sally* was greatly distressed, as indeed were all the School, for she dearly loved her Father, and Mrs. *Two-Shoes*, and all the Children dearly loved her. It is generally said, that we never know the real Value of our Parents or Friends till we have lost them; but poor *Sally* felt this by Affection, and her Mistress knew it by Experience. All the School were in Tears, and the Messenger was obliged to return; but before he went, Mrs. *Two-Shoes*, unknown to the Children, ordered *Tom* Pidgeon to go home with the Man, and bring a Letter to inform her how Mr. *Jones* did. They set out together, and the Pidgeon rode on the Man's Head, (as you see here)

for the Man was able to carry the Pidgeon, though the Pidgeon was not able to carry the Man, if he had, they would have been there much sooner, for *Tom* Pidgeon was *very good*, and never staid on an Errand.

Soon after the Man was gone the Pidgeon was lost, and the Concern the Children were under for Mr. *Jones* and little *Sally* was in some Measure diverted, and Part of their Attention turned after *Tom*, who was a great Favourite, and consequently much bewailed. Mrs. *Margery*, who knew the great Use and Necessity of teaching Children to submit chearfully to the Will of Providence, bid them wipe away their Tears, and then kissing *Sally*, you must be a good Girl, says she, and depend upon GOD Almighty for his Blessing and Protection; for *he is a Father to the Fatherless, and defendeth all those who put their Trust in him*.[43] She then told them a Story, which I shall relate in as few Words as possible.

The History of Mr. Lovewell, *Father to Lady* Lucy.

Mr. *Lovewell* was born at *Bath*, and apprenticed to a laborious Trade in *London*, which being too hard for him, he parted with his Master by Consent, and hired himself as a common Servant to a Merchant in the City. Here he spent his leisure Hours not as Servants too frequently do, in Drinking and Schemes of Pleasure, but in improving his Mind; and among other Acquirements, he made himself a complete Master of Accompts.[44] His Sobriety, Honesty, and the Regard he paid to his Master's Interest, greatly recommended him in the whole Family, and he had several Offices of Trust committed to his Charge, in which he acquitted himself so well, that the Merchant removed him from the Stable into the Counting-house.

Here he soon made himself Master of the Business, and became so useful to the Merchant, that in regard to his faithful Services, and the Affection he had for him, he married him to his own Niece, a prudent agreeable young Lady; and gave him a Share in the Business. See what Honesty and Industry will do for us. Half the great Men in *London*, I am told, have made themselves by this Means, and who would but be honest and industrious, when it is so much our Interest and our Duty.

After some Years the Merchant died, and left Mr. *Lovewell* possessed of many fine Ships at Sea, and much Money, and he was happy in a Wife, who had brought him a Son and two Daughters, all dutiful and obedient. The Treasures and good Things, however, of this Life are so uncertain, that a Man can never be happy, unless he lays the Foundation for it in his own Mind. So true is that Copy in our Writing Books, which tells us, that *a contented Mind is a continual Feast.*

After some Years successful Trade, he thought his Circumstances sufficient to insure his own Ships, or, in other Words, to send his Ships and Goods to Sea without being insured by others, as is customary among Merchants; when, unfortunately for him, four of them richly laden were lost at Sea. This he supported with becoming Resolution; but the next Mail brought him Advice, that nine others were taken by the *French*, with whom we were then at War;[45] and this, together with the Failure of three foreign Merchants whom he had trusted, compleated his Ruin. He was then obliged to call his Creditors together, who took his Effects, and being angry with him for the imprudent Step of not insuring his Ships, left him destitute of all Subsistence. Nor did the Flatterers of his Fortune, those who had lived by his Bounty when in his Prosperity, pay the least Regard either to him or his Family. So true is another Copy, that you will find in your Writing Book, which says, *Misfortune tries our Friends.* All these Slights of his pretended Friends, and the ill Usage of his Creditors, both he and his Family bore with Christian Fortitude; but other Calamities fell upon him, which he felt more sensibly.

In his Distress, one of his Relations, who lived at *Florence*, offered to take his Son; and another, who lived at *Barbadoes*, sent for one of his Daughters. The Ship which his Son sailed in was cast away, and all the Crew supposed to be lost; and the Ship, in which his Daughter went a Passenger, was taken by Pyrates, and one Post brought the miserable Father an Account of the Loss of his two Children. This was the severest Stroke of all: It made him compleatly wretched, and he knew it must have a dreadful Effect on his Wife and Daughter; he therefore endeavoured to conceal it from them. But the perpetual Anxiety he was in, together with the Loss of his Appetite and Want of Rest, soon alarmed his Wife.

She found something was labouring in his Breast, which was concealed from her; and one Night being disturbed in a Dream, with what was ever in his Thoughts, and calling out upon his dear Children; she awoke him, and insisted upon knowing the Cause of his Inquietude. *Nothing, my Dear, nothing,* says he, *The Lord gave, and the Lord hath taken away, blessed be the Name of the Lord.*[46] This was sufficient to alarm the poor Woman; she lay till his Spirits were composed, and as she thought asleep, then stealing out of Bed, got the Keys and opened his Bureau, where she found the fatal Account. In the Height of her Distractions, she flew to her Daughter's Room, and waking her with her Shrieks, put the Letters into her Hands. The young Lady, unable to support this Load of Misery, fell into a Fit, from which it was thought she never could have been recovered. However, at last she revived; but the Shock was so great, that it entirely deprived her of her Speech.

Thus loaded with Misery, and unable to bear the Slights and Disdain of those who had formerly professed themselves Friends, this unhappy Family retired into a Country, where they were unknown, in order to hide themselves from the World; when, to support their Independency, the Father laboured as well as he could at Husbandry, and the Mother and Daughter sometimes got spinning and knitting Work, to help to furnish the Means of Subsistence; which however was so precarious and uncertain, that they often, for many Weeks together, lived on nothing but Cabbage and Bread boiled in Water. But God never forsaketh the Righteous, nor suffereth those to perish who put their Trust in him. At this Time a Lady, who was just come to England, sent to take a pleasant Seat ready furnished in that Neighbourhood,[47] and the Person who was employed for the Purpose, was ordered to deliver a Bank Note of an hundred Pounds to Mr. *Lovewell*, another hundred to his Wife, and fifty to the Daughter, desiring them to take Possession of the House, and get it well aired against she came down, which would be in two or three Days at most. This, to People who were almost starving, was a sweet and seasonable Relief, and they were all sollicitous to know their Benefactress, but of that the Messenger himself was too ignorant to inform them. However, she came down sooner than was expected, and with Tears embraced them again and again: After which she told the Father and Mother she had heard from their Daughter, who was her Acquaintance, and that she was well and on her Return to

England. This was the agreeable Subject of their Conversation till after Dinner, when drinking their Healths, she again with Tears saluted them, and falling upon her Knees asked their Blessings.

Tis impossible to express the mutual Joy which this occasioned. Their Conversation was made up of the most endearing Expressions, intermingled with Tears and Caresses. Their Torrent of Joy, however, was for a Moment interrupted, by a Chariot which stopped at the Gate, and which brought as they thought a very unseasonable Visitor, and therefore she sent to be excused from seeing Company. But this had no Effect, for a Gentleman richly dressed jumped out of the Chariot, and pursuing the Servant into the Parlour saluted them round, who were all astonished at his Behaviour. But when the Tears trickled from his Cheeks, the Daughter, who had been some Years dumb, immediately cried out, *my Brother! my Brother! my Brother!* and from that Instant recovered her Speech. The mutual Joy which this occasioned, is better felt than expressed. Those who have proper Sentiments of Humanity, Gratitude, and filial Piety will rejoice at the Event, and those who have a proper Idea of the Goodness of God, and his gracious Providence, will from this, as well as other Instances of his Goodness and Mercy, glorify his holy Name, and magnify his Wisdom and Power, who is a Shield to the Righteous, and defendeth all those who put their Trust in him.

As you, my dear Children, may be sollicitous to know how this happy Event was brought about, I must inform you, that Mr.

Lovewell 's Son, when the Ship foundered, had with some others got into the long Boat, and was taken up by a Ship at Sea, and carried to the East Indies, where in a little Time he made a large Fortune; and the Pirates who took his Daughter, attempted to rob her of her Chastity; but finding her Inflexible, and determined to die rather than to submit, some of them behaved to her in a very cruel Manner; but others, who had more Honour and Generosity, became her Defenders; upon which a Quarrel arose between them, and the Captain, who was the worst of the Gang, being killed, the rest of the Crew carried the Ship into a Port of the *Manilla* Islands, belonging to the *Spaniards*;[48] where, when her Story was known, she was treated with great Respect, and courted by a young Gentleman, who was taken ill of a Fever, and died before the Marriage was agreed on, but left her his whole Fortune.

You see, my dear *Sally*, how wonderfully these People were preserved, and made happy after such extreme Distress; we are therefore never to despair, even under the greatest Misfortunes, for GOD Almighty is All-powerful, and can deliver us at any Time. Remember *Job*, but I think you have not read so far, take the Bible, *Billy Jones*, and read the History of that good and patient Man. At this Instant something was heard to flap at the Window, *Wow, wow, wow*, says Jumper, and attempted to leap up and open the Door, at which the Children were surprised; but Mrs. *Margery* knowing what it was, opened the Casement, as *Noah* did the

Window of the Ark, and drew in *Tom* Pidgeon with a Letter, and see here he is.

As soon as he was placed on the Table, he walked up to little *Sally*, and dropping the Letter, cried, *Co, Co, Coo*, as much as to say, *there read it*. Now this poor Pidgeon had travelled fifty Miles in about an Hour, to bring *Sally* this Letter, and who would destroy such pretty Creatures. – But let us read the Letter.

My dear Sally,

GOD Almighty has been very merciful, and restored your Pappa to us again, who is now so well as to be able to sit up. I hear you are a good Girl, my Dear, and I hope you will never forget to praise the Lord for this his great Goodness and Mercy to us – What a sad Thing it would have been if your Father had died, and left both you and me, and little *Tommy* in Distress, and without a Friend: Your Father sends his Blessing with mine – Be good, my dear Child, and God Almighty will also bless you, whose Blessing is above all Things.

> *I am, my Dear Sally,*
> *Your ever affectionate Mother,*
> MARTHA JONES.

* * *

CHAP. III.

Of the amazing Sagacity and Instincts of a little Dog.

SOON after this, a dreadful Accident happened in the School. It was on a *Thursday* Morning, I very well remember, when the Children having learned their Lessons soon, she had given them Leave to play, and they were all running about the School, and diverting themselves with the Birds and the Lamb; at this Time the Dog, all of a sudden, laid hold of his Mistress's Apron, and endeavoured to pull her out of the School. She was at first surprized, however, she followed him to see what he intended. No sooner had he led her into the Garden, but he ran back, and pulled out one of the Children in the same manner; upon which she ordered them all to leave the School immediately, and they had not been out five Minutes, before the Top of the House fell in. What a miraculous Deliverance was here! How gracious! How good was God Almighty, to save all these Children from Destruction, and to make Use of such an Instrument, as a little sagacious Animal to accomplish his Divine Will. I should have observed, that as soon as they were all in the Garden, the Dog came leaping round them to express his Joy, and when the House was fallen, laid himself down quietly by his Mistress.

Some of the Neighbours, who saw the School fall, and who were in great Pain for *Margery* and the little ones, soon spread the News through the Village, and all the Parents, terrified for their Children, came crowding in Abundance; they had, however, the Satisfaction to find them all safe, and upon their Knees, with their Mistress, giving God thanks for their happy Deliverance.

ADVICE *from the* MAN *in the* MOON.

Jumper, Jumper, Jumper, what a pretty Dog he is, and how sensible? Had Mankind half the Sagacity of *Jumper*, they would guard against Accidents of this Sort, by having a public Survey, occasionally made of all the Houses in every Parish (especially of those, which are old and decayed) and not suffer them to remain in a crazy State, 'till they fall down on the Heads of the poor Inhabitants, and crush them to Death. Why, it was but Yesterday, that a whole House fell down in *Grace-church-street*, and another in *Queen's-street*,[49] and an hundred more are to tumble, before this Time twelve Months; so Friends, take Care of yourselves, and tell the Legislature, they ought to take Care for you. How can you be so careless? Most of your Evils arise from Carelesness and Extravagance, and yet you excuse yourselves, and lay the Fault upon Fortune. Fortune is a Fool, and you are a Blockhead, if you put it in her Power to play Tricks with you.

> *Yours,*
> *The* MAN *in the* MOON.

You are not to wonder, my dear Reader, that this little Dog should have more Sense than you, or your Father, or your Grandfather.

Though God Almighty has made Man the Lord of the Creation, and endowed him with Reason, yet in many Respects, he has been altogether as bountiful to other Creatures of his forming. Some of the Senses of other Animals are more acute than ours, as we find by daily Experience. You know this little Bird,

Sweet Jug, Jug, Jug, 'tis a Nightingale. This little Creature, after she has entertained us with her Songs all the Spring, and bred up her little ones, flies into a foreign Country, and finds her Way over the Great Sea, without any of the Instruments and Helps which Men are obliged to make Use of for that Purpose. Was you as wise as the Nightingale, you might make all the Sailors happy, and have twenty thousand Pounds for teaching them the Longitude.[50]

You would not think *Ralph* the Raven half so wise and so good as he is, though you see him here reading his book. Yet when the Prophet *Elijah*, was obliged to fly from *Ahab* King of *Israel*, and hide himself in a Cave, the Ravens, at the Command of God Almighty, fed him every Day, and preserved his Life.

And the Word of the Lord came unto Elijah, *saying, Hide thyself by the Brook* Cherith, *that is before* Jordan, *and I have commanded the Ravens to feed thee there. And the Ravens brought him Bread and Flesh in the Morning, and Bread and Flesh in the Evening, and he drank of the Brook,* Kings, B.I. C.17.[51]

And the pretty Pidgeon when the World was drowned, and he was confined with *Noah* in the Ark, was sent forth by him to see whether the Waters were abated. *And he sent forth a Dove from him, to see if the Waters were abated from off the Face of the Ground. And the Dove came in to him in the Evening, and lo, in her Mouth was an Olive Leaf plucked off: So* Noah *knew that the Waters were abated from off the Earth.* Gen. viii. 8. 11.[52]

As these, and other Animals, are so sensible and kind to us, we ought to be tender and good to them, and not beat them about, and kill them, and take away their young ones, as many wicked Boys do. Does not the Horse and the Ass carry you and your burthens; don't the Ox plough your Ground, the Cow give you Milk, the Sheep cloath your Back, the Dog watch your House, the Goose find you in Quills to write with, the Hen bring Eggs for your Custards and Puddings, and the Cock call you up in the Morning, when you are lazy, and like to hurt yourselves by laying too long in Bed? If so, how can you be so cruel to them, and abuse God Almighty's good Creatures? Go, naughty Boy, go; be sorry for what you have done, and do so no more, that God Almighty may forgive you. *Amen*, say I, again and again. God will bless you, but not unless you are merciful and good.

The downfall of the School, was a great Misfortune to Mrs. *Margery*; for she not only lost all her Books, but was destitute of a Place to teach in; but Sir William *Dove*, being informed of this, ordered the House to be built at his own Expence, and 'till that could be done, Farmer *Grove* was so kind, as to let her have his large Hall to teach in.

The House built by Sir *William*, had a Statue erected over the Door of a Boy sliding on the Ice, and under it were these Lines, written by Mrs. *Two-Shoes*, and engraved at her Expence.

On SIN. A SIMILE.

As a poor Urchin on the Ice,
When he has tumbl'd once or twice,
With cautious Step, and trembling goes,
The drop-stile Pendant on his Nose,[53]
And trudges on to seek the Shore,
Resolv'd to trust the Ice no more:
But meeting with a daring Mate,
Who often us'd to slide and scate,
Again is into Danger led,
And falls again, and breaks his head.
So Youth when first they're drawn to sin,
And see the Danger they are in,

Would gladly quit the thorney Way,
And think it is unsafe to stay;
But meeting with their wicked Train,
Return with them to sin again:
With them the Paths of Vice explore;
With them are ruin'd ever more.

✳   ✳   ✳

CHAP IV.

What happened at Farmer Grove's; and how she gratified him for the Use of his Room.

WHILE at Mr. *Grove's*, which was in the Heart of the Village, she not only taught the Children in the Day Time, but the Farmer's Servants, and all the Neighbours, to read and write in the Evening; and it was a constant Practice before they went away, to make them all go to Prayers, and sing Psalms. By this Means, the People grew extremely regular, his Servants were always at Home, instead of being at the Ale-house, and he had more Work done than ever. This gave not only Mr. *Grove*, but all the Neighbours, an high Opinion of her good Sense and prudent Behaviour: And she was so much esteemed, that most of the Differences in the Parish were left to her Decision; and if a Man and Wife quarrelled (which sometimes happened in that Part of the Kingdom) both Parties certainly came to her for Advice. Every Body knows, that *Martha Wilson* was a passionate scolding Jade, and that *John* her husband, was a surly ill-tempered Fellow. These were one Day brought by the Neighbours for *Margery* to talk to them, when they fairly quarrelled before her, and were going to Blows; but she stepping between them, thus addressed the Husband; *John*, says she, you are a Man, and ought to have more Sense than to fly in a Passion, at every Word that is said amiss by your Wife; and *Martha*, says she, you ought to know your Duty better, than to say any Thing to aggravate your Husband's Resentment. These frequent Quarrels, arise from the Indulgence of your violent Passions; for I know, you both love one another, notwithstanding what has passed between you. Now, pray tell me *John*, and tell me *Martha*, when you have had a Quarrel the over Night, are you not both sorry for it the next Day? They both declared that they were: Why then, says she, I'll tell you how to prevent this for the future, if you will both promise to take my Advice. They both promised her. You know, says she, that a small Spark will set Fire to Tinder, and that Tinder properly placed will fire a House; an angry Word is with you as that Spark, for you are both as touchy as Tinder, and very often make your own House too hot to hold you. To prevent this, therefore, and to live happily for the future, you must solemnly agree, that if one speaks an angry Word, the other will not answer, 'till he or she has distinctly called over all the Letters in the Alphabet, and the other not reply, 'till he has told twenty; by this Means your Passions will be stifled, and Reason will have Time to take the Rule.

This is the best Recipe that was ever given for a married Couple to live in Peace: Though *John* and his Wife frequently attempted to quarrel afterwards, they never could get their Passions to any considerable Height, for there was something so droll in thus carrying on the Dispute, that before they got to the End of the Argument, they saw the Absurdity of it, laughed, kissed, and were Friends.

Just as Mrs. *Margery* had settled this Difference between *John* and his Wife, the Children (who had been sent out to play, while that Business was transacting) returned some in Tears, and others very disconsolate, for the Loss of a little Dormouse they were very fond of, and which was just dead. Mrs. *Margery*, who had the Art of moralizing and drawing Instructions from every Accident, took this Opportunity of reading them a Lecture on the Uncertainty of Life, and the Necessity of being always prepared for Death. You should get up in the Morning, says she, and so conduct yourselves, as if that Day was to be your last, and lie down at Night, as if you never expected to see this World any more. This may be done, says she, without abating of your Chearfulness, for you are not to consider Death as an Evil, but as a Convenience, as an useful Pilot, who is to convey you to a Place of greater Happiness: Therefore, play my dear Children, and be merry; but be innocent and good. The good Man sets Death at Defiance, for his Darts are only dreadful to the Wicked.

After this, she permitted the Children to bury the little Dormouse, and desired one of them to write his Epitaph, and here it is.

Epitaph on a Dormouse, *really written by a little* Boy.[54]

I.

In Paper Case,
Hard by this Place,
Dead a poor Dormouse lies;
And soon or late,
Summon'd by Fate,
Each Prince, each Monarch dies.

II.

Ye Sons of Verse,
While I rehearse,
Attend instructive Rhyme;
No Sins had *Dor*,
To answer for,
Repent of yours in Time.

✳   ✳   ✳

CHAP. V.

The whole History of the Considering Cap, set forth at large for the Benefit of all whom it may concern.

THE great Reputation Mrs. *Margery* acquired by composing Differences in Families, and especially, between Man and Wife, induced her to cultivate that Part of her System of Morality and Œconomy, in order to render it more extensively useful. For this Purpose, she contrived what she called a Charm for the Passions; which was a considering Cap, almost as large as a Grenadier's,[55] but of three equal Sides; on the first of which was written, I MAY BE WRONG; on the second, IT IS FIFTY TO ONE BUT YOU ARE; and on the third, I'LL CONSIDER OF IT . The other Parts on the out-side, were filled with odd Characters, as unintelligible as the Writings of the old *Egyptians*; but within Side there was a Direction for its Use, of the utmost Consequence; for it strictly enjoined the Possessor to put on the Cap, whenever he found his Passions begin to grow turbulent, and not to deliver a Word whilst it was on, but with

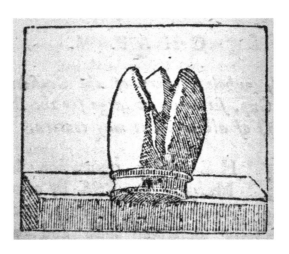

great Coolness and Moderation. As this Cap was an universal Cure for Wrong-headedness, and prevented numberless Disputes and Quarrels, it greatly hurt the Trade of the poor Lawyers, but was of the utmost Service to the rest of the Community. They were bought by Husbands and Wives, who had themselves frequent Occasion for them, and sometimes lent them to their Children: They were also purchased in large Quantities by Masters and Servants; by young Folks, who were intent on Matrimony, by Judges, Jurymen, and even Physicians and Divines; nay, if we may believe History, the Legislators of the Land did not disdain the Use of them; and we are told, that when any important Debate arose, *Cap, was the Word*, and each House looked like a grand Synod of *Egyptian* Priests. Nor was this Cap of less Use to Partners in Trade, for with these, as well as with Husband and Wife, if one was out of Humour, the other threw him the Cap, and he was obliged to put it on, and keep it till all was quiet. I myself saw thirteen Caps worn at a Time in one Family, which could not have subsisted an Hour without them; and I was particularly pleased at Sir *Humphry Huffum's*, to hear a little Girl, when her Father was out of Humour, ask her Mamma, *if she should reach down the Cap* ? These Caps, indeed, were of such Utility, that People of Sense never went without them; and it was common in the Country, when a Booby made his Appearance, and talked Nonsense, to say, *he had no Cap in his Pocket*.

Advice from FRIAR BACON.[56]

What was *Fortunatus*'s Wishing Cap, when compared to this?[57] That Cap, is said to have conveyed People instantly from one Place to another; but, as the Change of Place does not change the Temper and Disposition of the Mind, little Benefit can be expected from it; nor indeed is much to be hoped from his famous Purse: That Purse, it is said, was never empty, and such a Purse, may be sometimes convenient; but as Money will not purchase Peace, it is not necessary for a Man to encumber himself with a great deal of it. Peace and Happiness depend so much upon the State of a Man's own Mind, and upon the Use of the considering Cap, that it is generally his own Fault, if he is miserable. One of these Caps will last a Man his whole Life, and is a Discovery of much greater Importance to the Public than the Philosopher's Stone.[58] Remember what was said by my Brazen Head, *Time is, Time was, Time is past*: Now the *Time is*, therefore buy the Cap immediately, and make a proper Use of it, and be happy before the *Time is past*.

Yours, ROGER BACON.

CHAP. VI.

How Mrs. Margery was taken up for a Witch, and what happened on that Occasion.

AND so it is true? And they have taken up Mrs. *Margery* then, and accused her of being a Witch, only because she was wiser than some of her Neighbours! Mercy upon me! People stuff Children's Heads with Stories of Ghosts, Faries, Witches, and such Nonsense when they are young, and so they continue Fools all their Days. The whole World ought to be made acquainted with her Case, and here it is at their Service.

The Case of Mrs. MARGERY.

Mrs. *Margery*, as we have frequently observed, was always doing Good, and thought she could never sufficiently gratify those who had done any Thing to serve her. These generous Sentiments, naturally led her to consult the Interest of Mr. *Grove*, and the rest of her Neighbours; and as most of their Lands were Meadow, and they depended much on their Hay, which had been for many Years greatly damaged by wet Weather, she contrived an Instrument to direct them when to mow their Grass with Safety, and prevent their Hay being spoiled. They all came to her for Advice, and by that Means got in their Hay without Damage, while most of that in the neighbouring Villages was spoiled.

This made a great Noise in the Country, and so provoked were the People in the other Parishes, that they accused her of being a Witch, and sent Gaffer *Goosecap*, a busy Fellow in other People's Concerns, to find out Evidence against her. This Wiseacre happened to come to her School,[59] when she was walking about with the Raven on one Shoulder, the Pidgeon on the other, the Lark on her Hand, and the Lamb and the Dog by her Side; which indeed made a droll Figure, and so surprized the Man, that he cried out, a Witch! a Witch! upon this she laughing, answered, a Conjurer! a Conjurer!

and so they parted; but it did not end thus, for a Warrant was issued out against Mrs. *Margery*, and she was carried to a Meeting of the Justices, whither all the Neighbours followed her.[60]

At the Meeting, one of the Justices, who knew little of Life, and less of the Law, behaved very idly; and though no Body was able to prove any Thing against her, asked, who she could bring to her Character? *Who* can you bring against my Character, Sir, says she, there are People enough who would appear in my Defence, were it necessary; but I never supposed that any one here could be so weak, as to believe there was any such Thing as a Witch. If I am a Witch, this is my Charm, and (laying a Barometer or Weather Glass on the Table) it is with this, says she, that I have taught my Neighbours to know the State of the Weather. All the Company laughed, and Sir *William Dove*, who was on the Bench,[61] asked her Accusers, how they could be such Fools, as to think there was any such Thing as a Witch. It is true, continued he, many innocent and worthy People have been abused and even murdered on this absurd and foolish Supposition; which is a Scandal to our Religion, to our Laws, to our Nation, and to common Sense; but I will tell you a Story.

There was in the West of *England* a poor industrious Woman, who laboured under the same evil Report, which this good Woman is accused of. Every Hog that died with the Murrain, every Cow that slipt her Calf, she was accountable for:[62] If a Horse had the Staggers, she was supposed to be in his Head; and whenever the Wind blew a little harder than ordinary, *Goody Giles* was playing her Tricks, and riding upon a Broomstick in the Air. These, and a thousand other Phantasies, too ridiculous to recite, possessed the Pates of the common People: Horse-shoes were nailed with the Heels upwards, and many Tricks made use of, to mortify the poor Creature; and such was their Rage against her, that they petitioned Mr. *Williams*, the Parson of the Parish, not to let her come to Church; and at last, even insisted upon it: But this he overruled, and allowed the poor old Woman a Nook in one of the Isles to herself, where she muttered over her Prayers in the best Manner she could. The Parish, thus disconcerted and enraged, withdrew the small Pittance they allowed for her Support, and would have reduced her to the Necessity of starving, had she not been still assisted by the benevolent Mr. *Williams*.

But I hasten to the Sequel of my Story, in which you will find, that the true Source from whence Witchcraft springs is *Poverty*, *Age*, and *Ignorance*; and that it is impossible for a Woman to pass for a Witch, unless she is *very poor*, *very old*, and lives in a Neighbourhood where the People are *void of common Sense*.

Some Time after, a Brother of her's died in *London*, who, though he would not part with a Farthing while he lived, at his Death was obliged to leave her five thousand Pounds, that he could not carry with him.–This altered the Face of *Jane* 's Affairs prodigiously: She was no longer *Jane*, alias *Joan Giles*, the ugly old Witch, but Madam *Giles*; her old ragged Garb was exchanged for one that was new and genteel; her greatest Enemies made their Court to her, even the Justice himself came to wish her Joy; and though several Hogs and Horses died, and the Wind frequently blew afterwards, yet Madam *Giles* was never supposed to have a Hand in it; and from hence it is plain, as I observed before, that a Woman must be *very poor*, *very old*, and live in a Neighbourhood, where the People are *very stupid*, before she can possibly pass for a Witch.

'Twas a Saying of Mr. *Williams*, who would sometimes be jocose, and had the Art of making even Satire agreeable; that if ever *Jane* deserved the Character of a Witch, it was after this Money was left her; for that with her five thousand Pounds, she did more Acts of Charity and friendly Offices, than all the People of Fortune within fifty Miles of the Place.

After this, Sir *William* inveighed against the absurd and foolish Notions, which the Country People had imbibed concerning Witches, and Witchcraft, and having proved that there was no such Thing, but that all were the Effects of Folly and Ignorance, he gave the Court such an Account of Mrs. *Margery*, and her Virtue, good Sense, and prudent Behaviour, that the Gentlemen present were enamoured with her, and returned her public Thanks for the great Service she had done the Country. One Gentleman in particular, I mean Sir *Charles Jones*, had conceived such an high Opinion of her, that he offered her a considerable Sum to take the Care of his Family, and the Education of his Daughter, which, however, she refused; but this Gentleman, sending for her afterwards when he had a dangerous Fit of Illness, she went, and behaved so prudently in the Family, and so tenderly to him and his Daughter, that he would not permit her to leave his House, but soon after made her Proposals of Marriage. She was truly sensible of the Honour he intended her, but, though poor, she would not consent to be made a Lady, till he had effectually provided for his Daughter; for she told him, that Power was a dangerous Thing to be trusted with, and that a good Man or Woman would never throw themselves into the Road of Temptation.

All Things being settled, and the Day fixed, the Neighbours came in Crouds to see the Wedding; for they were all glad, that one who had been such a good little Girl, and was become such a virtuous and good Woman, was going to be made a Lady; but just as the Clergyman had opened his Book, a Gentleman richly dressed ran into the Church, and cry'd, Stop! stop! This greatly alarmed the Congregation, particularly the intended Bride and Bridegroom, whom he first accosted, and desired to speak with them apart. After they had been talking some little Time, the People were greatly surprized to see Sir *Charles* stand Motionless, and his Bride cry, and faint away in the Stranger's Arms. This seeming Grief, however, was only a Prelude to a Flood of Joy, which immediately succeeded; for you must know, gentle Reader, that this Gentleman, so richly dressed and bedizened with Lace,[63] was that identical little Boy, whom you before saw in the Sailor's Habit; in short, it was little *Tom Two-Shoes*, Mrs. *Margery's* Brother, who was just come from beyond Sea, where he had made a large Fortune, and hearing, as soon as he landed, of his Sister's intended Wedding, had rode Post, to see that a proper Settlement was made on her; which he thought she was now intitled to, as he himself was both able and willing to give her an ample Fortune. They soon returned to the Communion-Table, and were married in Tears, but they were Tears of Joy.

There is something wonderful in this young Gentleman's Preservation and Success in Life; which we shall acquaint the Reader of, in the History of his Life and Adventures, which will soon be published.

* * *

CHAP. VII. and Last.
The true Use of Riches.

THE Harmony and Affection that subsisted between this happy Couple, is inexpressible; but Time, which dissolves the closest Union, after six Years, severed Sir *Charles* from his Lady; for being seized with a violent Fever he died, and left her full of Grief, tho' possessed of a large Fortune.

We forgot to remark, that after her Marriage, *Lady Jones* (for so we must now call her) ordered the Chappel to be fitted up, and allowed the Chaplain a considerable Sum out of her own private Purse, to visit the Sick, and say Prayers every Day to all the People that could attend. She also gave Mr. *Johnson* ten Guineas a Year, to preach a Sermon, annually, on the Necessity and Duties of the marriage State, and on the Decease of Sir *Charles*; she gave him ten more, to preach yearly on the Subject of Death; she had put all the Parish into Mourning for the Loss of her Husband; and to those Men who attended this yearly Service, she gave Harvest Gloves, to their Wives Shoes and Stockings, and to all the Children little Books and Plumb-cakes: We must also observe, that she herself wove a Chaplet of Flowers, and before the Service, placed it on his Grave-stone; and a suitable Psalm was always sung by the Congregation.

About this Time, she heard that Mr. *Smith* was oppressed by Sir *Timothy Gripe*, the Justice, and his Friend *Graspall*, who endeavoured to deprive him of Part of his Tythes; upon which she, in Conjunction with her Brother, defended him, and the Cause was tried in *Westminster-hall*,[64] where Mr. *Smith* gained a Verdict; and it appearing that Sir *Timothy* had behaved most scandalously, as a Justice of the Peace, he was struck off the List, and no longer permitted to act in that Capacity. This was a Cut to a Man of his imperious Disposition, and this was followed by one yet more severe; for a Relation of his, who had an undoubted Right to the *Mouldwell* Estate, finding that it was possible to get the better at Law of a rich Man, laid Claim to it, brought his Action, and recovered the whole Manor of *Mouldwell*; and being afterwards inclined to sell it, he, in Consideration of the Aid Lady *Margery* had lent him during his Distress, made her the first Offer, and she purchased the Whole, and threw it into different Farms, that the Poor might be no longer under the Dominion of two over-grown Men.

This was a great Mortification to Sir *Timothy*, as well as to his Friend *Graspall*, who from this Time experienced nothing but Misfortunes, and was in a few Years so dispossessed of his Ill-gotten Wealth, that his Family were reduced to seek Subsistance from the Parish, at which those who had felt the Weight of his Iron Hand rejoiced; but Lady *Margery* desired, that his Children might be treated with Care and Tenderness; *for they*, says she, *are no Ways accountable for the Actions of their Father.*[65]

At her first coming into Power, she took Care to gratify her old Friends, especially Mr. and Mrs. *Smith*, whose Family she made happy. – She paid great Regard to the Poor, made their Interest her own, and to induce them to come regularly to Church, she ordered a Loaf, or the Price of a Loaf, to be given to every one who would accept of it. This brought many of them to Church, who by degrees learned their Duty, and then came on a more noble Principle. She also took Care to encourage Matrimony; and in order to induce her Tenants and Neighbours to enter into that happy State, she always gave the young Couple something towards House-keeping; and stood Godmother to all their Children, whom she had in Parties, every *Sunday* Evening, to teach them their Catechism, and lecture them in Religion and Morality; after which she treated them with a Supper, gave them such Books as they wanted, and then dispatched them with her Blessing. Nor did she forget them at her Death, but left each a Legacy, as will be seen among other charitable Donations when we publish her Will, which we may do in some future Volume. There is one Request however so singular, that we cannot help taking some Notice of it in this Place; which is, that of her giving so many Acres of Land to be planted yearly with Potatoes, for all the Poor of any Parish who would come and fetch them for the Use of their Families; but if any took them to sell they were deprived of that Privilege ever after. And these Roots were planted and raised from the Rent arising from a Farm which she had assigned over for that purpose. In short, she was a Mother to the Poor, a Physician to the Sick, and a Friend to all who were in Distress. Her Life was the greatest Blessing, and her Death the greatest Calamity that ever was felt in the Neighbourhood. A Monument, but without Inscription, was erected to her Memory in the Church-yard, over which the Poor as they pass weep continually, so that the Stone is ever bathed in Tears.

On this Occasion the following Lines were spoken extempore by a young Gentleman.

> *How vain the Tears that fall from you,*
> *And here supply the Place of Dew?*
> *How vain to weep the happy Dead,*
> *Who now to heavenly Realms are fled?*
> *Repine no more, your Plaints forbear,*
> *And all prepare to meet them there.*

THE END.

APPENDIX.

The Golden Dream; or, the Ingenuous Confession.

To shew the Depravity of human Nature, and how apt the Mind is to be misled by Trinkets and false Appearances, Mrs. *Two-Shoes* does acknowledge, that after she became rich, she had like to have been too fond of Money; for on seeing her Husband receive a very large Sum, her Heart went pit pat, pit pat, all the Evening, and she began to think that Guineas were pretty Things. To suppress this Turbulence of Mind, which was a Symptom of approaching Avarice, she said her Prayers earlier than usual, and at Night had the following Dream; which I shall relate in her own Words.

"Methought, as I slept, a Genii stept up to me with a *French* Commode,[66] which having placed on my Head, he said, now go and be happy; for from henceforth every Thing you touch shall turn to Gold. Willing to try the Experiment, I gently touched the Bed-post and Furniture, which immediately became massy Gold burnished, and of surprizing Brightness. I then touched the Walls of the House, which assumed the same Appearance, and looked amazingly magnificent. Elated with this wonderful Gift, I rang hastily for my Maid to carry the joyful News to her Master, who, as I thought, was then walking in the Garden. *Sukey* came, but in the Extacy I was in, happening to touch her Hand, she became instantly an immovable Statue. Go, said I, and call your Master; but she made no reply, nor could she stir. Upon this I shrieked, and in came my dear Husband, whom I ran to embrace; when no sooner had I touched him, but he became good for nothing; that is, good for nothing but his Weight in Gold; and that you know could be nothing, where Gold was so plenty. At this instant up came another Servant with a Glass of Water, thinking me ill; this I attempted to swallow, but no sooner did it touch my Mouth, than it became a hard solid Body, and unfit for drinking. My Distress now grew insupportable! I had destroyed, as I thought, my dear Husband, and my favourite Servant; and I plainly perceived, that I should die for want in the midst of so much Wealth. Ah, said I, why did I long for Riches! Having enough already, why did I covet more? Thus terrified, I began to rave, and beat my Breast, which awaked Sir *Charles*, who kindly called me from this State of Inquietude, and composed my Mind."

This Scene I have often considered as a Lesson, instructing me, that a Load of Riches bring, instead of Felicity, a Load of Troubles; and that the only Source of Happiness is *Contentment*. Go, therefore, you who have too much, and give it to those who are in want; so shall you be happy yourselves, by making others happy. This is a Precept from the Almighty, a Precept which must be regarded; for *The Lord is about your Paths, and about your Bed, and spieth out all your Ways.*[67]

An Anecdote, respecting TOM TWO-SHOES, *communicated by a Gentleman, who is now writing the History of his Life.*

IT is generally known, that *Tom Two-Shoes* went to Sea when he was a very little Boy, and very poor; and that he returned a very great Man, and very rich; but no one knows how he acquired so much Wealth but myself, and a few Friends, who have perused the Papers from which I am compiling the History of his Life.

After *Tom* had been at Sea some Years, he was unfortunately cast away, on that Part of the Coast of *Africa* inhabited by the *Hottentots*.[68] Here he met with a strange Book, which the *Hottentots* did not understand, and which gave him some Account of *Prester John's* Country;[69] and being a Lad of great Curiosity and Resolution he determined to see it; accordingly he set out on the Pursuit, attended by a young Lion, which he had tamed and made so fond of him, that he followed him like a Dog, and obeyed all his Commands; and indeed it was happy for him that he had such a Companion; for as his Road lay through large Woods and Forests, that were full of wild Beasts and without Inhabitants, he must have been soon starved or torn in Pieces, had he not been both fed and protected by this noble Animal.

Tom had provided himself with two Guns, a Sword, and as much Powder and Ball as he could carry; with these Arms, and such a Companion, it was mighty easy for him to get Food; for the Animals in these wild and extensive Forests, having never seen the Effects of a Gun, readily ran from the Lion, who hunted on one Side, to *Tom*, who hunted on the other, so that they were either caught by the Lion, or shot by his Master; and it was pleasant enough, after a hunting Match, and the Meat was dressed, to see how Cheek by Joul they sat down to Dinner.

When they came into the Land of *Utopia*,[70] he discovered the Statue of a Man erected on an open Plain, which had this

Inscription on the Pedestal: *On* May-day *in the Morning, when the Sun rises, I shall have a Head of Gold.* As it was now the latter End of *April*, he stayed to see this wonderful Change; and in the mean time, enquiring of a poor Shepherd what was the Reason of the Statue being erected there, and with that Inscription, he was informed, that it was set up many Years ago by an *Arabian* Philosopher, who travelled all the World over in Search of a real Friend; that he lived with, and was extremely fond of a great Man who inhabited the next Mountain; but that on some Occasion they quarrelled, and the Philosopher, leaving the Mountain, retired into the Plain, where he erected this Statue with his own Hands, and soon after died. To this he added, that all the People for many Leagues round came there every *May* Morning, expecting to see the Stone-head turned to Gold.

Tom got up very early on the first of *May* to behold this amazing Change, and when he came near the Statue he saw a Number of People, who all ran away from him in the utmost Consternation, having never before seen a Lion follow a Man like a Lap-dog. Being thus left alone, he fixed his Eyes on the Sun, then rising with resplendent Majesty, and afterwards turned to the Statue, but could see no Change in the Stone. – Surely, says he to himself, there is some mystical Meaning in this! This Inscription must be an Ænigma, the hidden Meaning of which I will endeavour to find; for a Philosopher would never expect a Stone to be turned to Gold; accordingly he measured the Length of the Shadow, which the Statue gave on the Ground by the Sun shining on it, and marked that particular Part where the Head fell, then getting a *Chopness* (a Thing like a Spade) and digging, he discovered a Copper-chest, full of Gold, with this Inscription engraved on the Lid of it.

Thy Wit,
Oh Man! whoever thou art,
Hath disclos'd the Ænigma,
And discover'd the Golden Head.
Take it and use it,
But use it with Wisdom;
For know,
That Gold, properly employ'd,
May dispense Blessings,
And promote the Happiness of Mortals;
But when hoarded up,
Or misapply'd,
Is but Trash, that makes Mankind miserable.
Remember
The unprofitable Servant,
Who hid his *Talent* in a Napkin;[71]
And
The profligate Son,
Who squander'd away his Substance and
fed with the Swine.[72]
As thou hast got the Golden Head,
Observe the *Golden Mean*,[73]
Be *Good* and be happy.

This Lesson, coming as it were from the Dead, struck him with such Awe, and Reverence for Piety and Virtue, that, before he removed the Treasure, he kneeled down, and earnestly and fervently prayed that he might make a prudent, just and proper Use of it. He then conveyed the Chest away; but how he got it to *England*, the Reader will be informed in the History of his Life. It may not be improper, however, in this Place, to give the Reader some Account of the Philosopher who hid this Treasure, and took so much Pains to find a true and real Friend to enjoy it. As

Tom had Reason to venerate his Memory, he was very particular in his Enquiry, and had this Character of him; – that he was a Man well acquainted with Nature and with Trade; that he was pious, friendly, and of a sweet and affable Disposition. That he had acquired a Fortune by Commerce, and having no Relations to leave it to, he travelled through *Arabia, Persia, India, Libia* and *Utopia* in search of a real Friend. In this Pursuit he found several with whom he exchanged good Offices, and that were polite and obliging, but they often flew off for Trifles; or as soon as he pretended to be in Distress, and requested their Assistance, left him to struggle with his own Difficulties. So true is that Copy in our Books, which says, *Adversity is the Touchstone of Friendship.* At last, however, he met with the *Utopian* Philosopher, or the wise Man of the Mountain, as he is called, and thought in him he had found the Friend he wanted; for though he often pretended to be in Distress, and abandoned to the Frowns of Fortune, this Man always relieved him, and with such Chearfulness and Sincerity, that concluding he had found out the only Man to whom he ought to open both his Purse and his Heart, he let him so far into his Secrets, as to desire his Assistance in hiding a large Sum of Money, which he wanted to conceal, lest the Prince of the Country, who was absolute, should, by the Advice of his wicked Minister, put him to Death for his Gold. The two Philosophers met and hid the Money, which the Stranger, after some Days, went to see, but found it gone. How was he struck to the Heart, when he found that his Friend, whom he had often tried, and who had relieved him in his Distress, could not withstand this Temptation, but broke through the sacred Bonds of Friendship, and turned even a Thief for Gold which he did not want, as he was already very rich. Oh! said he, what is the Heart of Man made of? Why am I condemned to live among People who have no Sincerity, and who barter the most sacred Ties of Friendship and Humanity for the Dirt that we tread on? Had I lost my Gold and found a real Friend, I should have been happy with the Exchange, but now I am most miserable. After some Time he wiped off his Tears, and being determined not to be so imposed on, he had Recourse to Cunning and the Arts of Life. He went to his pretended Friend with a chearful Countenance, told him he had more Gold to hide, and desired him to appoint a Time when they might go together, and open the Earth to put it into the same Pot; the other, in Hopes of getting more Wealth, appointed the next Evening. They went together, opened the Ground, and found the Money they had first placed there, for the artful Wretch, he so much confided in, had conveyed it again into the Pot, in order to obtain more. Our Philosopher immediately took the Gold, and putting it into his Pocket, told the other he had now altered his Mind, and should bury it no more, till he found a Man more worthy of his Confidence. See what People lose by being dishonest. This calls to my Mind the Words of the Poet:

> *A Wit's a Feather, and a Chief's a Rod,*
> *An honest Man's the noblest Work of God.*[74]

Remember this Story, and take Care whom you trust; but don't be covetous, sordid and miserable; for the Gold we have is but lent us to do Good with. We received all from the Hand of God, and every Person in Distress hath a just Title to a Portion of it.

A LETTER *from the* PRINTER *which he desires may be inserted.*

SIR,

I Have done with your Copy, so you may return it to the *Vatican*, if you please; and pray tell Mr. *Angelo* to brush up the Cuts, that, in the next Edition, they may give us a good Impression.

The Foresight and Sagacity of Mrs. *Margery* 's Dog calls to my Mind a Circumstance, which happened when I was a Boy. Some Gentlemen in the Place where I lived had been hunting, and were got under a great Tree to shelter themselves from a Thunder Storm; when a Dog that always followed one of the Gentlemen leaped up his Horse several Times, and then ran away and barked. At last, the Gentlemen all followed to see what he would be at; and they were no sooner gone from the Tree, but it was shivered in Pieces by Lightning! 'Tis remarkable, that as soon as they came from the Tree the Dog appeared to be very well satisfied, and barked no more. The Gentleman after this always regarded the Dog as his Friend, treated him in his Old Age with great Tenderness, and fed him with Milk as long as he lived.

My old Master *Grierson* had also a Dog, that ought to be mentioned with Regard; for he used to set him up as a Pattern of Sagacity and Prudence, not only to his Journeymen, but to the whole Neighbours. This Dog had been taught a thousand Tricks, and among other Feats he could dance, tumble, and drink Wine and Punch till he was little better than mad. It happened one Day, when the Men had made him drunk with Liquor, and he was capering about, that he fell into a large Vessel of boiling Water. They soon got him out, and he recovered; but he was very much hurt, and being sensible, that this Accident arose from his losing his Senses by Drinking, he would never taste any strong Liquor afterwards. – My old Master, on relating this Story, and shewing the Dog, used to address us thus, *Ah, my Friends, had you but half the Sense of this poor Dog here, you would never get fuddled, and be Fools.*

I am, Sir, Your's, &c.

W.B.[75]

The BOOKS usually read by the Scholars of Mrs. TWO-SHOES, are these, and are sold at MR. NEWBERY's, at the *Bible* and *Sun* in St. *Paul's* Church-yard.

1. The *Christmas-Box*, Price 1d.
2. The History of *Giles Gingerbread*, 1d.
3. The *New-Year's-Gift*, 2d.
4. The *Easter-Gift*, 2d.
5. The *Whitsuntide-Gift*, 2d.
6. The *Twelfth-Day-Gift*, 1s.
7. The *Valentine's-Gift*, 6d.
8. The FAIRING or *Golden Toy*, 6d.
9. The *Royal Battledore*, 2d.
10. The *Royal Primer*, 3d.
11. The *Little Lottery-Book*, 3d.
12. The *Little Pretty Pocket-Book*, 6d.
13. The *Infant Tutor, or pretty Little Spelling-Book*, 6d.
14. The *Pretty Book for Children*, 6d.
15. *Tom Trapwit's Art of being Merry and Wise*, 6d.
16. *Tom Trip's History of Birds and Beasts*, Price 6d.

17. *Food for the Mind, or a New Riddle Book*, 6d.
18. *Fables in Verse and Prose by Æsop, and your old Friend Woglog*, 6d.
19. The *Holy Bible abridged*, 6d.
20. The *History of the Creation*, 6d.
21. *A new and noble History of England*, 6d.
22. *Philosophy for Children*, 6d.
23. *Philosophy of Tops and Balls*, 1s.
24. *Pretty Poems for Children 3 Foot high*, 6d.
25. *Pretty Poems for Children 6 Foot high*, 1s.
26. *Lilliputian Magazine, or Golden Library*, 1s.
27. *Short Histories for the Improvement of the Mind*, 1s.
28. The *New Testament*, adapted to the Capacities of Children, 1s.
29. The Life of our Blessed SAVIOUR, 1s.
30. The Lives of the Holy *Apostles* and *Evangelists*, 1s.
31. The Lives of the *Fathers* of the *Christian* Church for the first four Centuries, 1s.
32. A Concise *Exposition* of the Book of *Common Prayer*, with the Lives of its *Compilers*, 1s.
33. The *Museum* for Youth, 1s.
34. An Easy *Spelling Dictionary* for those who would write correctly, 1s.
35. A *Pocket Dictionary* for those who would know the precise Meaning of all the Words in the *English* Language, 3s.
36. A Compendious History of *England*, 2s.
37. The Present State of *Great Britain*, 2s.
38. A Little Book of Letters and Cards, to teach young Ladies and Gentlemen how to write to their Friends in a polite, easy and elegant Manner, 1s.
39. The Gentleman and Lady's Key to *Polite Literature*; or, A *Compendious Dictionary* of Fabulous History, 2s.
40. The News-Readers Pocket-Book; or, A *Military Dictionary*, 2s.
41. A Curious Collection of Voyages, selected from the Writers of all Nations, 10 Vol. Pr. bound 1l.
42. A Curious Collection of Travels, selected from the Writers of all Nations, 10 Vol; Pr. bound 1l.

By the KING's Royal Patent,
Are Sold by J. NEWBERY, at the *Bible* and *Sun* in *St. Paul's Church-Yard.*

1. Dr. *James's Powders* for Fevers, the Small-Pox, Measles, Colds, &c. 2s. 6d.
2. Dr. *Hooper's Female Pills*, 1s.
3. Mr. *Greenough's Tincture* for Teeth, 1s.
4. *Ditto* for the Tooth-Ach, 1s.
5. *Stomachic Lozenges* for the Heart-burn, Cholic, Indigestion, &c. 1s. 6d.
6. The *Balsam of Health*, or, (as it is by some called) the Balsam of Life, 6d.
7. The *Original Daffy's Elixir*, 1s. 3d.
8. Dr. *Anderson's Scots Pills*, 1s.
9. The *Original British Oil*, 1s.
10. The *Alterative Pills*, which are a safe, and certain Cure for the King's Evil, and all Scrophulous Complaints, 5s. the Box, containing 40 Doses. – *See a Dissertation on these Disorders sold at the Place above-mentioned*, Price 6d.

THE
FAIRING:
OR, A
GOLDEN TOY,
FOR
CHILDREN
OF ALL
SIZES and DENOMINATIONS.

In which they may see all the Fun of the Fair,
And at Home be as happy as if they were there.

ADORNED WITH

Variety of Cuts from original Drawings

LONDON:

Printed for T. Carnan and F. Newbery,
jun. at No. 65, in St. Paul's Church-Yard,
(*but* not *for* F. Newbery, *at the Corner of*
Ludgate Street, who has no Share *in the late*
Mr. JOHN NEWBERY's *Books for Children*.).[1]

MDCCLXXVII.

(Price Six-pence, bound and gilt.)

Tom Trip *with old Ringwood and Jouler and Tray,*
Is riding to Town for a Fairing...............*Huzza!*

TO THE

TRUE and GENUINE

LOVERS *of* NOISE,

THIS BOOK,

WHICH WAS CALCULATED FOR THEIR

AMUSEMENT,

AND WRITTEN FOR THEIR USE,

IS MOST HUMBLY INSCRIBED

BY

YOU KNOW WHO.

The PREFACE.

To the Critics of the eighteenth Century

Ha! ha! ha! ha! ha! Who do I laugh at? Why, at you, Mr. Critic; who should I laugh at? A Critic is like a *Currycomb*,[2] and gives pleasure before he occasions Pain.

This book you say is written without either rule or method, or rhyme, or reason. Pray, Sir, give me leave to ask you, What rule there is for *Rioting*?[3] What method is there in *Confusion*? What rhyme in a *Rattle-Trap*? Or what reason in a *Round-a-bout*? Why none? And yet these are the Essentials of a Fair.[4]

Sir, if I understand the Matter, and, as Mr. Alderman *Bridle Goose* says, if I don't understand it Nobody does.[5] I say, Sir, if I understand the Matter (for we are now upon the Matter, and 'tis no Matter how soon we have done). A Metaphor is a Kind of a Simile, and a Simile a Kind of Description, and a Description a Kind of Picture; and as all of them are intended to convey to the Mind an Image of the Things they represent, what they represent must be like themselves; and as this Book is a Metaphor, or Simile, or Description, or Picture of a Fair, it must be like a Fair, and like nothing else; that is, it must be one entire Whole, but a whole Heap of Confusion.

Sir, I am sure I am right. You may take my Word for it; and that will put an End to the Controversy; and I heartily wish all our Controversies about nothing (which is indeed the Subject-matter of most Controversies) were determined in this Manner.

Pray, put this Book in the front of your Library, and take particular care to keep it clean.

✳ ✳ ✳

THE
FAIRING.

CHAP I.

Which begins in a Manner not prescribed by the Ancients.

HALLO Boys, hallo Boys. – *Huzza! Huzza! Huzza!*

Come *Tom*, make Haste, for the Fair is begun. See, here is *Jack Pudding* with the Gridiron on his Back, and all the Boys hallooing.[6]

Make Haste, make Haste; but don't get into the Crowd; for little Boys are often trod upon, and even crushed to death by mixing with the mob. If you would be safe, my dear, always avoid a Crowd. Look yonder, *Dick Wilson* there has done the very thing I cautioned you against. He is got into the middle of that great mob.

A silly Chit![7] that boy is always thrusting his Nose into Difficulties. Surely, there never was such an impertinent little Monkey. How shall we get him out? See how the Rogue scuffles and roars.

He deserves all the Squeezing he has, because he will never take Advice, and yet I am sorry for him. But what comes here? Oh, this is Mr. Pug riding upon a Man's Head, in order to draw a Crowd together.

One Monkey makes many, says the Proverb, and here it is verified. See, how the Rogue cracks Nuts, and throws the Shells at the people. Who tapped me on the Shoulder? Oh, *Sam*, what are you come puffing and blowing! Why, you look as busy as a Fool in a Fair.

Well, what News do you bring from this Region of Nonsense? I have not seen it, and should be glad to know what is done, without the Trouble of attending.

✳ ✳ ✳

CHAP. II.

Sam Gooseberry's *Account of the wonderful things in the Fair.*

Why there is such a Mobbing at the other Side of the Fair, says *Sam*, as you never saw in your Life, and one fat fellow has got among them that has made me laugh immoderately. Stand further, good

Folks, says he, what a mob is here! Who raked all this filthy Crowd together? Honest Friend, take away your elbow. What a beastly crew am I got among? What a smell! Oh, and such squeezing. Why, you over-grown Sloven, says a footman, that stood by, who makes half so much noise and crowding as you! reduce your own fat paunch to a reasonable compass, Sirrah, and there will be Room enough for us all. Upon this, the whole company set up a shout, and, crowding round my Friend *Tunbelly*, left an opening through which I made my escape, and have brought off *Dick Wilson* with me, who, by being heartily squeezed, and having twelve of his ten Toes trod off, is now cured of his impertinent curiosity. But you desire an account of the Fair, and I mean to gratify you.

The first Thing I saw, which gave me Pleasure, was old *Gaffer Gingerbread*'s Stall, with little *Giles* behind it.[8] See him, see him!

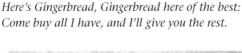

> *Here's Gingerbread, Gingerbread here of the best:*
> *Come buy all I have, and I'll give you the rest.*

The Man of the World for Gingerbread. What do you buy, what do you buy? says the old Gentleman; please to buy a Gingerbread Wife, Sir? Here is a very delicate one. Indeed, there is too much Gold upon her Nose; but that is no Objection to those who drive *Smithfield* bargains,[9] and marry their wives by weight. Will you please to have a gingerbread husband, Madam? I assure you, you may have a worse; or please to have a watch, Madam? Here are watches for Belles, Beaux, Bucks and Blockheads, who squander away that most inestimable of all Treasures *Time*, and then cry for it. Pray read the Motto to the dial-plate, Madam; you never saw a finer dial-plate in your Life, or a Motto that is more significant, and that deserves so much of your serious Consideration.

> *When Time is gone,*
> *Eternity comes on.*

Here, Giles, speak to it, says the old Gentleman.

Giles begins. This watch, Madam, is only a Penny with all the Gold about it. The Moral, Madam, you have into the Bargain, which, if rightly understood and properly applied, is of more value than a thousand Watches.

> *When Time is gone,*
> *Eternity comes on.*

Time is to eternity, as this grain of sand to the whole world; nay, it is not so much, yet we neglect and squander away that Time, which is given us to secure a glorious Eternity; which is in us the most extreme folly and madness. Let us think on the difference between living for ever in happiness or in misery, and we shall become better and happier even in this life: for it will always give us extreme pleasure to be assured, that we have secured to ourselves Happiness hereafter. This, madam, is some sort of security even against death. Observe what *Cardinal Wolsey* says:

> Farewel, a long farewel to all my greatness!
> This is the state of man: to-day he puts forth,
> The tender leaves of hope, to-morrow blossoms,
> And bears his blushing honours thick upon him;
> The third day comes a frost, a killing frost;
> And when he thinks, good easy man, full surely
> His greatness is a ripening, nips his root;
> And then he falls as I do. I have ventur'd,
> Like little wanton boys that swim on bladders,

These many summers in a sea of glory;
But far beyond my depth: my high blown pride
At length broke under me; and now has left me
Weary and old with service, to the mercy
Of a rude stream that must for ever hide me.
Vain pomp and glory of this world, I hate ye.
O! had I serv'd my God with half the zeal
I serv'd my king, he would not in mine age
Have left me naked to mine enemies.[10]

At this instant the father came up with Battledores in his hand.[11] These, Gentlemen, says he, are my Battledores, which are to be tied to the Breast Button, and worn as so many Monitors to the Head, and to the Heart: The first is to be worn by Men of all denominations, as it contains lessons of universal Utility.

Speak to it, *Giles.*

Giles got up, and delivered the History of *Honesty* and *Knavery*, and of *Industry* and *Indolence*, as follows:

THE HISTORY OF
HONESTY and KNAVERY.

HONESTY and *Knavery* were both apprenticed in the same town, to the same trade, and being both out of their time at the same instant, they opened different shops, and set up for themselves the same day.[12] According to the Practice of Shop-keepers in the Country, they dealt in every thing, even in drapery, grocery, wine, and medicines. *Honesty* opened shop in a decent manner, bid his customers welcome, sold them the best goods he could buy for money, at a moderate profit, and would abate nothing of what he asked: But *Knavery* tricked up his shop in a very gay manner, fawned upon his customers, bought such goods as he could afford to sell cheap, and make frequent abatements, taking more or less, as he could agree with his customers. By this means he allured the minds, and stole the hearts of the people; so that poor *Honesty* had only the wise men that would deal with him, and those bore no Proportion to the rest. Among other articles, they both dealt in Wine, of which *Honesty* took care to procure the best, even at any price; because he knew, that the health, and indeed the lives of his customers, depended much on the quality, as well as quantity of what they drank; but *knavery* bought any stummed stuff that he could get cheap,[13] and to puff it off, hung out a fine large Bush.[14] *Honesty* was advised to do the same; but he only shook his Head, and made this answer, *Good Wine needs no Bush*, and so it happened; for many of the Customers who dealt with *Knavery*, died with the Stuff he had given them to drink, whereas *Honesty* lost none of his friends: They grew heartier and better, while the other were declining, which was soon perceived; and the People all left *Knavery*, notwithstanding his fine Bush, and would deal only with *Honesty*. Thus by a steady perseverance, and doing what was prudent and just, and without any Artifice whatsoever, he gained the whole Trade to himself, and did not leave *Knavery* one customer; which so provoked him, who was always an Enemy before, that in the night he broke open the house of *Honesty*, and stole most of his goods; but they were found upon him, and he was tried and transported to a Country at a great Distance, from whence I hope he will never return to disturb poor *Honesty* again.

On this Circumstance is founded the old and true maxim, that *Good Wine needs no Bush.*

To this Battledore, *Giles* joined a *Gingerbread Paradox*, which here follows, with its explanation.

PARADOX.

Industry and Indolence *were born on the same Day, and died on the same Day*, which was just at the Age of Sixty; *yet* Industry *lived fifteen years longer than the other.* How can this be? Why I'll tell you.

Industry, being a notable Fellow, made it a Rule to get up early every Morning, for he had learned this maxim of his father:

> *Early to Bed and early to rise,*
> *Is the Way to be healthy, wealthy, and wise.*[15]

So up he jumped at Six o'Clock, and sometimes sooner; but as for *Indolence*, he always lay in bed till Noon, and when up, he found himself so weakened by laying long in Bed, that he had seldom strength or spirits to do any business.

Now, as sleep is a kind of death, for when sleeping, we have not the use of our reason, *industry* may with truth be said to have lived six hours a day more than *indolence*, which in the course of sixty years, must gain him fifteen: Besides this, he enjoyed good Health; but *Indolence* was always sickly. *Industry* gained a good Estate from a small beginning, and left all his relations and friends money to make them happy; but *indolence* idled away a large one, which had been gotten by his father, and had at last not enough to support himself. In short, *Industry* died among a circle of his friends, who really lamented his death, and buried him in a very decent manner: but *Indolence* died in a Ditch, and was buried by the Parish. *Idleness*, said *Solomon, will cloath a man with rags.*

The next Battledore, says *Giles*, is intended for the Ladies, and this is the Lesson.

Pride *is a turbulent companion, that robs us of our Peace; but* Prudence *proves the way to Happiness.*

THE HISTORY OF
Miss PRIDE and Miss PRUDENCE.

THERE was in the country two girls, called Miss *Pride* and Miss *Prudence.*

Miss Pride was a pert tawdry Hussey, who tricked herself up in all the ribbons, lace and finery she could get; but Miss *Prudence* only dressed herself neat and decent. When thus furbelowed out,[16] Miss *Pride* tossed up her Head with an insolent Air, took no Notice of any one she saw; and if she had lost her Way, would rather go wrong, than ask, a common Person to set her right: Miss *Prudence* too could hold up her Head, but then it was only to keep impertinent Fellows and Fools at a Distance; for to all others she ever spoke cordially, *Good Night, Neighbour*; *Good morning to you, Sir*: *How do you do, Madam?* and was very complaisant and obliging. Miss *Pride* was addressed by several Gentlemen in the Neighbourhood, and among others, by a Person of great Fortune and Accomplishments; but she gave herself such Airs, and made such a Fuss about Fortune and Settlement, Coaches and Card-money,[17] that the Gentleman grew sick of her Affectation, and left her without taking his Leave, which was to her no little Mortification. After this, he addressed Miss *Prudence*, who behaved with Civility and Politeness, and told him she had little Inclination to alter her Condition, but that she thought herself obliged to him for the good Opinion he had conceived of her. And when they came to treat about Fortune and Settlement, observed to him, that she should not be over exact about these Things; for his having the Character of a worthy Man, weighed more with her than all his Riches. In a little Time, Miss *Prudence* was married to this Gentleman of the first Fortune and best Accomplishments in the kingdom, which so stung Miss *Pride*, that she hated *Prudence* ever after.

At this Instant up bustled the old Gentleman. Here, *Giles*, says he, take these Battledores for the Politicians. This is an Age of

Politicks, Boy; even Tinkers are become *Machiavels*,[18] and Coblers settle the State of the Nation. Read it, *Giles*.

The BATTLEDORE, *to be worn on the Breast Button of the Waistcoat next the Heart.*

   I. No Title or Employment is honourable, which has not its Foundation in Virtue.

  II. In Cases of Humanity and Mercy, consult your Heart; and in Cases of Justice, your Head.

 III. Where the Public Weal is concerned, consult your Understanding, and if you have none, borrow.

 IV. Serve your Friend, but consider yourself, and spare your Country.

  V. When the Cause of your Country calls you to Arms, shew your Courage, if you have any; but shew it so that none may impeach your Prudence.

 VI. Are you a Man of Learning? Shew it not so much by your Skill in the *Roman* Language, as by a Practice of the *Roman* Virtue. – Their great Generals fought bravely to sustain the public Glory, and then retired to their own Ploughs, to avoid an Increase of the Public Expence.

On this Side of the Gingerbread, quoth *Giles*, you will observe, that my Father has given you a curious Picture of a Gentleman, with a bag at his Back, coming from his Fields, where he has been at Plough.

This is the famous and most truly noble *Quintus Cincinnatus*, a brave *Roman*, whose Actions are worthy the Attention and Imitation of every *Briton*.[19] This Man, at a Time when the City of *Rome* was like to be destroyed by the Dissentions and Commotions of the People, was by the Senate elected Consul, and Messengers being dispatched for him to repair to *Rome*, and take on him that honourable and important Office, they found this illustrious *Roman* meanly dressed, and at Plough for the Subsistence of his Family; for he had sold almost all his Estate to reimburse those who had been bound for his Son, who was fled to *Hetruria*.[20] The Messengers saluted him by the Name of Consul, invested him with the purple, and with the Ensigns of Magistracy, and then desired him to set out for *Rome*, where his Presence was greatly wanted; when so far was he from being lifted up by his new Dignity, or from the Thoughts of living grandly at the public Expence, that he paused for a Time, and said, with Tears in his Eyes, *For this Year my poor little Field will be unsown, and we shall be in Danger of being reduced to Want.* On his Arrival at *Rome*, he restrained the Tribunes, ingratiated himself with the Commons, and at the Expiration of the Consulate, returned to his rural Cot, and his laborious Life. But *Gracchus Clælius*, exciting the *Æqui* and *Volsci* to revolt, greatly distressed the *Roman* Army; upon which *Cincinnatus* was chosen Dictator, and engaging *Clælius*, he forced his whole Army to yield at Discretion, and obliged them to pass under the Yoke, which was two Spears set up, and a third laid across in the Form of a Gallows. After taking a considerable Town from the Enemy, he returned to *Rome*, with a more magnificent Triumph than any which had been before him. He then resigned his Office, and when the Senate and his Friends would have enriched him with the public Lands, Plunder and Contributions, he nobly refused them, and returned to his Hut and his Plough.

The sensible Manner in which little *Giles* introduced these Stories, drew all the People to his Father's Stall, and among the rest the *Merry Andrew*.[21]

See here he is with the Hunch at his Back. The Crowd that came with him obliged us to leave the Place; but just as we was going, *Giles* called out, Gentlemen, buy a House before you go. *'Tis better to buy than to build.* You have heard of the Cock that crowed in the Morn, that waked the Priest all shaven and shorn, that married the Man all tattered and torn, that kissed the Maiden all forlorn, that milked the Cow with a crumpled Horn, that tossed the Dog, that worried the Cat, that killed the Rat, that eat the Malt, that lay in the House that *Jack* built.[22]

This is the house that Jack built.

If there is any Part you do not like you may eat it; and I sell it for a Penny. Buy Gentlemen, buy and don't build. How many of my Friends have ruined themselves by building. The insufferable Folly of building a fine House, has obliged many a Man to lie in the Street. Observe what the Poet says on this Subject;

> *The man who builds, and wants wherewith to pay,*
> *Provides a Home, from which to run away.*
> *In* Britain *what is many a lordly Seat,*
> *But a Discharge in full for an Estate.*[23]

A little further we saw one with the Wheel of Fortune before him playing with Children for oranges. See here he is again. What do you say? Twenty may play as well as one. Ay, and all may lose, I suppose. Go away, Sirrah, what do you teach Children to game? Gaming is a scandalous Practice. The Gamster, the Liar, the Thief, and the Pickpocket, are first Cousins; and ought all to be turned out of Company.

You know little *Tom Simpson*, who comes to our School? Poor fellow, he has scarcely a Shoe to his Foot, and would often go without a Dinner, if he was not fed by the rest of the Boys, who, to be sure, are very good to him, as indeed they ought to be: For it is our Duty to help those who are in Distress, whether we know them or not. *He that giveth unto the Poor*, saith the Wise Man, *lendeth unto the Lord; who will in his good Time repay him seventy fold*. This little Boy's Grandfather was once the richest Man in all our Country, beloved by his Neighbours, and happy in a Wife, and a Number of fine Children, who were all very good. Yet this Gentleman, this Sir *William Simpson*, (my Father used to shed Tears when he told the Story) this Sir *William Simpson*, I say, was ruined by a Set of Sharpers in one Night.[24] They first persuaded him to play for small Sums, which they let him win, then plied him with Liquor till he was drunk, (how beastly and dangerous a Vice is Drunkenness!) and when he was in Liquor, they won Park after Park, and Farm after Farm, till they got his whole Estate. (What is bad enough for such villains?) He, poor Wretch, when he came to reflect on his Folly, and found that he had ruined his dear Wife and Children, ran mad, and was confined in *Bedlam*.[25] Lady *Simpson*, unable to support herself under such a Load of Misfortunes, died with Grief, and the Children, poor Babes, were all sent to the Parish.[26]

At this Instant up came *Dick Sudbury* crying. Here he is:

And what do you think he cries for? Why he has been at the Gaming-Table, or, in other Words at the Wheel of Fortune, and lost all the Money that was given him by his Father and Mother, and the Fairings that he received from Mr. *Long*, Mr. *Williams*, and Mrs. *Goodenough*: At first he won an Orange, put it in his Pocket, and was pleased; then he won a Knife, whipt it up, and was happy; after this, he won many other Things, till at last Fortune turned against him, as at one Time or other she always does against those who go to her Wheel and seek her Favours, and he was choused of all his Money,[27] and brought nothing away with him but a Half-penny Jew's Harp.[28] Why do you bellow so you Monkey? Go away, and learn more Sense for the future.

> *Would you be wealthy, honest* Dick,
> *Ne'er seek Success at Fortune's Wheel;*
> *For she does all her Votaries trick,*
> *And you'll sad Disappointment feel.*
> *For Wealth, in Virtue put your Trust,*
> *Be faithful, vigilant and just.*

Never game, or if you do, never play for Money. Avoid a Gamester as you would a mad Dog, or as you would a Wolf that comes to devour you.

What do you justle me for?[29] That Fellow is drunk now; see how he staggers along; and how like a Fool he looks! Drunkenness turns a Man into a Beast, and reduces him beneath the Notice even of a Boy. Let us put him in the Stocks; that was the Place intended for those who barter their Reason for a Pot of Beer, and waste that which others want. In with him! In with him!

See, here's drunken Will,
Who did nothing but swill,
Pray hiss at the Fool as you pass;
He has spent all his Pence
He has lost all his Sense,
And is now dwindled down to an Ass.

Heyday! who comes here? Oh, this is the Mountebank:

He's come to cure ev'ry Sore,
And make you twice as many more.

But hear him! hear his Speech, and observe the *Merry Andrew.*

The DOCTOR's *Speech.*

Gentlemen and Ladies, I am the Doctor of all Doctors, the great Doctor of Doctors, who can doctor you all. I ease your Pains *gratis*, cure you for nothing, and sell you my Packet that you may never be sick again. [*Enter* Andrew, *blowing a scrubbing Broom*] Sirrah, where have you been this Morning?

Andrew. Been, Sir; why, I have been on my Travels, Sir, with my Knife Sir; I have travelled all round this great Apple. Besides this, I have travelled through the Fair, Sir, and bought all these Gingerbread Books at a Man's Stall, who sells Learning by Weight and Measure, Arithmetic by the Gross, Geometry by the Square, and Physic and Philosophy by the Pound. So I bought the Philosophy, and left the Physic for you, master.

Doctor. Why, Sirrah, do you never take Physic?[30]

Andrew. Yes, Master, sometimes.

Doctor. What Sort do you take?

Andrew. Any Sort, no Matter what Sort; 'tis all one to me.

Doctor. And how do you take it?

Andrew. Why, I take it; I take it; and put it upon the Shelf: And if I don't get well, I take it down again, and work it off with good Ale. But you shall hear me read in my Golden Book, Master.

> *He that can dance with a Bag at his Back,*
> *Need swallow no Physic, for none he doth lack.*
> Again,
> *He who is healthy and chearful and cool,*
> *Yet squanders his Money on Physic's a Fool.*

Fool, Master, Fool Master, Fool, Fool.

Doctor. Sirrah, you Blockhead, I'll break your Head.

Andrew. What, for reading my Book, Master?

Doctor. No; for your Impudence, Sirrah. But come, good People, throw up your Handkerchiefs, you lose Time by attending to that blundering Booby, and by-and-by, you'll be in a Hurry and we shall not be able to serve you. Consider, Gentlemen and Ladies, in one of these Packets is deposited a curious Gold Ring, which the Purchaser, whoever it may happen to be, will have for a Shilling, together with all the Packet of Medicines; and every other

Adventurer will have a Packet for one Shilling, which he may sell for ten Times that Sum.

Andrew. Master, Master, I'll tell you how to get this Ring, and a great deal of Money into the Bargain.

Doctor. How, Sirrah?

Andrew. Why, buy up all of them yourself, and you'll be sure of the Ring, and have the Packets to sell for ten Shillings a-piece.

Doctor. That's true; but you are covetous, Sirrah; you are covetous; and want to get Money.

Andrew. And, Master, I believe you don't want to get Physic.

Doctor. Yes, I do.

Andrew. Then 'tis to get rid of it. But,

> *He that can dance with a Bag at his Back,*
> *Need swallow no Physic, for none he doth lack.*

Huzza, hallo Boys, hallo Boys, hallo!

✶   ✶   ✶

CHAP. III.

Sam Sensible's *Account of what he had seen in the Fair; particularly a Description of the* Up-and-down, *the* North Country Droll, *and the* Puppet-Shew.

Iᴛ is strange! but some Children will never take Advice, and are always running to Dangers and Difficulties. That Chit *Wat Wilful*, has been riding upon the *Up-and-down*, and is fallen off, and almost killed. You know what I mean by the *Up-and-down*? It is a Horse in a Box; a Horse that flies in the Air, like that which the ancient Poets rode on. But here it is:

And here is poor Wat, and his Mother lamenting over him.

These lofty Flights, are fit only for Poets and Politicians. If he had taken her Advice all had been well; for as he was going to mount, *Wat*, says she, don't be so ambitious. Ambitious People always tumble; when once up, it is not easy to get with Safety down. Remember what your poor Father used to read about

Cardinal *Wolsey* and others, and don't think of mounting too high. But *Wilful* would, and so down he tumbled, and lies here a Warning-piece to the Obstinate and Ambitious. Had he taken his Mother's Advice, and rode upon the *Round-about* as *Dick Stamp* and *Will Somers* do, he might have whipped and spurred for an Hour without doing any Mischief, or receiving any Hurt. But he is a proud obstinate silly Boy.

LINES on the *Up-and-down*, by a
great Man at Court

This sinks to the Ground,
While that rises high;
But then you'll observe,
He'll sink by and by:
Just so 'tis at Court,
To-day you're in Place,
To-morrow, perhaps,
You're quite in Disgrace.[31]

But I have seen at the farther End of the Fair, *Tom*, a Droll,[32] which, I think, has good Sense, and some Knowledge of Mankind in it. The Words are printed, and I have brought them to you. Here they are:

The *Geography* of the *Mind,*
OR,
A *New Way* to know the *WORLD.*

Neighbour Tumble-turf, and *Neighbour Chopstick.*

Chopstick. GOOD Morrow to you, Neighbour *Tumble-turf;* pray can you lend me your Grey Mare to take a Ride some eight or ten Miles to-day?

Tumble-turf. Why really Goodman *Chopstick,* I am just going to carry some Bags of Corn to the Mill to get ground, for my Wife wants Flour sadly.

Chopstick. There is no grinding to-day, Neighbour; I heard *Cogg* the Miller tell *Dick Hobson,* that the Mill was in Back Flood.

Tumble-turf. Say you so, Neighbour, I am sorry for that. Then I must ride to Town, and get my Wife some Flour, or she'll be out of all Patience.

Chopstick. You need not do so, Neighbour; I have got Flour enough, and can lend you some Pecks of mine.

Tumble-turf. Your Flour may not please my Wife, she's very particular.

Chopstick. No Flour can please her so well; why it was ground out of the last Corn I bought of you, which you said was the best you ever had in your Life.

Tumble-turf. 'Twas special good, indeed, special good! Neighbour *Chopstick*, there is nobody so willing to lend as I am; but my Mare does not eat Hay well, and I am afraid she will not hold out.

Chopstick. No matter for that, Neighbour; I can get her two or three Feeds of Corn upon the Road.

Tumble-turf. Corn is very dear, Neighbour.

Chopstick. That's true; but when one is out upon Business, it don't signify, you know.

Tumble-turf. It is a soggy Time, and my Mare has been hard worked, Neighbour; besides, my Saddle is broke, and I have lent my Bridle.

Chopstick. It matters not; I have a Saddle and Bridle of my own.

Tumble-turf. But your Saddle will not fit my Mare, Neighbour.

Chopstick. Then I can borrow of Neighbour *Rogers*.

Tumble-turf. His is as bad as yours.

Chopstick. Then I can be fitted at the *'Squire*'s. The Groom is an honest Fellow.

Tumble-turf. Why, Neighbour *Chopstick*, there is nobody, you know, so ready to lend as I am, and you should have the Mare with all my Heart, but she has got the Skin rubbed off her Back as broad as my Hand.

Chopstick. I'll get the Groom to stuff the Saddle. Nobody stuffs a Saddle so well as *Dick Groom*: the poor Beast shan't be hurt.

Tumble-turf. Nobody is so willing to lend a Neighbour as I am, nobody so willing; but my Mare is in rough Order, her Mane wants pulling sadly.

Chopstick. That is soon done, Neighbor; I can do that myself, and *Dick Groom* will help me.

Tumble-turf. But now I think on't, she wants new Shoes.

Chopstick. There is Time enough for that; the Days are of a good Length, the Mare trots well, and we have a Blacksmith at Hand.

Tumble-turf. Aye, as you say, the Mare trots well, and the Days are of a likely Length both for Master and Man, but our Neighbour *Blacksmith* cannot shoe her easy. I always take her to Market, and get her shoed in Town by *Ned Hammerwell*. He shoes her to Pattern.[33]

Chopstick. My Road lies through the Town; it will be none out of the Way.

[*Enter* Tumble-turf's *Servant*.]

Tumble-turf. Here is Neighbour *Chopstick* wants to borrow my Mare, *Tom*, prithee, step, and see, if her Shoulder is not much wrung. [*Exit* Tom.] There is nobody so willing as I am to oblige a Neighbour when I can; but [*Re-enter* Tom.]

Tom. Wrung; aye, Master, she is wrung indeed; the Skin is rubbed off the poor Jade as broad as my Back: She is not fit to ride; besides, I promised her to Goodman *Ploughshare* to fetch a Quarter of Coals. You know he has but two of his own, and if he can't have ours his must be idle.

Tumble-turf. Why indeed, Neighbour *Chopstick*, I am sorry it happens so. There is nobody so willing to lend as I am; and I wish I could let you have the Mare, but we cannot disappoint Goodman *Ploughshare*, for we owe him some Help. I am sorry it happens so.

Chopstick. I am sorry too; because it will be a Loss to both of us. You must know, Neighbour, I have had a Line from *Sir Thomas Wiseacre*'s Steward, to come over directly. There is a Bargain of Timber to be sold, and if I miss, another Chapman may step between;[34] which will be twenty Guineas out of your Way; for if I buy, you will have the Job of carrying it. I spoke about it. Sir *Thomas* pays well, and twenty Guineas is a good deal of Money, you know; but as the Mare is ill, there is an End of the Matter.

Tumble-turf. Twenty Guineas, did you say?

Chopstick. Yes; twenty Guineas! But as the Mare is not fit to go, I must stay at home; and there is an End of the Matter, Neighbour.

Tumble-turf. Here *Tom*, tell Goodman *Ploughshare*, that he cannot have the Mare to-day; for Neighbour Chopstick wants her, and he must not be disappointed. Another Day will do for him.

Chopstick. But how can we manage about the Flour, and the Saddle and Bridle, and about getting her shod. Besides if the Mare is ill?

Tumble-turf. She is not so ill but she will carry you very well. She eat her Hay well this Morning. As to the Flour, my Wife can stay some Days. I have a new Saddle and Bridle; you shall be welcome to them, though they were never used. The Skin is not rubbed off broader than my Finger; and now I think on't, she was new shod but yesterday. She will carry you well, Neighbour *Chopstick*, and I wish you a good Journey and Success with all my Heart.

Chopstick. Thank you, neighbour.

Tumble-turf. A good Morning to you.

> *If you would borrow of a Friend,*
> *That has not Will nor Heart to lend;*
> *Let his own Interest take the Lead,*
> *His Interest best your Cause will plead;*
> *For, Sirs, it always happens so,*
> That Money makes the Mare to go.[35]

In the same Booth we were shown the comical Dogs and Monkies brought from the Theatre in the *Haymarket*,[36] which were introduced with this short Prologue:

> *Puppies and Coxcombs, all draw near,*
> *And Belles and Beaux, and Bucks come here;*
> *Observe, the Feats perform'd by you,*
> *The very Dogs and monkies do.*

The first Scene presented us with two Monkies at Dinner dressed like modern Beaux, and a third in a Livery waited on them at Table.[37] See here they are.

And they look as much like *Dick Dapperwit* and *Jemmy Jessemy*, as ever you saw two Creatures in your Life; but they bowed to the Company, drank to each other, and behaved better than most of our modern Gentlemen. Your servant, Mr. *Pugg.*

We were then presented with a Grand Ball, which consisted of Dogs and Monkies dressed like Gentlemen and Ladies, and they walked upon their hind Legs, bowed, curtesied, and danced Minuets,[38] as is usual in the Assemblies of the Polite.

The next Scene was made up of several Dogs, that performed a Kind of Harlequin Entertainment, which was very droll, and conveyed to the Spectators as much Knowledge as Harlequin Entertainments usually do.[39]

We were then taught to ride the Great Horse, by a Monkey, which was placed on a great Dog that was bitted and saddled, and pranced and performed all the Feats of a managed Horse.

Other Dogs then appeared walking on their hind Legs, dressed like Soldiers, with their Guns and Bayonets fixed, and ran up Ladders to storm a Castle, while the Guns were firing from the Top of the Works. After this my old Friend the learned Dog made his Appearance.[40] See here he is.

And he composed from the Letters before him the following Poem.

The DOG on his own Abilities

Let pride no more your Hearts possess,
But here your Ignorance confess:
For sure, you all must blush to see
Yourselves exceeded thus by me.
    I for the Lawyers often write,
I for the Doctors oft indite;
Billets I pen for Belles and Beaux,
And softest Sentiments disclose.
In Politics I oft engage,
And sometimes scribble for the Stage;
Then cringe to get my Pieces on,
As all my Brother Bards have done.

After this he spelt all our Names, told us the Time of the Day, and almost told our Fortunes.

We were hurried from hence to another Booth, and placed before a Juggler with his Cups and Balls. See here he is. *Quick, Presto be gone.*

This conjuring Cur shewed us three empty Cups and three Balls. The Cups he turned down upon the Table, and then taking the Balls and throwing them away, as he pretended, he commanded the Balls and the Cups, and on turning them up, lo they were there. But *Dick Wilkins*, who you know is a very arch sensible Boy, told the Company there was no Mystery in this; for there are four Balls, says he, instead of three, one of which he conceals between the two middle Fingers of his right Hand, and by the Spring of one Finger discharges it under the Cup, when he puts it down. Then taking another Ball to put into his left Hand to throw away, as you would imagine, he by rubbing his Thumb conveys that also between his two Fingers, and not into his left Hand, and throws that under the Cup likewise; and having put one under each Cup, he reserves the last Ball between his two Fingers for the next Trick he is to perform. Let me put down the Cups, Master, says *Dick*, and then try if you can command the Balls under them. This the Man refused, and all the Company laughed at the little Fellow's Sagacity.

The next Trick he shewed was a Bag, in which Eggs were multiplied to a surprising Degree. First, the Bag was shewn empty, & then Eggs were found in it, and so on till a great Number were produced; and after they were all laid, as he pretended, out came a live Hen, to the Joy and Amazement of the Company.

This is a very pretty Trick, says *Dick*, and may make a Fool stare, but I will tell you how it is done, my Friend. You have two Bags that are made just like; in one of the Bags there are many Foldings, and some Pockets in that Part of it next to you, in which the Eggs are concealed, and are dropped into the Bag as you would have them, through a Hole at the End of the Pocket, which has Room enough to admit of two Eggs passing. In the other Bag you have concealed a Hen; and when you pretend to throw an Egg up to the Ceiling to make it stick, you let drop that Bag, and catch up the other just like it, which hung on a Hook behind your Table, and then let out the Hen. The Man blushed, which was somewhat extraordinary in a Juggler, and the Company burst into a Fit of Laughter.

After this, our Conjurer placed a Die upon the Table, and desired one of the Company to throw it. A Lady threw it, and up came Number *Five*. This the Man covered with a leathern Cap, and then asking for a Groat's-worth of Half-pence,[41] he put them under the Table, and ordered them to pass through the Table, and remain under the Cap, This done, he removed the Cap, and behold the Die was gone, and the Half-pence there, which was very surprising. He then covered the Half-pence again with the Cap, and commanded them again through the Table, and we heard them chink in his Hand. Then taking up the Cap, the Half-pence were gone, and the Die there with the same Number upwards, that was thrown by the Lady. This appeared very extraordinary, and our Juggler exulted a good deal, saying it could be done by no other Cap, but that, which was *Fortunatus*'s wishing Cap.[42]

Say you so, says *Dick*; then listen to me, and I will tell you how this mighty Feat is performed. In the first Place, my Friend, you get eight Half-pence rivitted together, and then cut a square Hole in the Middle thro' all the Half-pence but the uppermost; and this Machine, or bundle of Half-pence, you conceal in the little Cap. Now, when the Die is thrown, you cover it with the Cap, having these Half-pence concealed under it, and the square Hole that was made in them admits the Die; so that the Half-pence stand upon the Table. Then taking those Half-pence, which you borrowed, you rattle them under the Table, and then lifting up the Cap lightly, you discover those Half-pence you had concealed there. When putting on the Cap again, you rattle the Half-pence you had borrowed under the Table, as if they dropped through into your Hands, and squeezing the Cap with your Finger and Thumb, so as to take up the Half-pence rivitted together as well as the Cap, you leave the Die with the same Number upwards which had been thrown; and no Wonder, for the Die has never once been moved, but has all the Time stood in the same Place.

The Man was so confounded at this Discovery, that he would shew no more Tricks; and all the Company laughed to find, that our little Philosopher had more Wit than the Conjurer.

From hence we went to see the Puppet Show, and that impudent rogue *Punch*, who came in, *Caw, waw, waw*, strutting and prancing, and turned his Backside to all the fine Ladies, as you may see.[43]

I have got, says he, I have got. What have you got? cried the Fidler. Why, I have got a Present for a naughty Boy, says he, and held up a Rod.

This brazen-faced Fellow, however, was soon sent out to make Room for Mr. *Whittington* and his Cat; of whom we will give you some Account.[44]

Dick Whittington was a very little Boy, when his Father and Mother died; so little indeed, that he never knew them, nor the Place where he was born. He strolled about the Country as ragged as a Colt, till he met with a Waggoner who was going to *London*, and who gave him Leave to walk all the Way by the Side of his Waggon, without paying any Thing for this Passage; which obliged little *Whittington* very much, as he wanted to see *London* sadly; for he had heard that the Streets were paved with Gold, and he was willing to get a Bushel of it.[45] But, how great was his Disappointment, poor Boy, when he saw the Streets covered with Dirt instead of Gold, and found himself in a strange Place without Food, without Friends, and without Money.

Though the Waggoner was so charitable, as to let him walk up by the Side of the Waggon for nothing, he took Care not to know him when he came to Town, and the poor Boy was in a little Time, so cold and so hungry, that he wished himself in a good Kitchen, and

by a warm Fire in the Country. In this Distress he asked Charity of several People, and one of them bid him, *Go work for an idle Rogue.* That I will, says *Whittington*, with all my Heart. I will work for you, if you will let me. The Man who thought this savoured of Wit and Impertinence (though the poor Lad intended only to shew his Readiness to work) gave him a Blow with a Stick, which broke his Head, so that the Blood ran down. In this Situation, and fainting for Want of Food, he laid himself down at the Door of one Mr. *Fitzwarren*, a Merchant, where the Cook saw him, and being an ill-natured Hussy, ordered him to go about his Business, or she would scald him. At this Time Mr. *Fitzwarren* came from the Exchange, and began also to scold at the poor Boy, bidding him go to work.[46]

Whittington answered, that he should be glad to work, if any Body would employ him, and that he should be able if he could get some Victuals to eat; but he had had nothing for three Days, and he was a poor Country Boy, and knew nobody, and nobody would employ him. He then endeavoured to get up, but was so very weak that he fell down again, which excited so much Compassion in the Merchant, that he ordered the Servants to take him in, and give him some Meat and Drink, and let him help the Cook do any dirty Work that she had to set him about. People are too apt to reproach those who beg with being idle; but give themselves no Concern to put them in a Way of getting Business to do, or considering whether they are able to do it; which is not Charity. I remember a Circumstance of this Sort, which Sir *William Thompson* told my Father with Tears in his Eyes, and is so affecting, that I shall never forget it.

When *Sir William* was in the Plantations Abroad, one of his Friends told him he had an indented Servant whom he had just bought,[47] that was his Countryman, and a lusty Man, but he is so idle, says he, that I cannot get him to work. Ay, says Sir *William*, let me see him; accordingly they walked out together, and found the Man sitting on a Heap of Stones. Upon this, Sir *William*, after enquiring about his Country, asked, why he did not go out to work? I am not able answered the Man. Not able, says Sir *William*, I am sure you look very well, give him a few Stripes. Upon this, the Planter struck him several times, but the poor Man still kept his Seat. They then left him to look over the Plantation, exclaiming against his Obstinacy all the Way they went. But how surprized were they, on their Return, to find the poor Man fallen off the Place where he had been sitting, and dead. The Cruelty, says Sir *William*, of my ordering the poor Creature to be beaten while in the Agonies of Death lies always next my Heart. It is what I shall never forget, and will for ever prevent my judgeing rashly of People who appear in Distress. How do we know what our own Children may come to? The Lord have Mercy upon the Poor, and defend them from the Proud, the Inconsiderate, and the Avaricious.

But we return to *Whittington*; who would have lived happily in this worthy Family, had he not been bumped about by the cross Cook, who must be always roasting or basting, and when the Spit was still, she employed her Hands upon poor *Whittington* till Mrs. *Alice*, his Master's Daughter, was informed of it, and took Compassion on the poor Boy, and made the Servants treat him kindly.

Besides the Crossness of the Cook, *Whittington* had another Difficulty to get over before he could be happy. He had, by Order of his Master, a Flock Bed[48] placed for him in the Garret, where there were such a Number of Rats and Mice,that they often ran over the poor Boy's Nose, and disturbed him in his Sleep. After some Time, however, a Gentleman, who came to his Master's House, gave Whittington a Penny for brushing his Shoes. This he put in his Pocket, being determined to lay it out to the best Advantage; and, the next Day, seeing a Woman in the Street with a Cat under her Arm, he ran up to her, to know the Price of it. The Woman, as the Cat was a good Mouser, asked a great deal of Money for it; but on *Whittington*'s telling her, he had but a Penny in the World, and that he wanted a Cat, *sadly*, she let him have it, and a fine Cat she is; pray look at her:

This Cat *Whittington* concealed in the Garret, for Fear she should be beat about by his mortal Enemy the Cook, and here she soon killed or frighted away the Rats and Mice, so that the poor Boy could now sleep as sound as a Top.

Soon after this, the Merchant, who had a Ship ready to sail, called for all his Servants, as his Custom was, in order that each of them might venture some Thing to try their Luck; and whatever they sent was to pay neither Freight nor Custom;[49] for he thought, and thought justly, that God Almighty would bless him the more for his Readiness to let the Poor partake of his good Fortune; *He that giveth to the Poor, lendeth to the Lord*,[50] who will return it seventy Fold.

All the Servants appeared but poor *Whittington*, who having neither Money nor Goods, could not think of sending any Thing to try his Luck; but his good Friend Mrs. *Alice* thinking his Poverty kept him away, ordered him to be called, and here he is.

She then offered to lay down some Thing for him: but the Merchant told his Daughter, that would not do; for it must be some Thing of his own. Upon which poor *Whittington* said, he had nothing but a Cat, which he had bought for a Penny that was given him. Fetch thy Cat, Boy, says the Merchant, and send her. *Whittington* brought poor Puss, and delivered her to the Captain with Tears in his Eyes, for he said, he should now be disturbed by the Rats and Mice as much as ever. All the company laughed at the Oddity of the Adventure, and Mrs. *Alice*, who pitied the poor Boy, gave him something to buy him another Cat.

While Puss was beating the Billows at Sea, poor *Whittington* was severely beaten at home by his tyrannical Mistress the Cook, who used him so cruelly, and made such Game of him for sending his Cat to Sea, that at last the poor Boy determined to run away from his Place, having packed up a few Things he had, he set out very early in the Morning on *Allhallows* Day.[51] He travelled as far as Holloway, and there sat down on a Stone, now called *Whittington's Stone*, to consider what Course he should take; but while he was

thus ruminating, *Bow* Bells,[52] of which there were then only six, began to ring; and he thought their Sounds addressed him in this Manner:

> *Turn again* Whittington,
> *Lord Mayor of Great* London.

Lord Mayor of London, said he to himself, *what would one not endure to be Lord Mayor of* London, *and ride in such a fine Coach!*[53] *Well, I'll go back again, and bear all the Pummelling and ill Usage of* Cicely, *rather than miss the Opportunity of being Lord Mayor.* So home he went, and happily got into the House, and about his Business, before Mrs. *Cicely* made her Appearance.

Here we must stop a little, to address the Children of six Feet high, and among them those formidable Heroes the Critics, whose awful Brows strike Terror into the Hearts of us little Authors.

Be it known then, to these Gentlemen, and to all the Knights of the Goose Quill, that we are not insensible of the Prescripts of *Apollo*, or ignorant of the Laws of the Drama. We know, that the Unities of Action, Time and Place,[54] should be preserved as well in the Drama of *Whittington*, as in those of *Cæsar* or *Alexander*; but by your Permission, Gentlemen, we must, in Imitation of some of our Poets, just step abroad while you sit upon the Bench, to let you know what has happened to the poor Cat; however, we are going no farther than the Coast of *Africa*, to that Coast where *Dido* expired for the Loss of *Æneas*,[55] and we shall be back with you presently.

How perilous are Voyages at Sea, how uncertain the Winds and the Waves, and how many Accidents attend a naval Life!

The Ship, with the Cat on board, was long beating about at Sea, and at last by contrary Winds driven on a Part of the Coast of *Barbary*, which was inhabited by *Moors* unknown to the *English*. These People received our Countrymen with Civility, and therefore the Captain, in order to trade with them, shewed them Patterns of the Goods he had on board,[56] and sent some of them to the King of the Country, who was so well pleased, that he sent for the Captain and the Factor to his Palace, which was about a Mile from the Sea. Here they were placed, according to the Custom of the Country, on rich Carpets flowered with Gold and Silver; and the King and Queen being seated at the upper End of the Room, Dinner was brought in, which consisted of many Dishes; but no sooner were the Dishes put down, but an amazing Number of Rats and Mice came from all Quarters, and devoured all the Meat in an Instant. The Factor in Surprize turned round to the Nobles, and asked, If these Vermin were not offensive; *Oh, yes*, said they, very offensive; and the King would give Half his Treasure to be free of them; for they not only destroy his Dinner, as you see, but they assault him in his Chamber, and even in Bed, so that he is obliged to be watched while he is sleeping for Fear of them.

The Factor jumped for Joy; he remembered poor *Whittington* and his Cat, and told the King he had a Creature on board the

Ship that would dispatch all these Vermin immediately. The King's Heart heaved so high, at the Joy which this News gave him, that his Turbant dropped off his Head![57] Bring this Creature to me, says he, Vermin are dreadful in a Court and if she will perform what you say, I will load your Ship with Gold and Jewels in exchange for her. The Factor, who knew his Business, took this Opportunity to set forth the Merits of Mrs. *Puss.* He told his Majesty, that it would be inconvenient for him to part with her, as when she was gone the Rats and Mice might destroy the Goods in his Ship; but that to oblige his Majesty he would fetch her. Run, run, said the Queen, I am impatient to see the dear Creature. Away flew the Factor, while another Dinner was providing, and returned with the Cat, just as the Rats and Mice were devouring that also. He immediately put down Mrs. *Puss*, who killed great Part of them, and the rest ran away.

The King rejoiced greatly to see his old Enemies destroyed by so small a Creature, and the Queen was highly pleased, and desired the Cat might be brought near, that she might look at her. Upon which the Factor called, *Pussey, Pussey, Pussey,* and she came to him; he then presented her to the Queen, who started back, and was afraid to touch a Creature, which had made such a Havock among the Rats and Mice; however, when the Factor stroaked the

Cat, and cried *Pussey, Pussey, Pussey*, the Queen also touched her, and cried *Puttey, Puttey, Puttey*, for she had not learned *English*. He then put her down in the Queen's Lap, where she purring, played with her Majesty's Hand, and then sung herself to Sleep.

The King having seen the Exploits of Mrs. *Puss*, and being informed, that she was with young, and would stock the whole Country, bargained with the Captain and Factor for the whole Ship's Cargo, and then gave them ten Times as much for the Cat as all the rest amounted to. With which, after taking Leave of their Majesties, and other great Personages at Court, they sailed with a fair Wind for *England*, whither we must now attend them.

> *The Morn ensuing from the Mountain Height,*
> *Had scarcely spread the Skies with rosy Light:*[58]

when Mr. *Fitzwarren* stole from the Bed of his beloved Wife, to count over the Cash, and settle the Business of the Day.

He had but just entered the Compting-house, and seated himself at the Desk, when somebody came, Tap, tap, tap, at the Door. Who's there? says Mr. *Fitzwarren*. A Friend, answered the other. What Friend can come at this unseasonable Time? says Mr. *Fitzwarren*. A real Friend is never unseasonable, answered the other. I come to bring you good News of the good Ship *Unicorn*. The Merchant bustled up in such a Hurry that he forgot his Gout; he instantly opened the Door, and who should be seen waiting, but the Captain and Factor with a Cabinet of Jewels, and Bill of Ladings;[59] for which the Merchant lifted up his Eyes, and thanked Heaven for sending him such a prosperous Voyage. They then told him of the Adventures of the Cat, and shewed him the Cabinet of Jewels, which they had brought for Mr. *Whittington*. Upon which he cried out with great Earnestness, but not in the most poetical Manner:

> *Go call him, and tell him of his Fame,*
> *And call him Mr.* Whittington *by Name.*

It is not our Business to animadvert upon these Lines: we are not Critics, but Historians. It is sufficient for us, that they are the Words of Mr. *Fitzwarren*; and tho' it is beside our Purpose, and perhaps not in our Power to prove him a good Poet, we shall soon convince the Reader that he was a good Man, which is a much better Character; for when some, who were present, told him, That this Treasure was too much for such a poor Boy as *Whittington*, he said, *God forbid that I should deprive him of a Penny: it is all his own, and he shall have it to a Farthing.* He then ordered Mr. *Whittington* in, who was at this Time cleaning the Kitchen, and would have excused himself from going into the Parlour, saying, the Room was rubbed,[60] and his Shoes were dirty and full of Hobnails. The Merchant, however, made him come in, and ordered a Chair to be set for him. Upon which, thinking they intended to make Sport of him, as had been too often the Case in the Kitchen, he besought his Master not to mock a poor simple Fellow, who intended them no Harm, but to let him go about his Business. The Merchant, taking him by the Hand, said, Indeed, Mr. *Whittington*, I am in earnest with you, and sent for you to congratulate you on your great Success. Your Cat has produced you more Money than I am worth in the World, and may you long enjoy it, and be happy. At length, being shewn the Treasure, and convinced by them that all of it belonged to him, he fell upon his Knees, and thanked the ALMIGHTY for his providential Care of such a poor miserable Creature. He then laid all the Treasure at his Master's Feet, who refused to take any Part of it, but told him, he heartily rejoiced at his prosperity, and hoped the Wealth he had acquired would be a Comfort to him, and make him happy. He then applied to his Mistress, and to his good Friend Mrs. *Alice,* who likewise refused to take any Part of his Money, but told him, she really rejoiced at his Success, and wished him all imaginable Felicity. He then gratified the Captain, Factor, and Ship's Crew, for the Care they had taken of his Cargo, and distributed Presents to all the Servants in the House, not forgetting even his old Enemy the Cook, though she little deserved it.

After this, Mr. *Fitzwarren* advised Mr. *Whittington* to send for the necessary People and dress himself like a Gentleman, and made him the Offer of his House to live in till he could provide himself with a better.

Now it come to pass, that when Mr. *Whittington*'s Face was washed, his Hair curled, his Hat cocked, and he was dressed in a rich Suit of Cloaths, that he turned out a genteel young Fellow; and as Wealth contributes much to give a man Confidence, he in a little Time, dropped that sheepish Behaviour, which was principally occasioned by a Depression of Spirits, and soon grew a sprightly, and a good Companion; insomuch that Mrs. *Alice,* who had formerly seen him with an Eye of Compassion; now viewed him with other Eyes; which, perhaps, was in some Measure occasioned by his Readiness to oblige her, and by continually making her Presents of such Things as he thought would be agreeable.

When the Father perceived they had this good Liking for each other, he proposed a Match between them, to which both Parties chearfully consented, and the Lord-Mayor, (See here he is)

Court of Alderman, Sheriffs, the Company of Stationers, and a Number of eminent Merchants attended the Ceremony, and were elegantly treated at an Entertainment made for that Purpose.

History tells us, that they lived happily, and had several Children, that he was Sheriff of *London* in the Year 1340, and then Lord Mayor; that in the last Year of his Mayoralty he entertained King *Henry* the Fifth and his Queen, after his Conquest of *France*. Upon which Occasion, the King, in Consideration of *Whittington*'s Merit, said, *Never had Prince such a Subject*; which being told to *Whittington* at the Table, he replied, *Never had Subject such a King*. He constantly fed great Numbers of the Poor. He built a Church and a College to it, with a yearly Allowance for poor Scholars; and near it erected an Hospital. He built *Newgate* for Criminals, and gave liberally to St. *Bartholomew*'s Hospital, and to other public Charities.[61]

REFLECTION.

This Story of *Whittington* and his Cat, and all the Misfortunes which happened to the poor Boy, may be considered as a Cure for Despair, as it teaches us, that GOD Almighty had always something good in Store for those, who endure the Ills that befall them with Patience and Resignation.

This was a most extraordinary Cat, says *Dick Wilson*, but she was nothing to Puss in Boots. I'll tell you her Story.

PUSS in BOOTS.[62]

A Miller, who had three Children, left them no other Fortune than his Mill, an Ass, and his Cat. The Division was soon made. There was no Occasion for a Lawyer. His Fees would soon have consumed their little Substance. The eldest had the Mill, the second the Ass, and the youngest the Cat.

The last was much concerned at having so poor a Lot. *My Brothers*, said he, *may gain an honest living by joining their little Fortunes, but as for me, when I have eaten my Cat, and made me a Muff of her Skin, I must die with Hunger.* Puss, who seemingly sat unconcerned, heard him thus complain, and with a grave and solemn Look replied, Don't be so much concerned, my good Master;

you need only give me a Bag, and get me a Pair of Boots, that I may scamper thro' the Dirt and the Brambles, and you will see, that you have not so bad a Share as you imagine.

Though the Master of the Cat had but little Dependence on what he said, yet, as he had seen him perform so many cunning Tricks to catch Rats and Mice, as his hanging himself up by the Heels, and hiding himself in the Meal, pretended to be dead, he did not despair of his affording him some Assistance. When Puss had obtained what he asked, he booted himself like a little Man, and, throwing the Bag over his Shoulder like a School-boy, he held the Strings with his fore Paws, and ran to a warren, in which were many Rabbits; he put some Bran and Sow-thistles into his Bag,[63] and stretched himself out as if he was dead, waited till some young Rabbits, unacquainted with the Deceits of the World, came to examine the Bag, and eat what he had put into it.

Scarce had he laid down, when a young foolish Rabbit entered the Bag, and Master Puss immediately drawing the String, killed it without Mercy; then proud of his Prey, went to the Palace, and desired to speak with the King. Being admitted, he bowed to his Majesty, saying, I have brought you, Sir, a Rabbit, which my Lord the Marquis of *Carabas* (for that was the Title he was pleased to give his Master) begs your Majesty to accept. Tell thy Master, said the King, that I thank him, and receive it with Pleasure.

Another Time he concealed himself in the Standing Corn, still holding his Bag open, and when a Brace of Partridges ran into it, he drew the String and took them both; after which he went to present them to the King, as he had done the Rabbit. His Majesty also received the two Partridges with Pleasure, and ordered him some Money to drink.

Then Puss continued two or three Months carrying his Majesty from Time to Time Game, which he pretended his Master had caught. One Day, when he knew the King was going to take an Airing, along the Bank of the River, with his Daughter, the most beautiful Princess upon Earth, he said to his Master, If you will follow my Advice, you will make your Fortune; you need only bathe in the River where I shall shew you, and leave the rest to me. The Marquis of *Carabas* followed his Cat's Advice, though he did not think it would be of any Advantage.

While he was bathing, the King passed by, and Puss began to cry with all her Might, Help, help, my Lord Marquis of *Carabas* will be drowned. At this the King looking out at the Coach-Window, and knowing Puss, who had so often brought him Game, ordered his Guards to run to the Assistance of my Lord the Marquis.

While they were pulling the poor Marquis out of the River, Puss coming up to the Coach, told the King, that while his Master was bathing, some Rogues had carried away his Cloaths, though he had called out Thieves, Thieves, as loud as he was able; but the cunning Cat had only hid them under a great Stone. The King instantly commanded the Officers of the Wardrobe to run and fetch one of the best Suits for my Lord the Marquis.

My Lord was no sooner dressed than waiting on the King, he was received in the most gracious Manner; and as he was well made, very handsome, and the fine Cloaths set him off to Advantage, the Princess was perfectly charmed with him; and the King insisted on his stepping into the Coach to take the Air with him.

The Cat, overjoyed at seeing his Design thus happily begin to succeed, ran before, and perceiving some Countrymen mowing a Meadow, said, My honest Lads, if you don't tell the King, that the Meadow you are mowing belongs to the Marquis of *Carabas*, you shall be all cut as small as Herbs for the Pot. The King did not fail asking the Mowers to whom the Meadow belonged; when they all cried, To the Marquis of *Carabas*; for they were sadly afraid of the Cat. Your Majesty sees, said the Marquis, that it never fails to produce a plentiful Crop.

Master Puss, who kept running before, came up to some Reapers, and said to them, My honest Lads, if you don't tell the King, that all this Corn belongs to my Lord the Marquis of *Carabas*, you shall be cut as small as Herbs for the Pot. The King, who passed by a Moment after, was desirous of knowing to whom all that Corn belonged, and asking the Reapers, they all answered, May it please your Majesty, it all belongs to my Lord the Marquis of *Carabas*. At which the King, addressing himself to the Marquis, expressed his Satisfaction, and complimented him on the Occasion.

The Cat still running before the Coach, gave the same Charge to all he met; and the King was astonished at the great Estates belonging to my Lord the Marquis of *Carabas*.

Puss at length came to the stately Castle, which belonged to the richest Oger that ever was known; for all the Lands through which the King had passed were his Property. The Cat who knew who this Oger was, and what strange Things he could perform, desired to speak with him, saying, that he could not pass near his Palace without doing himself the Honour of paying his Respects to him. The Oger received him with as much Civility as an Oger could, and made him sit down. I have been assured, said the Cat, that you have the Power of assuming what Form you please, and can transform yourself into a Lion or an Elephant. This is true, returned the Oger, and to convince you, I will become a Lion. Puss was so terrified at seeing a Lion before him, that he crept into a Hole, but not without great Difficulty, on Account of his Boots: But on seeing the Oger had resumed his natural Form, he ventured out, and confessed, that he had been very much frightened. I have been also assured, said the Cat, that you have the Power of assuming the Form of the smallest Animals, and that you can change yourself into a Mouse; but I must confess that I think that impossible. Impossible! cried the Oger, see here, and instantly changing himself into a Mouse, skipped along the Floor. This the Cat no sooner perceived, than, springing upon him, he catched him in his Mouth and eat him up.

In the mean Time the King seeing the Oger's Palace, was resolved to go into it; and Puss, who heard the Rattling of the Coach over the Drawbridge, ran out, and said, Your Majesty is welcome to the House of my Lord the Marquis of *Carabas*. How! my Lord, said the King, is this Palace also yours? Nothing can be finer than this Court, and the stately Buildings that surround it. If you please, we will walk into it. The Marquis presented his Hand to the Princess, and following the King, entered a spacious Hall, where they found a magnificent Collation, which the Oger had provided for his Friends; who were that Day to have paid him a Visit, but did not dare come, because the King was there. His Majesty was charmed with the good Qualities of the Marquis, and the Princess was violently in Love with him, which the King perceiving, and considering his great Wealth, said, after drinking five or six Glasses, I have such an Esteem for you, my Lord, that it shall be owing to yourself alone, if you are not my Son-in-law. The Marquis bowing very respectfully, accepted the Honour done him, and the same Day was married to the Princess; in Consequence of which Puss became a great Lord, and never more ran after Mice, but for his Diversion.

As soon as *Dick* had finished his Story, *Sam Sensible* took him up with some Warmth. What, says he, do you intend to fob us off with a Fairy Tale, in which there is not the least Appearance of Probability? I don't consider, whether it is probable or not, says *Dick*; but I think my Puss is as good as your's; for in Matters of this Sort we are not so much concerned about the Truth of the Story, as the Moral it conveys; and tho' my Puss in Boots may be extravagant, she, in an indirect and pleasing Manner, tells me, that a Man should not despair, because Fortune seems to frown on him; that a good Address and fine Cloaths captivate the Ladies; and that Flattery may catch a King and kill a Giant, as we see in the Case of the Oger. This calls to my Mind the Saying of *Diogenes*, who being asked, what Beast was the most dangerous in Case it was to bite one, answered, *If you mean the Bite of a wild Beast, it is that of a Slanderer; if of a tame one, it is that of a Flatterer.*[64] All the Company laughed at the Defence *Dick* made for Mrs. Puss in Boots; but as her Story was so fantastical and out or Nature, Preference was given to the Cat of Mr. *Whittington*; and it was agreed, that Fairy Tales should never be read but on Fair Days, when People are inclined to have their Heads stuffed with Nonsense.

Here a great Noise in the Fair interrupted *Sam Sensible*, and cut the Thread of his Narration.

At this instant came up two Ballad-singers; and see here they are.

A New LOVE SONG
By the Poets of GREAT-BRITAIN

I.

THERE was a little Man,
Who wooed a little Maid,
And he said, Little Maid, will you wed, wed, wed?
I have little more to say,
So will you, aye or nay,
For the least said is soonest amended, ded, ded.

II.

Then reply'd the little Maid,
Little Sir, you've little said,
To induce a little Maid for to wed, wed, wed.
You must say a little more,
And produce a little Ore,
Ere I make a little Print in your Bed, Bed, Bed.

III.

Then the little Man reply'd,
If you'll be my little Bride,
I'll raise my Love Notes a little higher, higher, higher,
Tho' my Offers are not meet,
Yet my little Heart is great,
With the little God of Love all on Fire, Fire, Fire.

IV.

Then the little Maid reply'd,
Shou'd I be your little Bride,
Pray what must we have for to eat, eat, eat?
Will the Flame that you're so rich in
Light a Fire in the Kitchen,
Or the little God of Love turn the Spit, Spit, Spit?

V.

Then the little Man he sigh'd,
And some say a little cry'd,
For his little Heart was big with Sorrow, Sorrow, Sorrow.
I am your little Slave,
And if the Wealth I have
Be too little, little, little, we will borrow, borrow, borrow.

VI.

Then the little Man so gent,[65]
Made the little Maid relent,
For to kill him with Love was a Sin, Sin, Sin.
Tho' his Offers were but small,
She took his little All,
She could have but the Cat and her Skin, Skin, Skin.[66]

* * *

CHAP. IV.

Of CONSEQUENCES: *Or, An Account of Things not to be accounted for, but from Experience.*

WHO made all that Noise just now? You don't know; no, I believe you don't, indeed. But, I will tell you. Why, it was *Tom Trip*, who beat *Woglog* the great Giant.[67] He has got his Dog *Jouler* with him, and *Tinker*, and *Towser*, and *Rockwood*, and *Ringwood*, and *Rover*, all coupled together, and they draw him you see in a little Chariot. Here he comes; make Room, make Room for him! Your Servant, Mr. *Trip*; what brought you to Town, pray? Oh, you will not tell us, you say! Well; then I will tell these Gentlemen and Ladies; for I think it may be of Use to them. Master *Trip*, you must know, will ride an hundred Miles at any Time to see any little Boy or Girl, who is remarkably good. He is the little Gentleman, who used to go round with Cakes and Custards to all the Boys and Girls, who had learned Mr. *Newbery's* little Books, and were good; and having heard, that Master *Billy*, and Miss *Kitty Smith*, were on a Visit at the Duke's, he is come a long Way to see them. Well, it seems very strange, that this little Boy and Girl should be so well beloved; that every Body should want to see them; but, if you consider how good they are, it will not seem strange at all. We are naturally found of those that are good. Even naughty Children, who teaze others, love those best who are good-natured, and will not teaze them. And so it is through Life; a Knave likes an honest Man better than one of his own Stamp, and would rather deal with him, because he knows that the honest Man will not deceive him. There was a Town in some Country beyond the Sea, where the People were so wicked as to be all Thieves; yet two *Englishmen*, who were honest, went over, and lived among them very well; for as those People were afraid to trust each other, they all of them dealt with these two *Englishmen*. However, they dealt with them, not because they were *Englishmen*, but because they were honest Men; and they lived very well, and got rich even among a Parcel of Rogues. So true is that Copy in our Writing-Books, which says, *Honesty is the best Policy*; and that other Copy, which says, *Good Boys gain many Friends, but naughty Boys none*. If all People were *good*, all would be *happy*; and there would be no such Thing as Fear in the World. We should have no Occasion for Locks and Bolts, and Bars, and Jails, and Whips and Rods; and the Lawyers might burn all their Books; for they would be useless, But, I must run and see, how Master *Smith* receives *Tommy Trip*. – Stay a little, and I will be with your presently.

* * *

CHAP V.
Of Dress and Draggle-tails;[68] *a Lesson for* GREAT CHILDREN.

WELL, there was great Joy at their Meeting. Master *Smith* embraced little *Trip*, and, then taking him by the Hand, introduced him to the young Marquis, who received him very politely; that is, he received him so as to make him happy; for the Business of Politeness is to make People easy, happy, and agreeable. After some Time, he led him to the Duke and Duchess, who took great Notice of him, I assure you: But at this Instant, an Adventure ensued, which made us laugh heartily. And what do you think it was? Why, as we were then walking on the Green, a Lady came up dressed in one of the Sweep-street Gowns, which was held up by the Duke's great Dog, *Keeper*. See here he is.

This Lady flirted through the Company without speaking, and very familiarly brushed by the Duchess. Her Grace stood astonished, and the Duke was agreeably surprised, to see his favourite Dog *Keeper* so well employed. When this Lady stood still, the Dog ran to another, *bow, wow*, and took up her Train, and after that he took up the Trains of two Ladies at once; who, as they wanted to go different Ways, pulled and could not think what was the Matter, and when they looked round and saw him, were frightened prodigiously, and called out for Help.

The whole Company soon gathered round laughing; and the Extravagants, who wanted to bring this foolish Fashion into the Country, felt the Ridicule, and walked off the Green. Well! 'tis amazing, says the Duchess, that young Women should think to make themselves amiable by drawing six Yards of silk in the Dirt after them. It is more amazing, answered the Duke, that Ladies should hope to get themselves good Husbands by Extravagance and Nastiness;[69] for what can be more filthy than drawing their Negligees thus in the Dirt? But the Lass, continued the Duke, who has so agreeably ridiculed this foolish Fashion, I must be better acquainted with; so pray let her drink a Dish of Tea with us at the Inn. A Card was immediately sent, and Madam was introduced to her Grace, where she behaved with so much Decorum, that the Company took her for a Person of Fortune; but when the Duchess had prevailed on her to throw off the Veil, who should she be but Mrs. *Dolly* the Dairy Maid, whom the young Marquis and Master *Smith* had engaged in this Scheme for the Benefit and Instruction of her Neighbours and fellow Servants; and had taught the Dog to support her Train. The Duchess laughed immoderately at the Conceit, and gave her a new Suit of Cloathes; and the Duke said, she was a notable Baggage, and ordered her five Guineas. It is impossible to say how much the young Marquis and Master *Smith* were caressed on this Occasion by the Duke, Duchess, and indeed the whole Company; nor did poor *Keeper* go without his Reward, *bow, wow, wow*, for he had a good Dinner ordered him, and was after that frequently suffered to come into the Parlour, till, in a Fit of Jealousy, he pulled little *Pompey* out of Lady's Lap, and attempted to take his Place.[70] However, he soon recovered of this Disgrace; for having been taught by the Servants to fetch and carry, and perceiving that the Duchess, when she went out, had dropped her Watch, he took it up and brought it to her; upon which she patted his Head, and took him again into Favour.

There's an honest Fellow for you!

After this, we were led to the Duke's House, where his Grace moralized on the Day's Diversion.

REFLECTION.

A Fair, says he, may be compared to a Journey through Life, where Mankind are always busy, but too frequently in Schemes that are idle and ridiculous. You now seem tired of the Fair; and are sensible, I hope, from the little Satisfaction these Baubles give you, that there is no real Pleasure, but in living a virtuous, peaceable and good Life.

Note, When *Keeper* had once learned his Business, he would be employed; so that when Ladies came to the Duke's dressed in the Modern Mode, the Dog always run to take up their Trains; upon which his Grace usually laughed, and said, his Dog was a great Enemy to Extravagance. We are told, that a noted Schemer took Advantage of his Circumstance, and bred a Number of Curs to support the Ladies Negligees at *Vauxhall* and *Ranelagh*,[71] which he let out at a Shilling a Week, and their Board, and made much Money by it. But why so hard upon the Ladies, you'll say! Are not the Men in their Dress as whimsical and ridiculous? Most undoubtedly. It is not many Years since, some of these Creatures put Wire or Iron Wigs upon leaden Heads, and had their borrowed Locks powdered with Blue, instead of White, which Fashion would certainly have prevailed, if Mrs. *Midnight*, at the little Theatre in the *Haymarket*, had not dressed her Raggamuffins in blue Perriwigs.[72]

✶　✶　✶

APPENDIX

Containing an Account of what was done on the other Side of the Fair.

WHILE we were thus entertained with *Tommy Trip*, *Dolly*, and the Dog *Keeper*, a Gentleman on the other Side of the Fair had his Pocket picked of his Watch, Pocket Book, and a large Sum of Money. – How absurd and foolish it is for People to carry any Thing which is valuable into a Mob or a Fair with them? Those who are going where there is a Crowd, should always leave their Pocket-Books, Watches, and whatever is of great Value, at Home, and take with them no more Money than what they really want.

An odd Way of hiding Money

Several Persons were taken up on Suspicion of picking the Gentleman's Pocket, and among the rest a poor Solider that came to beat up for Volunteers;[73] who told the Mayor that he was innocent, and that he had not had a Farthing of Money in his Pockets for many Years. Upon this he was searched and several Pieces of Silver being found upon him, the Mayor was about to commit him; but another Soldier stept up, and said that Money was his. Yours, answered the Mayor, how came your Money in this Man's pocket? Why, I will tell your Worship, said the Soldier, this Man here, who is my Comrade, loves strong Beer so well, and Money

so little, that his Pay is always spent before he gets it; and I can safely say, that he has not seen Six-pence of his own these seventeen Years; which has been greatly to my Disadvantage; for as we were Chums, and lay in the same Room, and Sometimes in the same Bed together, the Money I put into my Pocket the over Night was generally gone in the Morning, and I was left pennyless and in want; to prevent which, I have for some Time past slipt my Money privately into his Pocket, where it has lain very securely and not been touched; for tho' he has often searched my Pockets for Money, I knew he would never think of looking in his own. – The Mayor laughed at the Conceit, and the Man was discharged, but was directed to behave himself better for the future, and to keep his fingers out of his Friend's Pocket.

The Benefit of learning to Read well.

While they were searching after the Gentleman's Watch and Pocket-Book, for which a great Reward was offered, Miss *Sullen* and Miss *Meanwell* happened to go through the Fair; and the first, who was an obstinate ill temper'd Girl, and never would learn her Book, picked up a Piece of Paper printed on a Copper Plate,[74] which she looked at, and then threw it in the Dirt, saying, it was only a Bit of an old Almanack:[75] for she was so great a Dunce that she could not read it. This did not satisfy Miss

Meanwell, who was a sensible and good-natured, as the other was cross and ignorant. She took the Paper out of the Dirt, and on reading it, found it was a Bank Note of twenty Pounds; upon which she sent to the Bell-man (See here he is)

to cry it, that the right owner might have it again, which you know was very honest; and hearing that it had been taken out of the Gentleman's Pocket Book, who was not at the Mayor's, and had got his Book again, she carried it to him; and told him the Manner in which she got it; and that she had sent the Bell-man to cry it. The Gentleman was so pleased with her prudent Behaviour, and in particular with her Honesty, that he gave her the Note for a Fairing.[76] Only think of that, twenty Pounds for a Fairing! You see,

Honesty is the best Policy, as my Copy-book says. Had she concealed this Note, and not generously brought it to the right Owner, and told the Truth, it would have been taken from her in a disgraceful Manner, and she would not have had it for a Fairing. Twenty Pounds! Only think how many pretty Things a young Lady may buy with *Twenty Pounds*. She wished for a little Horse to carry her Home; but the Mayor would not let her lay out her Money in that Manner, and the Gentleman told her, as she was so good, and so honest, and learned her Book so well, she should go Home in his Coach.

Miss *Sullen*, now put in for her Share, and said indeed she would have half; for she found the Note first. Aye, said the Mayor, and was such a Dunce you could not read it, but threw it down in the Dirt again. No, no, if such a great Girl as you, who have been so long at School, can't read, you don't deserve Fairings, or any Thing else. So pretty Miss *Meanwell* had the Whole, and the Coach, to carry her Home into the Bargain; and having bought a Parcel of little Books for her Brothers and Sisters, she galloped away with the good News to her Father and Mother; who we may suppose, kissed her a thousand Times.

To a Good GIRL

So, pretty Miss *Prudence*, you're come to the Fair;
And a very good Girl they tell me you are.
Here, take this fine Orange, this Watch, and this Knot;[77]
You're welcome, my Dear, to all we have got;
For a Girl that's so good, and so pretty as you,
May have what she pleases – Your Servant, Miss *Prue*.

To a Naughty GIRL

SO, pert Mistress *Prate-apace*, how came you here?
There's nobody wants to see you at the Fair.
Not an Orange, an Apple, a Cake, or a Nut,
Will any one give to so saucy a Slut.
For such naughty Girls we here have not Room,
You're proud and ill-natur'd – Go Hussey, go home.

To a Good BOY

THERE was a good Boy who went to the Fair,
And the People rejoic'd because he came there.
They all gave him Fairings, because he was good,
And they let him have all the fine Things that he wou'd.
He went to the Puppet-show, then to the Play:
Make Room for the very good Boy there. – Huzza.

To a Naughty BOY

THERE was a bad Boy who rode to the Fair,
And all the Folks hiss'd because he came there.
They sent home his Horse
Because he was cross.
Not a Thing could he get of all he did lack,
And they laid his own Whip upon his own Back.
Go home, Sirrah.

The END.

BOOKS for the Instruction and Amusement of Children. Printed for T. CARNAN, and F. NEWBERY, Junior, at Number 65, in *St. Paul's Church-Yard*, London.

THE Renowned History of Little Goody TWO-SHOES, afterwards called Mrs. MARGERY TWO-SHOES; with the Means by which she acquired her Learning and Wisdom, and in Consequence thereof, her Estate. Price *Six Pence* bound, and adorned with Cuts.

The INFANT TUTOR: Or, An easy Spelling Book for little Masters and Misses; made pleasing with a Variety of Stories and Fables, and embellished with Cuts. Price *Six Pence* bound.

BE MERRY and WISE: Or, The *Cream* of the *Jests* and *Marrow* of *Maxims*, for the Conduct of Life; published for the Use of all little good Boys and Girls, by *T. Trapwit*, Esq. Adorned with Cuts. Price *Six Pence* bound. – *Would you be agreeable in Company, and useful to Society, carry some merry Jests in your Mind, and honest Maxims in your Heart.* GROTIUS.

FABLES in VERSE, for the Improvement of the Young and the Old. By *Abraham Æsop*, Esq. To which are added, FABLES in *Verse* and *Prose*, with the Conversation of Birds and Beasts, at their several Meetings, Routs and Assemblies. By *Woglog* the Great Giant. Illustrated with a Variety of curious Cuts, and an Account of the Lives of the Authors. Price 6d. bound.

The HOLY BIBLE abridged: Or, The History of the Old and New Testament, illustrated with Notes, and adorned with Cuts, for the Use of Children. Price *Six Pence* bound. – *Suffer little Children to come unto me, and forbid them not.* – St. Luke.

A New History of ENGLAND, from the Invasion of *Julius Cæsar* to the Reign of King George II. Adored with Cuts of all the Kings and Queens who have reigned since the *Norman* Conquest. Price 6d. bound. – *The Memory of Things past ought not to be extinguished by Length of Time, nor great and admirable Actions remain destitute of Glory.* – HERODOTUS.

The VALENTINE'S GIFT: Or, the whole History of *Valentine's Day*: Containing the Way to preserve *Truth*, *Honour* and *Integrity* unshaken. – *Very necessary in a trading Nation.* Price Six Pence bound.

The Little FEMALE ORATORS: Or, Nine Evenings Entertainment; with Observations. Embellished with Cuts. Price Six Pence.

HYMNS for the AMUSEMENT of CHILDREN. Embellished with Cuts, Inscribed to Prince FREDERICK, Bishop of OSNABRUG. Price 6d bound.

Notes

The Lilliputian Magazine

1. Thomas Carnan (1737–88) was the second son of William Carnan, a Reading printer. When William Carnan died shortly after Thomas' birth, the printing business passed to John Newbery, William's journeyman, who in 1739 married William's widow, Mary Carnan, becoming Thomas' step-father. Although Thomas would eventually inherit part of Newbery's business, when *The Lilliputian Magazine* was first published in 1751, Thomas would have been only 14 years old. Newbery appears to have been using his name as a means of disguising his own involvement; it was a tactic he had already used with several other titles, including the periodical *The Midwife; or Old Woman's Magazine* (1750–3) edited by Christopher Smart.

2. Jill E. Grey speculates that this dialogue, along with the fable and the lines from Alexander Pope that follow, might have formed the substance of the 'Proposal' for the *Lilliputian* that William Strachan printed for John Newbery in January 1751. Strachan's ledgers record that he printed 8000 copies; they were presumably distributed in order to attract subscribers. Grey, 'The Lilliputian Magazine – A Pioneering Periodical?', *Journal of Librarianship*, 2 (1970), 107–15 (pp.110–11).

3. *Emblem*: a picture or short fable expressing a moral or religious allegory, such as John Bunyan's *Book for Girls and Boys* (1686), republished as *Divine Emblems* (1724). Emblem-books were a common form of seventeenth- and early eighteenth-century children's literature

4. Alexander Pope, *An epistle to the Right Honourable Richard Lord Viscount Cobham* (1734). The original reads ''Tis Education forms the vulgar mind'.

5. *Stays*: a laced underbodice, stiffened with strips of whale-bone or other material, worn to give shape to the figure.

6. *Bob*: 'An ornamental pendant; an ear-drop' (*OED*): an earring.

7. Probably the church of St. George the Martyr on Borough High Street at the junction with Long Lane and Marshalsea Road, about 700 meters from the south end of London Bridge. The church had been rebuilt in 1734–6.

8. *Norwood*: Today a suburb, about five miles south of central London. In the mid-eighteenth century, the area was still largely covered by the sparsely populated Great North Wood.

9. The 'History of Florella' bears a number of similarities to Samuel Richardson's novel *Pamela; or, Virtue Rewarded* (1740–1). See 'Introduction'.

10. *Execution*: 'The enforcement by the sheriff, or other officer, of the judgment of a court...chiefly, the seizure of the goods or person of a debtor in default of payment' (*OED*).

11. Lilliput is the fictional island empire described in the first part of Jonathan Swift's *Travels into Several Remote Nations of the World*, better known as *Gulliver's Travels* (1726). From very shortly after its first publication, other authors began to adopt the name for a variety of purposes.

12. It was proverbial that Alexander the Great 'when he had conquer'd the World, wept that there were no more Worlds to conquer' (*Æsop's fables. With instructive morals and reflections, abstracted from all party considerations, adapted to all capacities* (London: J. Osborn Jnr., 1740), p. 5).

13. No further parts were actually published.

14. *Barnet*: A Hertfordshire town, ten miles north of central London.

15. *To a tittle*: 'with minute exactness, to the smallest particular' (*OED*).

16. *Cock throwing*: a blood sport widely practiced in eighteenth-century Britain in which people took turns to throw sticks at a cockerel tied to a stake, often betting on when the cock would die. William Hogarth depicts boys engaged in cock throwing in the first print in his *Four Stages of Cruelty* (1751).

17. Cock throwing was a traditional activity for Shrove Tuesday when 'fritters' (now more commonly called 'pancakes') were eaten. Samuel Pepys mentions both of these activities in his diary for 26 February 1660–1.

18. Jonah, 4: 11.

19. Deuteronomy, 22: 6–7.

20. According to legend, cock throwing commemorated the occasion when 'the Crowing of a Cock prevented our *Saxon* Ancestors from massacring their Conquerors...the *Danes*, on the Morning of a *Shrove-Tuesday*, whilst asleep in their Beds.' *Clemency to brutes; the substance of two sermons preached on a Shrove-Sunday, with a particular view to dissuade from that species of cruelty annually practised in England, the throwing at cocks* (London: R. and J. Dodsley, 1761), p.26.

21. On 4 February 1752, 'A precept was issu'd by the lord mayor to all constables and other officers within London and its liberties, to apprehend all idle and disorderly persons...who shall be found on *shrove* Tuesday or any other day throwing at cocks, &c.' *The Gentleman's Magazine*, 22 (1752), p.89.

22. *Open his pipes and maunder*: vocally complaining.

23. This dance was, for some reason, omitted from later editions of the *Lilliputian Magazine*. The notated music reproduced here has (like the accompanying text) been taken from the 1752 edition (see 'Note on the Texts'). Christopher Smart co-edited and contributed to *The Student, or, The Oxford and Cambridge Monthly Miscellany*, running from 1750–1 and published by John Newbery.

24. *Polly Newbery*: probably John Newbery's daughter Mary (Polly), who was born in 1740.

25. *Pippins*: apples, often of a variety used for cooking.
26. *Sack*: an archaic name for Spanish wine.
27. Answers appear on p.67.
28. Christopher Hunter (born 1748) was Smart's nephew, and later the author of a 'Life of Christopher Smart' that prefaced the first volume of *The poems of the late Christopher Smart* (1791).
29. Probably Margaret 'Peg' Wolfington (1720?–60), one of the most celebrated actresses of the 1740s and 1750s in London and Dublin. She was acclaimed for 'breeches roles', for which she dressed in male clothes, and was notorious for her relationships with a number of lovers, including David Garrick, and for feuds with other actresses.
30. Margaret (Peggy) Smart was Christopher's older sister, around 30 years old at the time of the publication of *The Lilliputian Magazine*.
31. This is the earliest known publication of verses that would become a staple of later eighteenth- and nineteenth-century poetry anthologies, songbooks and hymnals. In these republications it was frequently titled 'The Hymn of Eve'. It probably formed part of Thomas Arne's oratorio *The Death of Abel*, first performed in 1744 but was apparently expanded to include this extra material for performances in 1755. See Betty Rizzo and Robert Mahoney, *Christopher Smart: An Annotated Bibliography 1743–1983* (New York: Garland, 1984), no.525, where Smart's authorship of the piece is asserted. Smart certainly wrote songs for performance and knew many musicians, including Charles Burney, Arne's apprentice.
32. *Tantwivy*: more usually 'tantivy', meaning at full gallop.
33. Woglog the Great Giant would appear in several subsequent children's books published by John Newbery and others but this was apparently his first appearance, he being 'introduced to amuse and to terrify, by turns, the young students' according to James Pettit Andrews, *Addenda to Anecdotes, &c. Antient and Modern. With Observations* (London : printed for John Stockdale, 1790), p.18.
34. *Town-bull*: 'a bull formerly kept in turn by the cow-keepers of a village' (*OED*).
35. This 'Scripture History' is paraphrased from *Genesis*, 37–45.
36. *Messes*: portions of food.
37. Strange animals and fish were commonly exhibited as curiosities in eighteenth-century England. Indian princes were a rarer sight, but on several occasions, delegations of native American dignitaries visited England and attracted widespread attention. A delegation of Cherokee 'kings' and 'princes' visiting in 1730, for example, were granted audiences with the King and were followed around London by large crowds.
38. In 1752, England adopted the Gregorian calendar already in use in most of Europe, in place of the Julian Calendar. This necessitated certain calendric adjustments, including a new start date for each year (1 January rather than 25 March). To avoid confusion, from 1752 dates could be qualified with 'New Style' (or N.S.) or 'Old Style'

(O.S.) to designate whether they accorded to the Julian or Gregorian calendars.

39. One of the most enduringly popular of the plays produced by David Garrick (1717–79), actor and theatre manager at the Theatre Royal, Drury Lane, London, was the pantomime *Queen Mab*, first presented at Christmas 1750. Its music was written by Christopher Smart's friend Charles Burney, and Smart wrote a flattering summary of the pantomime in his periodical *The Midwife, or Old Woman's Magazine* (1 (1750), 145–51). Queen Mab, according to Mercutio in William Shakespeare's *Romeo and Juliet*, is 'no bigger than an agate-stone | On the fore-finger of an alderman' (I.iv.56–7). Smart described the 'Fairy Dance' that closed Garrick's *Queen Mab* as being 'perform'd by several little Boys and Girls'.

40. *Bason...key*: variant spellings of 'basin' (a dock in which the water is kept at a constant level) and quay.

41. A 'jack' could refer to any of many machines consisting solely or essentially of a roller or winch, such as a lifting jack, or a 'smoke-jack', 'a machine for turning the spit in roasting meat; either wound up like a clock or actuated by the draught of heated air up the chimney' (*OED*).

42. Matthew, 22: 37–9; Mark, 12: 29–31; and Luke, 10: 27.

43. *Seals*: usually pieces of wax on which designs have been impressed attached to a document, but figuratively 'a token or symbol of a covenant; something that authenticates or confirms' (*OED*).

44. The Court of Common Council, elected from the Freemen of the various London wards and presided over by the Lord Mayor, had by the eighteenth century become the effective governing body of the City of London.

45. *Cheapside*: A major street in the City of London running from the Bank of England to St. Paul's Cathedral, and in the eighteenth century still the main market and shopping street of London.

46. Each ward of the City of London elects a Freeman to be an alderman, sitting in the Court of Aldermen and carrying out various governmental, judicial and ceremonial roles.

47. To be 'out of his time' was to have completed his apprenticeship, usually set at seven years, and to have become a journeyman.

48. *Reins...neck*: once a horse has been trained it need no longer be under tight control but can be directed by reins laying lightly on its neck.

49. Two sheriffs are elected annually by the liverymen of the guilds of the City of London. Being 'called to the chair' (more usually 'passed the chair') means that Tommy Thoroughgood has become Lord Mayor of London, an office to which a senior alderman who has already served as Sheriff is elected for the term of a year.

50. *Betook himself to the highway*: became a highway robber.

51. Probably Enfield, a town 15 miles north of London on Ermine Street, one of the main roads to the north and well-known as a haunt for highwaymen.

52. The Old Bailey Sessions House was the court exercising criminal jurisdiction over the whole of London and the surrounding area.

53. *Cast for his life*: condemned to death.

54. *100l*: £100 in pre-decimal British currency which was divided into *librae*, *solidi* and *denarii* (pounds, shillings and pence).

55. *Sugar-work*: a sugar factory.

56. *Amain*: 'Exceedingly, greatly' (OED).

57. *Hogshead*: a large cask with a set capacity, dependent on what commodity it held.

58. *Imprimis*: 'In the first place; first. Originally used to introduce the first of a number of items, as in an inventory or will' (*OED*).

59. *Indent themselves ... ill- treated*: in seventeenth- and eighteenth-century Britain many young people contracted themselves, or were contracted by others, to work for a fixed period (usually up to seven years) in exchange for food, lodging, clothing and transportation to the place of indenture, which was most often the American colonies.

60. Smart's authorship of this poem is confirmed by an advertisement for *The Lilliputian Magazine* in the *Daily Advertiser*, 102 (29 June 1751) which lists, as appearing in the *Magazine*, 'A Morning Hymn for all little, good Boys and Girls, which is also proper for People of riper Years, by Mr. Kitty Smart' (p.2).

61. 'The Peacock' has been attributed to Christopher Smart: see Moira Dearnley, *The Poetry of Christopher Smart* (London: Routledge and Kegan Paul, 1968), p. 299).

62. Drones are male honey bees, and do not gather pollen or nectar or help to build the hive and cannot sting. At the onset of colder weather they are often expelled from the hive by female bees.

63. In Roman mythology, Venus was goddess of love and beauty, and Mars the god of war. Cupid was their child. Jove, or Jupiter, was the king of the gods. Semele is a figure from Greek mythology. Dionysus, the god of wine, was the son of Semele and Zeus, the Greek equivalent of Jupiter.

64. *The Midwife; or, The Old Woman's Magazine*, a periodical edited by Christopher Smart under the name 'Mary Midnight', was issued in monthly parts, at 3d. each, from October 1750 to June 1753 and later published in three volumes. The title-page claimed that *The Midwife* was 'Printed for Mary Midnight and sold by T. Carnan', but since Carnan, John Newbery's step-son, was only fourteen in 1751, it is probable that his name was being used as a front by Newbery. Indeed, the second and third volumes were 'Printed for Thomas Carnan, at J. Newbery's'.

65. Answers on page 76.

66. *Musæum* at *Oxon*: the Ashmolean Museum in Oxford, opened in 1683.

67. In the Old Testament account, an angel presents itself before the ass that Balaam is riding causing it to stop: 'And Balaam said unto the ass, Because thou hast mocked me: I would there were a sword in mine hand, for now would I kill thee.' Numbers, 22: 29.

68. Sydrophel is a charlatan astronomer in Samuel Butler's mock-romance, *Hudibras* (1662–80).
69. Psalm 137 ('By the rivers of Babylon...') expresses the desire to return home of Jews in exile following the Babylonian conquest of Jerusalem in the sixth century BCE.
70. *Courtesy*: now more usually 'curtsy'.
71. Kanhoji Angria (or Angre) (1669–1729), was admiral of the Maratha navy, though regarded in Britain as a pirate. He successfully attacked European shipping from the 1690s until his death, operating off the coast of India, south of Mumbai.
72. The 'catechism' (a question-and-answer statement of Christian belief), the Book of Common Prayer and the New Testament were three of the basic stages of what John Locke, in *Some Thoughts Concerning Education* (1693), had called the 'ordinary Road' of education. By the mid-eighteenth century, publishers were producing books specifically for children to replace or supplement this basic curriculum, such as John Newbery's seven *Circle of the Sciences* books (1745–6), each of which taught a specific subject (grammar, arithmetic, rhetoric, etc.).
73. *Flocks*: 'A material consisting of the coarse tufts and refuse of wool or cotton, or of cloth torn to pieces by machinery' (*OED*).
74. English country dancing generally involved several couples dancing in a 'set'. New dances were often developed, usually employing new combinations of existing moves. Here the 'hay' (more usually 'hey') is a move in which one or more dancers weaves between the other dancers, and a 'cast off' is to turn outward and move along the outside of the set.
75. *Groat*: a coin of low value, worth four English pence.
76. Aretæus and Philoxenus are the names of two ancient world physicians.
77. Ecclesiasticus (also known as 'The Wisdom of Jesus the Son of Sirach'), 6: 16.

The History of Little Goody Two-Shoes

1. *Meanwell*: Many fictional characters had been called by this name before *Goody Two-Shoes*, such as 'Mary Meanwell', a correspondent to Richard Steele and Joseph Addison's *Spectator* (29 October 1711) who wrote on the subject of visiting protocols.
2. In England and Wales, the 'Overseer of the poor' was 'a parish officer responsible for organizing relief and employment for the poor, and later for some further parish and municipal duties' (*OED*). Duties usually included assessing and collecting the 'Poor Rate' tax, drawing up voting and jury lists, and organising apprenticeships and work for paupers. In theory, the office was appointed annually.
3. *Church-warden*: person elected in each parish to look after the church and church-yard.

4. Road maintenance was the responsibility of each parish. Churchwardens appointed a local man to serve as Surveyor of the Highways, usually for a year, whose job it was to ensure that parishioners worked on, or paid for, the upkeep of the roads.

5. *Justice of Peace*: magistrate appointed to preserve the peace and fulfil basic judicial functions in a particular district. More usually 'Justice of the Peace'.

6. *Throw up*: relinquish; that is to say that Sir Timothy was attempting to force Mr Meanwell to give up his lease on the farm so that it would return to its owner, Sir Timothy.

7. English Law is based on past decisions and, even in the mid-eighteenth century, the sum of these precedents, called 'common law', was extremely voluminous. In 1765, the probable year of *Goody Two-Shoes'* publication, Sir William Blackstone published the first volume of his *Commentaries on the Laws of England* (1765–69), the first successful treatise on common law suitable for non-lawyers.

8. *Seized for*: 'To take possession of (goods) in pursuance of a judicial order' (*OED*).

9. In 1746 Dr. James's Fever Powder was invented by the physician Robert James who appointed John Newbery as the exclusive sales agent. Although expensive at 2s. 6d. for a pair of doses, the Powder was extremely successful, being used, and often enthused about, by the aristocracy, monarchy and literati. Containing antimony and calcium phosphate as sweating agents, the powder was chiefly designed for use against fevers but it was advertised, and taken, as a defence against almost all disorders and even as a general pick-me-up. James and Newbery both made large sums through the sale of the powder, and its popularity continued into the nineteenth century. See 'Introduction' for more on Newbery's commercial activities.

10. Under the Poor Relief Act of 1662 the poor were allowed support (food, clothing, lodging) only if they were established residents of a particular parish. Those who could not prove residency were liable to be removed to their place of 'settlement', usually where they had been born.

11. *Curl-pated*: curly-haired.

12. Traditionally a tenth part of the annual agricultural production of a parish, tithes constituted the major part of most clergymen's income. By the mid-eighteenth century they were usually paid in cash rather than in kind. The 'small tithe' went directly to the clergyman but the larger 'great tithe' was often paid to a lay 'impropriator', usually a landowner whose estate was derived from one of the monasteries dissolved at the Reformation.

13. If Margery could show forty days of undisturbed residency in the parish she could acquire 'settlement rights' and her upkeep would become the responsibility of the parish.

14. *Sequel*: not necessarily a separate, subsequent text, but more generally anything that follows as the consequence of an event or course of action.

15. As well as the now more familiar 'short s', Margery's lower-case alphabet includes a 'long s' (ʃ), a standard feature of written and printed English until around 1800. It was used when the 's' came at the beginning or middle of a word. The letter 'J' was not universally considered as a separate letter in the eighteenth century, accounting for its omission from Margery's upper-case alphabet, although compare pp.102 and 120.

16. *Bodkin*: A small pointed instrument used to fasten up hair, pierce holes in cloth, draw cord through fabric, etc.

17. 'The Cuz's Chorus set to Music' and 'Some Account of the Society of Cuzes', along with a portrait of 'a good fat Cuz arrayed in the Robes of his Order', are to be found, tipped in rather incongruously, in *A Pretty Play-Thing for Children*, published by John Newbery in 1759 or 1760. Printers playfully referred to themselves 'Cuzes' in a beer-fuelled ceremony initiating their apprentices into the trade. The 'chorus' was an arrangement of letters and the syllables they formed set to a tune ('BA-ba, BE-be, BI-bi-bi-bi; | B o bo; Ba-be-bi-bo; B u bu; Ba-be-bi-bo-bu- | and so through the rest of the Consonants'). A musical score was printed in *A Pretty Play-Thing for Children* but, according to David Hounslow, it cannot easily be made to fit the lyric. Hounslow also convincingly argues that this section of *A Pretty Play-Thing for Children* was written by Christopher Smart: see his 'The Cuz's Chorus: Or, a Little Piece of Book-Trade Nonsense', *Quadrat*, 12 (2001), 3–7. The 'Cuzz's Chorus' was cut from many editions of *Goody Two-Shoes* published after c.1790.

18. These four prayers are adapted from text found in most eighteenth-century catechisms, which were themselves derived from scripture, here, 1 Peter, 2: 1, Matthew, 22: 37–9 (also Mark, 12: 30; and Luke, 10: 27), Exodus, 20: 12 (also Deuteronomy, 5: 16) and Matthew, 5: 44.

19. The English proverbs set out here, one running into another, had been in circulation for many years. 'He that will thrive must rise at five', for instance, appears in John Clarke's 1639 *Paroemiologia Anglo-Latina in usum scholarum concinnata. Or proverbs English, and Latine* (London: Robert Mylbourne), and had been included in a similar list of proverbs contained in *The Child's New Play-Thing*, published by Newbery's forerunner Mary Cooper in 1743.

20. *Plaister*: 'a solid medicinal or emollient substance spread on a bandage or dressing and applied to the skin' (*OED*).

21. *Groat*: a coin of low value, worth four English pence.

22. Many of these religious adages were commonplaces of eighteenth-century didactic literature, although they do not appear to have been previously printed in exactly this form. The first three lines, for instance, feature in *The Child's New Play-Thing* (London: M. Cooper, 1743), p.12, while lines 1 and 3 are written out on one of the home-made alphabet cards produced by Jane Johnson for her children in the late 1730s and 1740s (Johnson, J. mss., Lilly Library, Indiana University, Bloomington, Indiana, Set 1, no.48).

23. *Cunning little Baggage*: 'Baggage' was a name applied familiarly or play-fully to young women, 'especially in collocation with *artful, cunning, sly, pert, saucy, silly*, etc.' (*OED*); in the eighteenth century, 'cunning' usually meant 'clever' or 'skilful' rather than 'crafty'.
24. *Hussey*: 'The mistress of a household; a thrifty woman' (*OED*).
25. *Clerk*: the parish clerk was an officer of a church, in charge of the run-ning of the church and tasked with assisting the clergyman.
26. *Pet*: 'a fit of peevishness' (*OED*).
27. The existence or otherwise of ghosts had become a matter of substan-tial debate in the years immediately prior to the publication of *Goody Two-Shoes*. Much of the debate had focussed on the 'Cock Lane Ghost', whose scratching and knocking had drawn large crowds to the sup-posedly haunted house (located only a few hundred yards north of Newbery's shop) and been avidly discussed in the newspapers and other publications in early 1762. The fraud was eventually exposed in the summer. Oliver Goldsmith (who may have written all or part of *Goody*) had contributed to the debate, mocking Londoners' gullibility, with the pamphlet *The mystery revealed; containing a series of transactions and authentic testimonials, respecting the supposed Cock-Lane ghost* (1762).
28. *Isle*: aisle.
29. *creep-mouse Girl*: one 'that creeps like a mouse so as to escape notice; furtive, timid, shy' (*OED*).
30. *break ... Jewels*: in legal terms, to 'break' a house was to enter it, usually with force, by breaching part of its perimeter circuit.
31. William Shakespeare, *Richard III*, I.iii.333, derived from 1 Peter, 3: 9.
32. *turned Evidence*: 'said of an accomplice or sharer in a crime: to offer himself as a witness for the prosecution against the other persons implicated' (*OED*).
33. *Nurse Truelove's New-Year's-Gift: or, The Book of Books for Children* was one of John Newbery's first publications for children. It was printed in or before 1750, though apparently not advertised until 1753 (see Roscoe, *John Newbery and his Successors*, pp.204–5). One of its con-stituent stories was 'The history of Mrs. Williams and her plumb cake'.
34. A daily periodical conducted by Richard Steele and Joseph Addison, and largely written by them, in 1711–12 and 1714. This adaptation of Psalm 23 ('The Lord is my shepherd'), by Addison, appeared in his essay on trust in God in *Spectator* no. 441 (26 July 1712).
35. *Landskip*: landscape.
36. *throwing at Cocks*: see note 16 on p.224.
37. Proverbs, 30: 17.
38. On 16 June 1761 the *Public Advertiser* carried an article to advertise 'the last Week of exhibiting the learned Canary Bird in the Haymarket, St. James's' (p.3). As an unlicensed theatre, the Haymarket had previ-ously been the venue for other animal acts (see note 36 on p.237).
39. *Sleep ... Kind of Death*: the original source of these lines (if any) is untraced. Christopher Smart would later write about 'cordial sleep,

to death akin' in Hymn XXXVI: 'At Undressing in the Evening' in *Hymns for the Amusement of Children* (1771).

40. *Dam*: mother.

41. From a proverb in print as early as the seventeenth century, although its appearance here is cited by Peter and Iona Opie as its earliest use in this standard form in juvenile literature (*The Oxford Dictionary of Nursery Rhymes* (Oxford: Oxford University Press, 1997), p.147)

42. *Routs and Rackets*: respectively, 'a fashionable gathering; a large evening party or soirée of a type fashionable in the 18th and early 19th centuries' and 'a large, noisy, or exuberant social gathering or event; a party' (*OED*).

43. Adapted from Psalms, 68: 5.

44. *Accompts*: business accountancy.

45. Britain and France were in conflict for much of the eighteenth century, including during the War of the Spanish Succession (1702–13), the War of the Austrian Succession (1744–8) and the Seven Years' War (1756–63) which had ended shortly before the first publication of *Goody*.

46. Job, 1: 21.

47. *Seat*: the country-house residence of a gentleman or noble family.

48. Presumably what is now the Philippines, in the eighteenth century a Spanish colony. The capital was Manila, on Luzon Island.

49. See Introduction, p.xviii.

50. The Longitude Act of 1714 offered a reward of £20,000 to anyone who could invent a reliable means of determining longitude at sea to to within 30 miles. John Harrison was able to achieve this with an unprecedentedly accurate marine timekeeper, finished in 1760 and tested in 1761 and 1764.

51. 1 Kings, 17: 2–6.

52. Genesis, 8: 8 and 11.

53. *drop-stile*: a form of gate; but this is probably a printer's mistake for 'drop still', which later editions prefer.

54. Benjamin Cooke, organist and master of choristers at Westminster, Abbey set this poem to music: see *A Collection of Glees, Catches and Canons for Three, Four, Five and Six Voices* (London: for the author, c.1775), where it is 'said to be written by a little Boy from Newberrys [*sic*] Books'.

55. Until the adoption of the bearskin hat after the Battle of Waterloo, British grenadiers wore a tall cap much like a bishop's mitre.

56. Roger Bacon (c.1214–92?), Franciscan friar, scientist and philosopher. After his death, Bacon acquired almost legendary status as a magician. He was credited with manufacturing a brass head and enlisting the help of the Devil to make it speak. According to most versions of the legend, its only words were 'Time is – Time was – Time is past', but Bacon was asleep when these were spoken and the head disintegrated.

57. In the medieval romance of Fortunatus, often republished in cheap formats in eighteenth-century Britain, the hero acquires a magical

hat which can transport him instantly to anywhere in the world, as well as a magically replenishing purse from which he could draw daily supplies of gold.

58. The Philosopher's Stone is the legendary alchemical substance used to turn base metals into gold.

59. *Wiseacre*: a foolish person who thinks themselves wise.

60. Prosecutions for witchcraft continued into the eighteenth century, such as that of Jane Wenham, said to be the last person convicted of witchcraft in Britain, who was sentenced to death (but pardoned) in 1712. With growing scepticism about the veracity of witchcraft, the 1736 Witchcraft Act repealed previous legislation against such practices, making it instead an offence to pretend to have supernatural powers.

61. Margery has been brought before Justices of the Peace who collectively sit on the 'Bench'.

62. *Murrain*: cattle disease.

63. *Bedizened*: dressed up in finery, ornamented.

64. Westminster-hall is located in London, next to the Houses of Parliament, and was in the eighteenth century the seat of the highest courts in the country: Common Pleas, King's Bench, and Chancery.

65. Ezekiel, 18: 20.

66. *Commode*: 'A tall head-dress fashionable with women in the last third of the 17th and first third of the 18th centuries, consisting of a wire frame-work variously covered with silk or lace; sometimes with streaming lappets which hung over the shoulders' (*OED*).

67. Psalms, 139: 2–4 as quoted in Addison's essay no. 213, in *The Spectator* for 3 November 1711.

68. *Hottentots*: used from the seventeenth century to refer to Khoikhoi peoples of what are now South Africa and Namibia.

69. According to legend, Prester John ruled an undiscovered Christian kingdom in either Asia or Africa.

70. By the eighteenth century, 'Utopia' was a generic name for an ideal or imaginary community, derived from Thomas More's 1516 book of that name.

71. The parable of the talents: Luke, 19: 12–20.

72. The parable of the prodigal son: Luke, 15: 11–16.

73. The middle course between two extremes; moderation.

74. Alexander Pope, *An Essay on Man* (1733–4), iv, 182–3.

75. Charles Welsh speculates that 'W.B.' might be W. Bristow, Newbery's neighbour and publisher of several titles in which Newbery had an interest, including the *Public Ledger* (*A Bookseller of the Last Century* (London: Griffith, Farran, Okeden and Welsh, 1885), p.43).

The Fairing: Or, A Golden Toy for Children

1. In 1767, on the death of John Newbery, his son Francis (1743–1818) took over the flourishing publishing and patent medicine business.

Operating at 65, St. Paul's Church-Yard, he worked (until 1779) in a partnership with Thomas Carnan (1737–88), his half-brother and John Newbery's stepson. However, John Newbery had earlier set up his nephew, also called Francis Newbery (d. 1780), as a publisher. His shop was nearby, at 20 Ludgate Street, also sometimes called 20 St. Paul's Church-Yard or 'The Corner of St. Paul's Church-Yard'. A rivalry developed between these two businesses, each using their publications to disparage the other.

2. *Currycomb*: toothed instrument used for loosening dirt or hair on horses and stimulating the skin to produce natural oils.

3. *Rioting*: 'Originally excessive revelry or merriment; dissoluteness; debauchery. Later in weakened use, often without negative connotation of excess: revelry, lively festivities' (*OED*).

4. The 'round-about' and perhaps the 'rattle-trap' were fairground rides, although 'rattle-trap' could also mean either 'A small or worthless article; an appurtenance, a trapping; a knick-knack, curiosity, or trifle' or 'A talkative person, a chatterer' (*OED*).

5. In the third book of François Rabelais' *Gargantua and Pantagruel* (1532–64) as translated by Sir Thomas Urquhart in 1653, Bridlegoose is a judge who determines innocence and guilt by rolling dice. A 'Mr. Bridle-Goose, Master of the Menagerie' later appeared in an often-reprinted article in Christopher Smart's *The Midwife; or Old Woman's Magazine*, 1 (1750), 197 (see note 64, p.227) as one party in a learned dispute about which card game Alexander the Great played with the Queen of the Amazons. An alderman was a freeman of a city, here probably the City of London, elected to carry out various governmental, judicial and ceremonial roles.

6. *Jack Pudding...Gridiron*: Jack Pudding was a standard buffoon character appearing in street theatre, usually carrying a broom and a gridiron (a cooking utensil formed of parallel metal bars). Tobias Smollett describes a Jack Pudding (or equally, a Merry Andrew) as a 'facetious droll, who accompanies your itinerant physicians...and on a wooden stage entertains the populace with a solo on the salt-box, or a sonnata [sic] on the tongs and gridiron.' *The Adventures of Sir Launcelot Greaves*, 2 vols. (London: J. Coote, 1762), vol.1, p.76.

7. *Chit*: 'A person considered as no better than a child' (*OED*).

8. *The Renowned History of Giles Gingerbread* was published by John Newbery, probably in late 1764 (it was advertised alongside *The Fairing* and *Goody Two-Shoes*). In the book, Giles is taught to read with the use of gingerbread letters baked by his father, Gaffer Gingerbread: Giles is allowed to eat those letters he has learned.

9. *Smithfield bargains*: 'a sharp or roguish bargain...a marriage of interest, in which money is the chief consideration' (*OED*).

10. William Shakespeare, *Henry VIII*, III.ii.352–66 and 456–8. During the reign of King Henry VIII, Thomas Wosley (c.1473–1530) steadily rose to be the most powerful man in England, becoming Lord Chancellor, Archbishop of Canterbury and a cardinal. His downfall, following his

failure to secure an annulment of the King's first marriage, was swift: he was stripped of his offices and property and died a year later.

11. *Battledores*: derived from the name for the racket used in playing with a shuttlecock, a 'battledore' came also to mean a small bat on which were fixed printed alphabets and other short texts designed to teach children to read. From the 1740s, John Newbery and his business associate Benjamin Collins began to manufacture another product also called a battledore. Printed on card or paper folded to make a booklet of two pages with an overlapping flap at the front, these could feature more sophisticated texts, and pictures, alongside the alphabets.

12. *out of their Time*: completed the period for which they had been bound apprentice.

13. *stummed Stuff*: wine that was partly fermented or unfermented, or which had been mixed with partly fermented or unfermented grape-juice ('stum') in an attempt to renew it.

14. *puff...Bush*: To 'puff' was to praise something extravagantly, to publicise and 'to make the subject of a laudatory advertisement, review, etc.'; a 'bush' was 'a branch or bunch of ivy (perhaps as the plant sacred to Bacchus) hung up as a vintner's sign; *hence*, the sign-board of a tavern'. The phrase 'good wine needs no bush', meaning that good wine would procure customers without the need of advertising, was proverbial by the seventeenth century. (*OED*.)

15. See note 41 on p.232.

16. *furbelowed*: Originally a 'furbelow' was 'a piece of stuff pleated and puckered on a gown or petticoat; a flounce', but the term was increasingly used more generally of ladies' dress as 'a contemptuous term for showy ornaments or trimming' (*OED*).

17. *Card-money*: money allowed to someone to enable him or her to play cards; here, understood to be an amount paid by a husband to his wife as stipulated in their marriage settlement.

18. *Machiavels*: a person who acts on the principles thought to have been advanced by Noccolò Machiavelli, chiefly in *The Prince* (1532), but more generally, a cunning or scheming politician, or a politician in general.

19. Although historical details are disputed, Lucius Quincius Cincinnatus, a Roman patrician of the fifth century BCE, was celebrated both by the Romans and subsequently as the ideal of the virtuous, dutiful and modest citizen of early Rome. Rome being under attack by the Aequi, or a coup having been attempted by Spurius Maelius (accounts vary), Cincinnatus was called from the plough, appointed dictator, assembled an army, triumphed in battle, and returned to his ploughing, all within fifteen days. The account set out here closely follows that given in John Lockman's highly successful *A new Roman history, by question and answer* (third edition, London: T. Astley, 1749), pp.53–4 (in later editions of which John Newbery had a share), itself apparently derived from Laurence Echard's *The Roman history from*

the building of the city to the perfect settlement of the empire by Augustus Caesar (London: M. Gillyflower *et al.*, 1695), pp.104–6.

20. Cincinnatus' son, Caeso Quinctius, was, like his father, an opponent of the Plebeians in ancient Rome. In 461 BCE, Caeso was sentenced to death for disrupting the Plebeians' activities, but absconded while on bail, escaping to the Eturians (*'Hetruria'*). His father was left to pay an immense fine, and it was this burden that forced him to gain a living by himself working his land.

21. *Merry Andrew*: 'A person who entertains people with antics and buffoonery; a clown; a mountebank's assistant.' (*OED*). See above, note 6, p.234.

22. 'The House that Jack Built' would become an extremely popular rhyme but its first known printing (doubtlessly being referred to here by Giles) was in John Newbery's *Nurse Truelove's New-Year's Gift*, probably published in 1750 or shortly afterwards. See Roscoe, *John Newbery and his Successors*, pp.204–5 and *The Oxford Dictionary of Nursery Rhymes* (Oxford: Oxford University Press, 1997), pp.269–73.

23. From Edward Young, *Love of Fame, the Universal Passion*. Satire I, first published in 1725 (ll.171–4).

24. *Sharpers*: cheats or swindlers

25. *Bedlam*: the Hospital of St. Mary of Bethlehem in London which, since 1377, had been an asylum for the accommodation and treatment of mentally ill patients.

26. *sent to the Parish*: forced to rely on Poor Relief provided by their parish.

27. *choused*: duped, swindled or defrauded.

28. *Jew's Harp*: 'A musical instrument of simple construction, consisting of an elastic steel tongue fixed at one end to a small lyre-shaped frame of brass or iron, and bent at the other end at right angles; it is played by holding the frame between the teeth and striking the free end of the metal tongue with the finger' (*OED*).

29. *justle*: to push against or collide with.

30. *Physic*: medicine.

31. Compare the description of the game of leap-frog in John Newbery's first children's book, *A Little Pretty Pocket-Book* (*c.*1744; rpt. London: J. Newbery, 1760): 'This stoops down his Head, | Whilst that springs up high; | But then you will find, | He'll stoop by and by. | Moral. | Just so 'tis at Court; | To-day you're in *Place*; | To morrow, perhaps, | You're quite in Disgrace.' In earlier editions these lines were followed by: 'He that has got a good Place, let him keep it – but I am afraid your Milkmaid will not keep her Place, if she loses her Fail of Milk, which she deserves to do by coming thro' the Fair.'

32. *Droll*: 'A comic or farcical composition or representation; a farce; an enacted piece of buffoonery; a puppet-show' (*OED*).

33. *Pattern*: a model from which a thing is to be made; perhaps in this case a stored outline of the horse's shoe.

34. *Chapman*: a merchant or trader.

35. This verse and the dialogue that precedes it appears to be derived from a traditional nursery rhyme, 'Will you lend me your mare to ride a mile? | No, she is lame leaping over a stile. | Alack! and I must go to the fair! | I'll give you good money for lending your mare. | – Oh, oh! say you so? | Money will make the mare to go.' (See *The Oxford Dictionary of Nursery Rhymes* (Oxford: Oxford University Press, 1997), pp.349–50.) The last line had become a common phrase by at least the late-seventeenth century when a broadside entitled *Money makes the Mare to go, or, An Excellent new Song of the suttle shirking Sharpers, Mountebanks, Juglers, Gamesters, and many others of the like faculty* (*c*.1680) was published.

36. From December 1752 to March 1753, the Haymarket Theatre, London (which, until 1767 lacked an official patent for producing legitimate theatre) was the venue for what advertisements called 'A Pantomime Entertainment by the Animal Comedians, Brought from Italy by one Signor Ballard'. This dogs and monkeys act formed part of a nightly entertainment created and largely performed by Christopher Smart entitled 'Mrs Midnight's Concert', 'The Old Woman's Oratory' and various other titles (*Public Advertiser*, 12 December 1752, p.2).

37. The antics described in this section of *The Fairing* (dogs dressed as two beaux at a meal; dogs and monkeys dancing minuets; a monkey riding a large dog; dogs dressed as soldiers, storming a castle) were all apparently features of the 'Pantomime Entertainment by the Animal Comedians' performed in 1752–3 at the Haymarket Theatre as part of Smart's 'Mrs Midnight's Concert'. A number of contemporary engravings titled 'Mrs Midnight's Animal Comedians' depict each of these scenes (one version exists in the Bodleian Library, Douce Prints 2.49, f.41; another is reprinted from the Harvard University Theatre Library in Philip H. Highfill, Kalman A. Burnim, Edward A. Langhans (eds), *A Biographical Dictionary of Actors, Actresses, Musicians, Dancers, Managers and Other Stage Personnel in London 1660–1800*, vol. 14 (Carbondale: Southern Illinois University Press, 1991), p.119.)

38. *Minuets*: a slow, graceful dance.

39. From the early eighteenth century the 'Harlequinade', featuring the comic Harlequin and other stock characters appropriated from the Italian *Commedia dell'Arte* tradition, became a standard part of the English pantomime. The harlequinade closed the pantomime, which itself generally formed the afterpiece to serious plays and operas. Although chiefly comic spectacles, the pantomimes were often topically satirical.

40. Dogs trained to answer questions (generally by attending to unobtrusive signs indicating which of the cards laid before them they should pick out) were exhibited throughout the eighteenth century. Christopher Smart wrote an article about one of the most celebrated – 'Le Chien Savant, or the matchless learned French Dog, which is now exhibited to the Inspection of the Curious, at Mr. *Hally's*, Watchmaker, *Charing-Cross*' – in his *The Midwife: or, the Old Woman's Magazine*, 1

(1750), 202: 'This entertaining and sagacious Animal...does, by ranging Typographical Cards (in the same Manner that a Printer composes) read, write and cast Accompts, and by the same Method answers many Questions out of *Ovid's Metamorphosis*, in Geography, the *Roman*, *French*, and *English* History; reckons the Number of Persons present, if not above thirty; composes any Surname or capital Name, which is not too difficult to spell; solves small Questions in the four Rules of Arithmetick; tells, by looking at any Watch in the Company, what Hour it is, in a Manner quite particular and agreeable; distinguishes all the different current *English* Coins, and shews the Colour of any Person's Cloaths, by bringing the very Colour that most nearly resembles them, with several other amusing and extraordinary Performances. – To be seen without Loss of Time, from Ten in the Morning till Seven in the Evening, by any Number of Persons, at 2s. 6d. each.'

41. *Groat*: a coin of low value, worth four English pence.
42. *Fortunatus's wishing Cap*: see note 57 on p.232.
43. *Punch*: the violent, bawdy and anarchic Mr. Punch was the chief character (along with his wife Judy) in a puppet show common in England from the seventeenth century.
44. Based on a real fifteenth-century London mayor, the story of Dick Whittington was circulating in dramatic and ballad form by 1605. By the eighteenth century it had become popular as a chapbook, with a more elaborate narrative given in prose.
45. *Bushel*: a measure of capacity used for corn and other foodstuffs, or, more loosely, a large quantity.
46. The Royal Exchange was opened in 1570 as a 'bourse' in which merchants could meet to transact business. It had to be rebuilt twice after fires, reopening in 1669 and 1844.
47. *indented Servant...bought*: see note 59 on p.227.
48. *Flock*: 'coarse tufts and refuse of wool or cotton...used for quilting garments, and stuffing beds', and by extension 'something valueless or contemptible' (*OED*).
49. *Freight nor Custom*: respectively 'hire of a vessel for the transport of goods' and a 'toll, impost, or duty, levied...in the name of the king or sovereign authority upon merchandise exported from or imported into his dominions' (*OED*).
50. Proverbs, 19: 17.
51. All Saints' Day, 1 November.
52. The Whittington Stone, perhaps the base of a ruined wayside cross, is located near the foot of Highgate Hill, about four miles north of the centre of London and on the edge of the area usually called Holloway. The stone marks the spot where, according to tradition, Richard Whittington heard the bells of St. Mary-le-Bow, which were rung every night, calling him to return to London.
53. A lavish new coach especially for the Lord Mayor of London had been constructed in 1757 and has been used by successive Lord Mayors ever since.

54. Deriving the idea from Aristotle's *Poetics*, most dramatic critics in the early modern period held that a play should revolve around one main action, and should follow the effects of this action across a single day and in a single place.

55. In classical mythology, and in particular in Virgil's *Æneid*, *Æneas* left the siege of Troy to voyage around the Mediterranean before eventually founding the settlement that would become Rome. En route *Æneas* is given hospitality by Queen Dido of Carthage, a city in the Bay of Tunis.

56. *Patterns*: a sample.

57. *Turbant*: turban.

58. Virgil, *Æneid*, translated by John Dryden (1697), bk. XII, ll. 172–3.

59. *Bill of Ladings*: 'an official detailed receipt given by the master of a merchant vessel to the person consigning the goods, by which he makes himself responsible for their safe delivery to the consignee' (*OED*).

60. *rubbed*: made clean by means of repeated dry scrubbing.

61. The historical Richard Whittington (*c*.1350–1423) gained his fortune as a London mercer and moneylender, rising to become Sheriff in 1393 and Lord Mayor in 1397, 1406 and 1419. On his death he arranged for his entire estate to go to charity, including the rebuilding of Newgate prison, part of St. Bartholomew's Hospital and the church, almshouses and college of priests of St. Michael Paternoster Royal.

62. Although there were several earlier versions, 'Puss in Boots' first made its appearance in English in a 1729 translation of 'Le Maistre Chat, ou le chat botté' from Charles Perrault's *Histoires ou contes du temps passé* (1697).

63. *Sow-thistles*: 'the species of *Sonchus*; ... common European weeds characterized by their sharply-toothed thistle-like leaves and milky juice' (*OED*).

64. The quotation was attributed to Diogenes of Sinope (c.400–325 BCE), founder of the Cynics.

65. *gent*: noble or having the qualities associated with high birth, and by extension, courteous.

66. The Opies list this as the first known appearance in print of what would become, with some alterations, a popular song for children. It had probably circulated as a sung or printed ballad beforehand. Horace Walpole makes reference to it in May 1764, attributing it to a Sir Charles Sidley. See *The Oxford Dictionary of Nursery Rhymes* (Oxford: Oxford University Press, 1997), pp.341–3.

67. *Tom Trip ... Woglog the great Giant*: see note 33, p.225.

68. *Draggle-tails*: 'Skirts that drag on the ground in the mud' (*OED*).

69. *Nastiness*: in the eighteenth century, usually meaning lack of cleanliness.

70. *The History of Pompey the Little: or The Life and Adventures of a Lap-Dog*, a satirical novel by Francis Coventry, had been published in 1751.

71. *Vauxhall* and *Ranelagh*: two pleasure gardens south-west of London.
72. Most people used an off-white powder on their wigs, but black or blue was not unknown, as Oliver Goldsmith's Chinese visitor to Britain notes in *The Citizen of the World* (London: J. Newbery and W. Bristow, 1762: vol.1, p.9). Christopher Smart's entertainments, entitled (among other things) 'Mrs Midnight's Concerts', took place at the Little Theatre in Haymarket, London.
73. *beat up for Volunteers*: recruit for the army.
74. Books or papers requiring high-quality script or images (including bank notes) were printed using copper plates onto which the designs had been engraved or etched.
75. *Almanack*: a cheaply-printed annual publication containing a calendar plus meteorological and astrological predictions.
76. *Fairing*: souvenir of a fair (see Introduction).
77. *Knot*: tied ribbons worn as an ornament.